Whereabouts Unknown

Whereabouts Unknown

A NOVEL

RICHARD PROBERT

AUTHOR OF *THAT GOOD NIGHT*

BEAUFORT
BOOKS

Whereabouts Unknown

Copyright 2022 by Richard Probert
FIRST EDITION

9780825309786 Hardcover
9780825308574ebook

For inquiries about volume orders, please contact:
Beaufort Books, 27 West 20th Street, Suite 1103, New York, NY 10011
sales@beaufortbooks.com

Published in the United States by Beaufort Books
www.beaufortbooks.com

Distributed by Midpoint Trade Books
a division of Independent Publisher Group
https://www.ipgbook.com/

Book designed by Mark Karis

Printed in the United States of America

To Carmelita Britton for her encouragement, patience, tenacity, and all the things that wives of writers have to contend with.

To the Memory of my friend Bruce Butterfield.

Acknowledgements

Kim Probert-Grad, my daughter, who knows a thing or two about books and wasn't shy about sharing her thoughts about mine.

Mary Kaskin, Karen Kaderavick, Claudia Hornby, Victoria Heasley, who were willing to read earlier manuscripts, a job not suited to the faint-of-heart.

Scott Woolweaver, a professional violist who helped me with Anna's repertoire.

Frank Natali, Grazie per il tuo aiuto con l'Italiano.

Gary T. Redlinski, Vietnam veteran whose firsthand account of what is was like working in Graves Registration is much appreciated.

Joe Fedorko for his encouragement and for giving me a glimpse of life in the army.

Jim Owens, retired Executive Director of the Indiana Limestone Institute of America, Inc. for his help in understanding one of our nation's great natural resources.

Megan Trank, Managing Editor at Beaufort Books, as well as Olivia Fish, and Lita Robinson, for overseeing an editing process that was informative and challenging.

Doug Grad, my agent, for his steadfast support.

Beth

JUNE 15–18, 1993

1

I was still in a bathrobe that Mom had made for me, a heavy maroon corduroy thing with wide lapels and a tasseled sash. Why she picked yellow for the piping is anyone's guess. My parents were off to Indianapolis to visit Mom's friend Jenny and her husband, so I had the house to myself. I'd slept in, feeling I deserved every sleeping minute after working the graveyard shift at Walmart.

It was my second week on the job. I'd joined the store's Associates' Team two days after graduation from good old South Bloomington High School, home of the Panthers. (Never mind that our good-old-boy Hoosiers had wiped out their animal namesakes in the late 1800s.) I'd graduated Salutatorian, Class of 1993, which won me a full scholarship to Indiana University. IU is within walking distance of my front door, but God forbid living at home. That's why I'm working at Walmart: to earn enough money to move on campus.

I was munching on a mouthful of Cheerios when I heard a feeble knock at the front door. It was more of an apology than a knock, like maybe a kid selling something. The second knock was louder.

I got up from the kitchen table and went to the front door, parted the sheers, and peered out. And there stood Father Jamison. I guessed the good Father to be in his mid-twenties—looking more like Jughead from the comics than Friar Tuck. Lanky with a head of red hair that had a life all its own, his close-together blue eyes made it seem as if he was always studying something. Norman Rockwell would have loved this guy.

Behind him were two cops standing straight as a pin. Both had their hats cradled in their left arms, which they held across their chests, right arms cocked behind their backs. Four ladies dressed in black were on the sidewalk. I recognized Mrs. Archibald. She's in my mother's sewing circle at church.

I clutched my robe tight around me and opened the front door. I left the screen door hooked. Mrs. Archibald looked at me with a shy, hesitant, pained smile. The other ladies stood quietly with heads bowed. The cops didn't move a muscle. I said nothing, just looked at Father Jamison.

"Good Morning, Beth," he said in a shaky voice. "May I come in?"

Unhooking the screen door, I said, "Yeah...okay," then asked, "Is there something wrong?"

As he stepped through the door, Father Jamison looked at me softly. He had tears in his eyes. Almost whispering, he said, "I'm sorry, Beth. There's been a terrible accident. Your parents are… no longer with us." He reached out and took my hands in his.

We stood staring at each other. I couldn't talk. I looked around, out at the others standing silently. I didn't tear up or wail or anything like that. I guess you could say I was numb.

I don't know how long we stood there before he released my hands and they dropped to my sides.

"What's everybody doing here, Father?" I finally asked.

He explained that the policemen accompanied him because that was the law. I can't imagine what that law is all about. He said that the ladies were there to be with me. "In your time of need," is what he said. When I didn't reply, he turned to open the door and stepped back onto the porch. Looking back at me, he said, "I'll be right back."

I watched Father Jamison say something to the cops, who turned and left. One of them glanced back at me for a second with what looked like pity in his eyes. Then, with Mrs. Archibald in the lead, the ladies made their way up the four rickety steps in slow motion. They stood on the porch where the cops had been, and Father Jamison came back inside. "May Mrs. Archibald and her friends come in?" he asked.

"O…Okay, I guess so," I answered. My parents are dead. I didn't even say goodbye when they left this morning. I wasn't even awake.

They sat me on the sofa and took turns speaking quietly, telling me not to worry, that everything would be all right. One of them went into the kitchen and came back with my cup of unfinished coffee. She said she'd make more. When the ladies ran out of things to say, Father Jamison cleared his throat and asked me if I had a preference for a funeral home.

Like yeah, my favorites are… I thought, but just shook my head *no.* Then he asked me if I had any relatives living nearby. Somebody he could call?

I had a made-up list of relatives that had come in handy when I was in elementary school. When the other kids reported in after summer or Christmas break that they'd gone to their grandma's house, played with their cousins, or that their Uncle Ernie and Aunt Ruthie had come up from Virginia, I'd give my own bullshit report like a lieutenant: "My uncles and aunts came over with Grandma and Grandpa and stayed right through Christmas," I'd say, without missing a beat. In the summers I supposedly went to Louisiana to help my Uncle Chucky catch fish. I'd been to Alaska, Florida, and Pennsylvania—you name it, I'd been there. I lied so much I even began to believe myself. I still lie a lot, or…make things up, really. I don't know why I do that, I just do. Sorta filling in the blanks.

In school, I was always a loner. I avoided anything to do with sports or theatre, any of that rah-rah stuff. In junior high I did play the clarinet in the band, but once they started marching, I quit. In high school I joined the Diggers Club—a bunch of nerds rooting around in local history. That's how I know about the demise of panthers.

Back to Father Jamison's question about relatives—I told him the truth: I didn't have any. No uncles, aunts, or cousins. No grandparents.

"No one?"

"Nope. I'm it."

"Well Beth, I want you to know that you're not alone. We're here to help you get through all this." He asked me if I would like him to handle the funeral details, and when I told him that would be great, he said he would take care of it—that I should expect a call from the Tarski Funeral Home to go over the details, and to call him if I had any questions.

Before leaving, he took my hand in his and quietly said a prayer. I'm not the churchy type, but I admit it was comforting.

He said goodbye to the ladies. I walked him out onto the porch. He gave me a quick hug and left. I walked over to the porch railing and watched him get into his car and drive away. He didn't look back.

When I was little, I used to stand by that railing, peeling off strips of chalky white paint that was probably loaded with lead. That's what I found myself doing after Father Jamison left. I tossed the paint-chips over the rail. A car went by, thumping junk from oversized speakers. I watched a few crows soar over. There's a flock of them in the neighborhood. Late in the day, they group up, cawing to each other like they're reporting in. Watching the crows and looking at the dirty street in front of the house put tears in my eyes. I still didn't wail or anything like that, but my eyes filled up. My cheeks were a mess of tears.

I agreed to everything the ladies asked me to do. I took a shower and got dressed while they cleaned and straightened up the place. Tidied up the kitchen. Put fresh coffee on. Set out some plates. In an hour or so, the phone began ringing. Mrs. Archibald and the others busied themselves answering it and greeting visitors at the door, all the while stealing glances at me.

I didn't know very much about death. People wanted to pay their respects, I guess. Neighbors, church people…I didn't know most of them. They brought enough food to feed an army. What were they thinking? A week later, I'd be tossing out moldy everything. I was grateful that the ladies had taken over, ushering people to my side, setting out plates of food, not letting anybody bother me too much.

Word spread fast. Heidi and Jake came over but didn't stay too long. Heidi and I have been friends since she moved here in fourth grade. Jake's my steady boyfriend and my bodyguard. Literally. I picked him because he was the biggest (but not fat) guy in the school. Until Jake, boys were after me all the time. I was T and A all the way. Jake put a stop to it just by being my boyfriend. He knew what *no* meant, too.

By mid-afternoon, the house had emptied. The ladies cleaned up and made sure my dinner was all set before they started getting ready to go. Mrs. Archibald gave me her phone number. "Call me if you need anything, Beth. It's the least I can do for your poor mother." She swiped at a tear on her cheek and continued, "Mary Adamski is certainly in heaven, God bless her soul."

She didn't mention Emil. Emil was my father but he never let me call him Dad or Pa or anything but his name.

A little after they left, Father Jamison phoned to tell me that my parents were at Tarski's Funeral Home over on Orchard Hill Road, and that they'd be calling me soon.

"Father—what kind of accident was it?" I asked him. He'd never told me how they died.

"Oh, Beth, I'm so sorry," he said. "I should have told you, but…. Their car went out of control over near the abandoned quarry by Elwren. The police don't know what happened but they're investigating. The coroner said they must have died instantly. They didn't suffer, Beth." He paused, then asked, "Are you…okay there by yourself?"

I said I was fine, that in fact I needed some alone time.

Just before six o'clock, Mr. Tarski called from the funeral home. He told me that if I got some clothes ready for the viewing, he'd come over to pick them up in the morning. He promised to call first. After we hung up, I went into my room and changed out of my good dress into jeans and a T-shirt. I hadn't been further than the front porch all day and was feeling kind of pent up, so I went out to the backyard.

Here in Indiana, spring goes on and on. The grass needed mowing. The plants were going nuts. Mom's flower garden was showing its colors, not a weed in sight. I'll have to keep an eye on it. I walked over to our huge oak tree, probably left from when this was nothing but a farm. In the fall, it dropped acorns like hail. One time—I was probably around six—I picked up a bunch of them and put them in a drawer under the workbench in the garage. I forgot about them and I guess they began sprouting in there. When Emil tried to open the drawer a few months later, they'd swelled it up so tight it wouldn't budge. He cursed his way through destroying the drawer front with a crow bar before taking a leather belt to my backside. Child abuse? I guess it was, but I didn't know it at six years old. I blamed myself for being a "bad girl."

I thought about mowing the lawn but second-guessed myself. It probably wouldn't look right, me out there, being in mourning and all. I went back in the house and put the plate the ladies had left for me in the oven to warm, then headed for my parents' bedroom to find clothes for the funeral.

Their room had been off-limits to me for as long as I could remember. Emil was very strict about that. The minute I opened the door, my stomach turned upside down. On top of being really nervous, the smell of sweet perfume and sweat made me sick. I made it to the toilet just in time.

When I could pull myself up off my knees, I washed my face and stood in front of the mirror for a while. My hair was cut short and dyed purple with streaks of blonde. My parents didn't like it, but Heidi did and Jake thought it was cool. My manager at Walmart didn't say anything at all. Around the same time that I dyed my hair, I got my left nostril pierced and wore a small gold stud in it, which drove Emil up the wall. He called me a slut. Mom kept asking why I did it, but I really didn't have an answer to that. I got into this habit of rubbing the stud with my finger. That's what I was doing while I looked in the mirror.

I decided to put off going back into their bedroom for the clothes. I didn't think I could eat because I had just thrown up, but I realized I was really hungry and took my plate from the oven. The food—roast beef, green beans, and some kind of rice—tasted really good. For dessert, I had my choice of three different Jell-O things: cherry with marshmallows, lemon with peaches, or lime with bananas. I picked the lime. When I cleaned up, I saw that the trash bin had been emptied and lined with a new bag. The ladies had really taken their job seriously. *I'll have to send them a thank-you note.*

After dinner, I went back to the bedroom, but this time I was ready. I threw the door open and the next thing I did was open the blinds, then the windows. I was pretty antsy the whole time I was in there, thinking that Emil would walk in on me any second. I bet it had been a long time since birdsong had come into that room.

Mom's dresser had four drawers. The top was chest-high with a mirror stuck on the back. One of her homemade lace doilies covered the top. She was always making that kind of stuff—*tatting*, she called it. I picked up her hair brush. When I was little, she'd brush my hair with it. She'd treat it like it was something really special. I'd have to wait on the back porch while she went inside to get the brush. Sometimes, we'd sit under the oak tree and she'd sing a little song or tell me a story while she gently brushed my hair. I don't remember when she stopped doing all that, but I was probably the one who stopped it. Thought I was too old, I guess.

As I put the brush back on her dresser, I cried a little. I didn't touch anything else. I sat on the edge of the worn, sagging bed feeling sorry for myself. The bedspread was neat as a pin. Pink with white cotton tufts. I might have seen it before, but I couldn't really remember it. There was a book lying on Mom's nightstand, open to a passage that read: *This is the day the Lord hath made; We greet it with joy and gladness.*

"Oh, Mom," I cried out loud. I grabbed the box of tissues that sat next to the book and went through about a dozen of them before I settled down.

I was at a loss about what clothes to get. How was I supposed to know how to dress dead people? Emil was easy—he was never what people would call a sharp dresser. Mom tried though, and I wanted to pick something she'd like.

Emil's side of the closet was neat, probably because Mom kept it that way. A pair of wrinkled, oil-stained pants he wore a lot hung from a hook on the back of the door, looking like a rag. He didn't have much. A few shirts, some pants. His Knights of Columbus sport coat, one ugly dark brown suit. I took out the suit and laid it on the bed. His dress shoes were worn, heavy wingtips. I hated touching them.

Most of Mom's stuff was pretty dull, but in the back of the closet were a few dresses I'd never seen before. One of them was fitted with a flared bottom. Something you'd wear to do the rumba or something—real Latin-looking. God, I mean, Mom wearing this! That was a shocker. Just for fun, I held it up in front of me and twirled around in front of the mirror.

Another dress was vivid pink, with a cloth flower—now crushed like a truck ran over it—sewn to the bodice. This was not the dress to be buried in. The last one was blue with white pinstriping, pretty formal looking. I held it up to myself and it looked pretty good. Mom might like this one. I put it on the bed. I didn't think she'd want the ladies from church seeing the other ones. I hung them back in the closet.

Mom's dresser drawers were in perfect order, not like mine with bras, panties, socks, sweaters, my yearbook, all tossed into whatever drawer had room. The third one down was full of slips, and I took one out. As I did, I noticed something at the very bottom of the drawer: an envelope.

Yellowed and probably years old, I thought it might be a secret love letter, like the ones I used to get from a kid named Adam when I was in ninth grade. He knew how to get me going. I was crushed when he moved away. Jake doesn't write love letters.

When I examined the thing further, I realized it was two envelopes, one inside the other. The outside one was addressed to Mom here in Bloomington. The one inside was addressed to Mom, too, but to a place in Oolitic—a small town just south of here. Stamped in red was *Return to Sender. Addressee Unknown.* I couldn't find a date anywhere. Both envelopes had the same return address: Anna Robertson, RR I, Clayton, Wisconsin.

The letter came out of the envelope in pieces. It had been torn up, then taped back together, and the tape was in bits, like tiny shards of glass. At this point I was pretty weirded out. I took the paper fragments to the kitchen table to piece them together. It was like a puzzle, but I'm pretty good at puzzles so it didn't take me too long. In tidy cursive handwriting, the letter said:

Dear Mom and Dad,

I hope that my writing to you will help ease whatever pain or anger still remains. More than two years have passed since I left home and much has happened, all good, I am happy to say. I trust that you are well.

Jim and I are married and we have a two-year-old daughter named Sarah. Congratulations, you're grandparents! Soon to be again, too, as we're expecting another in October. A picture speaks louder than words, so I've included one of me, Jim, and Sarah in front of our cabin. Please contact me at the return address on the envelope.

Your Loving Daughter,

Anna

No date on the letter. And *Dad* not *Emil. Your Loving Daughter*!

What did it all mean?

2

I stared at that letter for a long time. Well, not just at the letter; I stared at the walls and ceiling and the worn linoleum floor. I stared at everything in the kitchen including a piece of water-stained, faded green wallpaper next to the sink. I used to stare at that spot when I was doing my homework. I guess I thought if I looked at something ugly, my mind would want to get back to the homework, but it never worked.

I kept bouncing my eyes between that ugly spot and the letter. Those words, *Your Loving Daughter, Anna,* were blinking at me. *Whose* loving daughter? Mom's and Emil's was the only thing I could figure out. The envelope was addressed to them, so what other explanation could there be?

I found myself getting pissed. My parents had just died, and here I was getting pissed at them. But didn't I have every right to? They had another daughter. I had a sister and they never told me. *Nice play, guys!*

Father Jamison had said they died instantly, and I didn't exactly understand what that meant either. *Instantly*-instantly?

Within ten seconds? A minute? No, a minute wouldn't be *instantly*; even ten seconds can be forever. Watching the sweeping second hand on the kitchen clock, I decided that two seconds would be the maximum time for dying instantly. One second seemed right, like a quick fade-out at the end of a dramatic movie scene.

I sat at the kitchen table practicing gently closing my eyes in one second then two second intervals. I decided that if I had a choice, I'd prefer to die with a two-second fade-out, which felt gentle and gave me time to exhale without pushing out the air.

Maybe if they had lived, they would have told me about my sister. Like, next week, or when I reached twenty-one. Or got married or something. Mom could have told me a hundred times. When she brushed my hair, for instance. Or when we made cookies, which we did a lot when I was little. Or yesterday, for Christ's sake! Any goddamn time. Why keep it a secret? If they hadn't gotten killed, I wouldn't know now—or maybe ever.

I wondered if Father Jamison knew. If Mom confessed or something. Even if he did, he'd never tell me.

Screw this!

I took the rest of the night to go through the house bit by bit, looking for the picture mentioned in the letter or anything else that might be hidden away that I wasn't supposed to know about. I went through everything in their bedroom and this time I didn't feel like Emil would walk in. I got my hopes up when I found a locked box on the floor in the back of the closet, behind Emil's stuff. The key was taped to the bottom, so I opened it right up. There wasn't much in there, no more letters and no photographs. There was an insurance policy—Prudential. Mr. Tarsky had said I'd probably find one, and that it would surely cover the cost of the burials. The only other things in the box were the deed to the house and an Indianhead penny, 1886. I put everything back, closed the lid, and left the key in the lock.

Mom's sewing room was so neat that it was easy to search. Zip. There was nothing in the basement but a musty smell. In my closet, there's a trapdoor to the attic. When I was little, I asked Emil about what was above the trapdoor and he told me monsters lived up there; that they'd kill me if I ever opened it, which I never did.

When I finally opened the trapdoor, I nearly peed in my pants for fear of monsters, and I'm eighteen. Daddies can really lay a trip that lasts. The attic was empty except for insulation.

I found a roll of Scotch tape and taped the letter back together, then eased it back in the envelope. I put it on top of my dresser and set the second envelope next to it. I went to bed thinking about Anna, like how she'd look. I said "Aunt Beth" out loud a few times to feel what it was like to be an aunt. It felt good. I acted out, "It's nice to meet you, too, Jim." Just before falling asleep, I pretend-hugged Sarah.

In the morning, it took me a few minutes to shake off that drowsy sleep leftover feeling. With my head clearing, I remembered that Mom and Emil were killed in a car accident. That fact blew the fog right out of my head. It was like one of those things that just doesn't seem possible but it was and then there's the likelihood that I have a sister named Anna. I was not close to my parents but then, I wasn't close to anyone. Still, they were my parents and...well, honestly I don't know how I feel. Sad? Of course I'm sad. But happy, too. Sort of a yin and yang thing. I might have a sister and that makes me happy. Just knowing that is like having all sorts of wonderful possibilities. With that, I got dressed, had a cup of coffee and gnawed on a sticky bun left here by one of the visitors from yesterday. Next on my list was to get ready for Mr. Tarsky, the guy from the funeral home.

I ironed Mom's dress, then packed it and her other stuff in a little tweed suitcase I found in the sewing-room closet. It looked new. I mean not like *today* new, but old-and-never-used new. It had a black plastic handle. The outside looked like heavy cloth, maybe tweed, but it was really made out of cardboard. Like a big version of a dolly suitcase I got from Santa Claus eons ago. I packed for her like she was going on a vacation, including underwear and jewelry. Mom didn't wear makeup very often but I stuck in some of her blush along with my own favorite eye shadow and lipstick, *Cherry Kiss*. I wanted her to look good. Real feminine, like when she'd dress up to go with her friends to concerts over at IU.

I put Emil's clothes into a box from the garage, adding a purple tie with hunting dogs printed on it, and white socks because I couldn't find any dark ones.

Mr. Tarsky was right on time. After he'd shaken my hand and told me how sorry he was, he motioned toward the sofa and we both sat down.

"Do you want wood?" he asked.

"Wood?" I drew a blank for a second, and then realized what he meant.

He told me that the newest thing was wooden coffins. That the metal ones were out of style. People just loved the wooden ones. *Real comfortable*, is how he put it. I asked him if there was a nice down pillow in there, but he just kept rambling on. He told me that mahogany was the best because it didn't rot and lasted a long time. It all sounded pretty pricey, but I never could get a word in to ask about the cost. I kept thinking of the wooden coffins they show on old westerns, a few rough boards whacked together.

Without my asking, Mr. Tarsky finally got down to business. He said he'd have to check for sure, but he thought with all expenses combined and for the best coffins, he could bury my parents for around twelve to fifteen thousand dollars.

Yeah, right! Mom had told me that women were often taken advantage of in business, like the time she had her car serviced at Randy's Auto Shoppe. She went there for an oil change and left with new shock absorbers, a flushed cooling system, a transmission adjustment, and all-around wheel balancing. She had turned down new tires because hers were only a year old and she didn't drive more than 10,000 miles a year, if that. When she told Emil about it, he and a few of his friends paid Randy a visit.

I decided to string Mr. Tarsky along to see how far he would go. "How deep will they be buried?" I asked him. "Is it cheaper if I don't go very deep? Maybe just set them on top of the ground?"

But there was no kidding this guy; he took his job dead serious. By the time he got done talking at me, I knew all about graves. Why the preferred depth is six feet, the advantages and disadvantages of mausoleums, how water tables affect caskets and their contents…everything. When he stopped to take a breath, I told him to put them in the cheapest coffins he had.

"I don't sell cheap!" he said.

"The least expensive then," I told him, and he ended up quoting me $9,200 for the whole deal. When I told him I'd talk it over with Father Jamison, he went down to $8,800, and

I said Okay, just to shut him up and be done with it.

I was real clear on how I wanted my mother made up. Mr. Tarsky said he'd do his best and that he'd call when he was done so I could see her before the viewing. He said that he'd make Emil look good, too, and that he didn't need socks or shoes.

I have to admit, Mr. Tarsky did a really good job. Mom looked great. No, she didn't look *natural*—I mean, there was no getting around the fact that she was dead—but she looked sort of pleased with herself, like death wasn't this huge disappointment. The blue dress was the perfect choice. Emil looked good, too, and together they were a handsome couple. I was actually proud to be their daughter.

It was the first funeral I'd ever been to, and it was my parents'. People were nice, especially the ladies from church. Mrs. Archibald played doting grandmother, and told me I was holding up really good.

Father Langley ran the service, not Father Jamison. He's a monsignor, so he really knows his stuff. He said a lot in Latin: *Requiem aeternam dona eis pacem* means *grant them eternal rest. Et lux perpetua* is *eternal light.* I had to know that stuff for my First Holy Communion. I remember the Requiem Mass because it really nails you. Fire and hell, Purgatory, and finally Heaven if it all works out. Sinners have it tough after they die.

Heidi came early with her mom, and they sat up front like they were family. That made me feel good. Jake came later and joined them, and the three of them rode along with me to the cemetery, in the big black car right behind the hearses. While Father Langley was saying things over the graves, I looked out over the cemetery and thought about my niece, Sarah. That made me smile without realizing it, and I think I got a few stares. I couldn't help it, though. I was busting to know more about my new family. I didn't know how old Sarah would be because there was no date on the letter, but I was thinking of her as a little girl. And Anna said she was pregnant, so there must be another niece or a nephew. That's what I was smiling about. Me, having a sister and being an aunt. There were plenty of tears, too. Like I said before, this was my first funeral and I didn't have a clue. It's really the end. I mean when the caskets were lowered into the ground, I cried pretty hard.

After the reception at the church—Mrs. Archibald had arranged it—I went to Heidi's house with Jake. Her parents are really nice, so I decided to tell them about finding the letter and learning that I had a sister. Heidi's mom was shocked. She held her hand over her mouth and even had tears in her eyes, and gave me the longest hug ever. She said it was terrible that I hadn't known something like that. Heidi's dad went right to the telephone and called information for Clayton, Wisconsin, but there was no listing.

During dinner, we devised a plan for finding out more. First thing was to go to the place in Oolitic, which was only thirty miles away. Wisconsin was the second thing—to try to find the cabin mentioned in the letter. Heidi suggested that, and said that she and Jake wanted to go along. I really didn't like the idea, but I didn't say anything because I didn't want to hurt anybody's feelings. Heidi's mom must have seen the look on my face, though, and said that pilgrimages are best done alone. Like I said before, she's really neat.

I figured, why wait? The next day I drove to Oolitic in Mom's car, a ten-year-old Plymouth Omni. "Powder blue, like new," she used to say.

Oolitic looked just like I remembered it from my Girl Scout trip there. I tried to find the address I had, but kept winding up at a sewage treatment plant. I went around the block three times to make sure, but there's nothing at 22 Welsh Street except that plant. I rolled down my window and asked some man walking by if he knew anything about the address. He told me there used to be some houses there, but they tore them down. He kept flipping his eyes between my chest and the stud in my nose, which pissed me off but I didn't say anything. Then he just walked away. I drove over to Main Street and parked outside of Lester's Hardware. It was built of limestone, of course, this being the place where they quarry the stuff. Lester's sold everything from candy bars to snout rings, but nobody in there knew anyone named Adamski.

Downtown Oolitic was really just a few stores. Near the end of Main, I noticed a sign pointing toward the Joe Palooka Monument. Apparently he had been created right here. I remembered the name from history class. Our teacher was crazy about old cartoons as a way to study history. The Joe Palooka character was a boxer who enlisted in World War II and became a hero. Now we have Homer Simpson. Go figure!

I parked the car, figuring I'd walk over to the monument, but I never made it. On my way, I met this lady walking her dog. I had to get out of the way, actually—the mutt was all teeth and growls. The lady apologized, wagging her finger and saying, "She's a nasty little doggie, isn't she?"

More like a fucking beast, I thought. I asked the lady if she knew anybody named Adamski, and, *bingo!*

"They used to live on Welsh Street," she said. "Moved away, I think." She kept talking as she dragged the nasty little doggie down the street and I followed her, making sure to keep clear of the thing. "I didn't know them really. Try Pete Paulson. Lives over there on Balkan Lane, third block, second house on the left!" She was yelling over the high-pitched yips and snarls. "Number twenty-seven!"

I yelled back a thank-you, but I doubt that she heard it.

3

Balkan Lane was storybook, with big trees lining both sides. The effect was like walking down an aisle. The houses were perfect, lawns mowed, hedges trimmed, not a weed among the flowers. Big porches, window boxes...I remembered a street like it in Bloomington, where I went once to sell magazines for our eighth-grade class. If you sold something like a million subscriptions you got a free trip to Disneyland. It would have been easier to win the Indy 500 on a hobby horse. I think I went to about three houses before I threw all of that magazine crap in somebody's garbage can and went home.

I followed the dog lady's directions to the guy's house—third block, second house on the left. I walked by it, cased it out, and waited for my nerves to settle. Paul something, she'd said. Maybe it was on the mailbox. I turned back toward the house and saw the number 27 fixed on a piece of wood just under the porch roof. Polished brass. I went up three or four porch steps wide enough to be bleachers. The porch ran the whole width of the house.

It was perfect—no peeling paint, like back home. The floor

was shiny gray with a fake-grass carpet bigger than my room. A glider faced the street. A couple of rocking chairs and some small tables were carefully placed, like it was a living room. I could've lived on that porch. I checked out the mailbox. *Pete and Neddy Paulson* was neatly printed on the front. I pushed the doorbell button, heard a quick *brrring,* and waited. No one came. I pushed it again, holding it this time.

After another minute, a man opened the inside door and stood behind the screen. He wasn't tall but he was wide. Almost the whole width of the door. His hair was really short and gray and he had a big nose, old-looking plastic-framed glasses, a flannel shirt, and wide suspenders.

"Yes, what is it?" he asked.

"Are you Mr. Paulson?"

"You sellin' something?"

That threw me. "No, sir," I said as politely as I could. "I was wondering if you ever heard of people named Adamski?"

He scrunched up his face. His eyebrows pulled in. He let out a long *Hmmm.* He stared at me like…well, I don't know. It was like he was reading me. Studying me like I was some kind of creature he'd never seen before. I must have started fiddling with my stud because he looked right at my nose. "Does that thing itch or something?"

It took me a moment to figure out what he meant. I think I blushed a little and was about to tell the old geezer that it was none of his business where I itch. But before I could say anything, he said, "Haven't heard that name in a long time." He opened the screen door like he was going to invite me in but he just stood there rubbing his chin and studying me. "You're not Anna, are you? You seem a bit young…."

I must have smiled because he got a big grin on his face. I told him that my name was Beth. "Anna's my sister," I said. Then I started to cry. It was the first time I'd heard somebody say her name—and the first time I said it aloud myself. I don't like to cry but sometimes you can't help it.

The man came out on the porch then, and kept saying, *my oh my* over and over again. He led me to one of the rockers and asked me if I liked lemonade. Before I could say anything, he was scurrying back into the house like his pants were on fire. I felt around in my pockets but didn't have a tissue or anything, so I did a quick swipe with my shirt sleeve and enjoyed the view of the street, rocking back and forth like an old granny. Being on that perfect porch felt really good, like I'd rocked in that chair a hundred times before. I wondered if Anna was ever on this porch.

The old man came out carrying a tin tray with two glasses filled with lemonade. He had a paper towel wrapped around each glass and held there with a rubber band. "Hope this is okay," he said, setting down the tray on a little table and sitting down in a chair across from me. "Since the missus passed away, I do what I can."

"I'm really sorry," I told him.

"It's been three years, but…you know…it's a hard thing to get over. I guess I never will."

"Mr. Paulson, do you know Anna?"

"You can call me Smithy, like everybody else. I was a blacksmith before I retired." He showed me his hands like I could read palms or something. They were the biggest I'd ever seen. "I've known Anna ever since she was a tyke. Sweet little lady. How is she doing?"

I took my time telling Smithy about my parents and the

letter. He was all ears. When I finished all he could say was, "My word," which he repeated a number of times while shaking his head back and forth, back and forth. After a short pause, he asked me what had led me to his house.

"I went to the address on the letter from Oolitic, but it's a sewage plant. Some guy told me that a lot of houses were torn down over there. Then this lady with a crazy dog told me that I should talk to you about the Adamskis."

Mr. Paulson—Smithy—laughed and said, "Jenny Grayson. She loves that dog. Why, nobody knows." He fell silent, stroked his chin, and then said, "They built that plant maybe fifteen or twenty years ago, right after your parents left town." He paused for a moment. "So, you were born in Bloomington?"

"I guess I was." I'd never thought anything different.

Smithy started rocking again, and staring out onto the street like he was trying to remember something. Then he stopped, looked me in the eye, and said, "To be truthful, Beth, well, by golly, I guess you have a right to know. Your sister Anna left high school and ran off with a fellow named Jim Robertson. That was probably before you were born. Jim, well, he was in his twenties so the whole thing raised a lot of eyebrows."

I was stunned and proud all at the same time. I guess the way I looked wound Paulson up because he went off on a blue streak.

"Jim had just come back from Vietnam. Most people who knew Jim and Anna were okay with it after the initial surprise, but not your parents. No sir, they could not get over it. Especially your father. He was mad as a hornet, and, well…how do I put this? He just went mean on that girl. Locked Anna up in the house and did everything he could to keep the two youngsters apart."

"Yeah, I can believe that," I said, and then went quiet again so he could tell me more.

"Well, Beth," he said, looking like a kid who couldn't keep a secret, "Jim wasn't going to have it. He broke in through Anna's bedroom window and off they went."

Romeo and Juliet. Maria and Tony. Helen and Paris. It was just so damn romantic! I'd thought about doing something similar for years—not with Jake or anybody, but just climbing out of my window and getting the hell out of there. And Anna did it! "Hot damn!" I said without thinking.

Smithy chuckled a little. We sat for a moment before he said, "Say, does that thing bother you much?"

"What thing?"

"In your nose."

I must have been at it again. "Not really. If I could keep my fingers off it, I'd never know it was there."

"Beats me why anybody would want to do that," he said. He was probably in his seventies or eighties so it wasn't a big surprise that he'd have a comment about my stud. If I'd wanted to be rude, I could have turned around and asked him why he was wearing double-wide suspenders and a flannel shirt on a hot, sunny day. Instead, I asked, "So what happened after they ran off? Did you ever hear from them again?"

At that, he lit up like a Christmas tree, leaned forward, and touched me on my knee like the good-old boy he was. I didn't like it one bit and pulled away really quick. Almost spilled the rest of my lemonade in the process. I overreacted, I know, but I'm pretty picky about who touches me.

After that, Smithy kept his hands to himself. "At first I'd hear from them. Jim'd send me letters and tell me how things were going." He stopped for a moment. "They had a daughter. Did you know that?"

"Yes," I said. "That was in Anna's letter, too. Her name's Sarah. They had another child on the way when she wrote. It's really neat to think I'm an aunt."

"Another on the way? Well, now, see, that's something I didn't know." He seemed to get a little sad. "We were pretty close, me and Jim," he told me. "Then something happened, I don't know what, but I stopped hearing from him. Just like that. I sent off a few letters, but never got any response."

I didn't know what to say so I just sat there and pretty soon, Smithy got back into storytelling mode. "Did you know that Jim was a stone carver?"

I shook my head. How would I know that? I never even knew he existed till a week ago.

"Yes, well…there aren't too many who can carve stone like Jim Robertson. Shoot, I wish I knew what happened to him."

I could tell the old man was struggling, that his memories were knocking him around. "If I find them," I said, then corrected myself. "I mean *when* I find them, I'll let you know."

"You'll find them all right." I think he was going to pat me on the back but decided against it. "You've got spunk!"

"Spunk? Is that like *punk* with an *s*?" I joked.

"No, no, it's a good thing. Like…grit. You've got *grit*, same as I had when I was young. Not everybody's got it, you know. It's something you're either born with or you're not—like an inner strength. Don't give up on your mission, young lady. It ain't every day that one comes along."

I must have been beaming. I mean, nobody had ever told me before that I had *spunk*. "Spunk," I said back to him.

"By golly, you've got it. You just got to believe in yourself."

"I do," I said, feeling like I was taking an oath. Maybe I was.

"That's a girl," he said as he stood. I watched him teeter a bit and felt like I should help, but I didn't want to embarrass him so I just waited. When he was on his feet, I stood up. "So you'll be going up to Wisconsin, then?" he asked.

"As soon as I can figure it all out," I said, and he immediately turned into a grandpa, full of advice.

"Drive slow and don't be staying just anywhere. Pick out a good safe place to rest up." As he took my empty glass, his eyes shone at me like he was some teenager. I bet he was something when he was my age—Jake times two.

I gave him a hug—I just couldn't help it—and felt the bones in his back. It was like his age was poking out, contradicting the flash in his eyes.

He led me to the front steps, where I promised to let him know what happened. "I have your address," I said.

"Well, let me give you my phone number," he said, disappearing into the house. He was back in a minute and handed me a folded piece of paper. I turned to leave, tucking the paper into my pocket.

"Tell those two lovebirds I said hello," he said, waving goodbye. I waved back before jumping in the car. I felt all puffed up like I was ready to take this on. My mission: finding Anna.

Jim

1953–1968

4

My dad was MIA in Korea. I was only three–years-old when Mom got the telegram, on January 26, 1953. To me at the time, *missing* was what happened when I couldn't find my toy truck. If dad was *missing,* maybe I could find him. I searched under my bed, in closets, everywhere. No Dad.

Mom told me that if anybody could find dad it would be President Eisenhower. She worshipped him. Of course, he didn't find Dad, either.

Before the telegram, Mom and I used to go out a lot. Mom taught Sunday school, so we went to church every week. We got groceries from Simons, where Mr. Simons always gave me candy. We'd take walks to a park that had swings. We didn't live in a typical neighborhood with blocks of houses and yards. We lived on Franklin Alley, which was in the southern part of Milwaukee, just east of Kinnickinnic Avenue. Originally, our building had been a horse-and-carriage barn. It was made of poured concrete faced with red brick. Even the steps were concrete, eighteen of them. Each one had a rubber tread glued to it. Somebody told me once that it was originally owned by the Pabst family. Upstairs had been for grooms and drivers and part of it had been used as a hay loft. Downstairs was where they kept the horses and carriages. Over the years the upstairs had been converted into an apartment and the downstairs into car storage. My dad, a mechanic, bought the building with the idea that we'd live upstairs while he used the downstairs as a car repair shop. Mom told me that once my dad's business was going, the plan was to buy a house.

After Mom got the telegram, we went out less and less. At first, people came to visit. They brought me toys and dropped off all sorts of goodies, from cookies to roasts. But after a while they stopped coming. Except for Hans Biettermeir, that is. Hans owned one of the shops in our alley, where he manufactured beer steins. When dad went missing, Hans took it upon himself to make sure that Mom and I were okay and would stop by every once-in-awhile to visit. Because he was on the Board of Trustees for the Lutheran School, he even got me a scholarship to go there, which I did from first grade through high school. Class of 1968.

Whenever we did go out somewhere, Mom would say we had to hurry home in case there was news about Dad. For a while, I'd get all keyed up, wanting more than anything to get back and see Dad standing there. But, just as I had given up looking under my bed and in closets, I gave up on that, too. Mom was another story. Now and then she took me to church, and sometimes we'd go for a short walk, but that was about it. We didn't have a car, so whatever we needed came from stores close by or by phone order from Simon's. There was always a piece of candy in the bottom of the bag.

I was about five years old when Mom started letting me go

out on my own. I'd stay in the alley and she'd keep pretty close tabs on me from one of the front windows. Workers up and down the alley knew what was going on, and they kept an eye on me too, inviting me into their shops. She came to trust all that, and in due time, I could come and go as I pleased, as long as I told her where I was going.

Besides Hans's Stein Works, other businesses on the alley included Bumpy's Truck Tire and Repair, Westen's Chrome Plating, and—just at the dead end—Sal's Memorials. Since all the workers knew me, I could spend my days pretending I was employed at one or another of the shops and they'd play along. Once in a while, Mom would even pack me a lunch—mayonnaise sandwiches were my favorite—so I could stay out all day.

Most of the guys were vets of World War II or Korea, but they never talked to me about all that, probably because of my missing dad.

Sal worked alone, and at first, I was scared of him. He hardly ever came outside his place, which wasn't noisy like the other businesses on the alley. When things were quiet, I could hear soft clinking coming from his shop.

There was nothing about Sal that seemed friendly. Other guys in the alley were always horsing around—grab-ass, they called it—but not him. I remember one guy saying that Sal was a nutcase.

Because it was at the end of the alley, I could just as easily cross the road and avoid Sal's Memorials altogether. But for some reason, Sal's place was like a magnet to me. Sometimes, I'd catch the old man looking at me through his front window and he'd nod his head a little. I'd never get a smile or a wave, just that tiny nod.

One sunny day in June, just around my ninth birthday, all that changed. School had been out for about a week. Some of my school friends came over once in a while, but their moms didn't like them coming to the alley. They thought the neighborhood was too rough, I guess. Sometimes I'd meet kids in the park, but most of the time I was alone.

Anyway, on this particular day I was walking toward Sal's place and the magnet was pulling me like crazy. Just as I was passing by, Sal came out and stood in the doorway. He stared right into my eyes—glared, really. His eyes caught mine and held on. Then he smiled a little and beckoned me forward. "Come," he said, like I was a puppy. Clutching the most beat-up lunch box I'd ever seen, he walked out and sat down on an old bench and leaned his back against the battered brick wall. "So, Jimmy Boy," he said in a thick Italian accent, "you want to sit down?" He patted the bench next to him. I didn't know how he knew my name or what the *Boy* part meant, but I had a good feeling. His voice was kind. Warm. He spoke as if he'd known me for years.

I sat.

The lid on Sal's old lunchbox was so twisted that there was a good space between it and the bottom. He'd stuck the stub of a pencil in the hasp to keep it closed. A piece of rubber stretched around the thing to keep it together. The handle was missing, so he carried it like my mom clutched her purse, like somebody was always ready to snatch it from her.

As he opened the box, I had to wonder what kind of ungodly meal that box held. As it turned out, it was the best food I'd ever eaten or will ever eat in a lifetime. Sharing that lunch with Sal was more than eating; it was heaven. I didn't know it then, but with each bite, I was etching a memory that would carry me through thick and thin. The crumbs that gathered on my shirt from a hard roll were like flecks of gold. Smoky hard salami and cold gnocchi felt as good to bite into as they tasted. When I asked Sal about the hunk of cheese he handed me, he called it *scamotz*, which made me laugh. He had me repeat the word three or four times before I got it right. When I was older, I learned that *scamotz* was really just mozzarella. Sal treated me like he'd known me all my life. His dark eyes—not so much warm as deep—always regarded me as if he was about to do or say something important. They said, *I know a lot you don't know, so listen.*

Sal wasn't tall—maybe five-foot-eight—but his shoulders seemed wider than a Euclid truck. His shadow was rectangular. He was as strong as a bull and his hands were padded thick with calluses. His hair, usually hidden under a cap, reminded me of short-cut crabgrass, only gray. I can't remember seeing him dressed in anything but green work pants with a matching long-sleeved shirt.

I found out later that at the time I met him he was already in his late seventies, a widower ready to retire. He told me once that he was sick of competing with "the guys who use stencils and air-compressors instead of chisels and mauls." Sal was too proud for that sort of thing. When he was a kid growing up in Italy, his parents had sent him off to apprentice as a stone carver, where he learned to do everything by hand, with patience and skill and not a stencil in sight.

After lunch that first day, Sal invited me into his shop. Unlike Bumpy's Tires and Weston's Chrome Shop, both of which were filthy, Sal's place was orderly. There was lots of dust and grit on the floor, but it smelled nice in there—earthy but not damp.

In one corner was an air-compressor the size of a small car. It sat inside a steel mesh cage like some miserable beast. Most of the time it was idle, but he'd occasionally use it to rough out a large carving like the top or bottom of a pilaster, or to break down a large chunk of marble or limestone. In another corner was a closet where he kept his tools—chisels and mallets that he called *mia bene scalpelli*, as if he were talking about something religious, like a communion cup or maybe even a saint. There were some drawers with chisels so precious to Sal that I wasn't allowed to touch them. Racks of stone lined the walls. A large stone-cutting saw sat near the back of the shop next to a double-sized garage door, along with hydraulic lifts and heavy, steel-wheeled dollies. A chain hoist ran on an I-beam that bisected the place.

Two sturdy work benches with wooden tops a foot or more thick sat in the middle of the floor. One of them was clean, but on the other sat a block of limestone about three feet all around. I followed him over to that bench. For a nine-year-old, sixty-five pound kid, looking up at that stone was like standing in the shadow of the great pyramid. Motioning to a heavy wooden box next to the bench, he said, "Stand on the box so you can see the top of the stone." I did as I was told. A line of shallow holes had been drilled down the center of the stone. Lying to the side were iron wedges. The first thing he had me do was put the wedges in the holes. Handing me a small hammer he said, "Now, Jimmy Boy, you're going to open the stone. Go right down the line, tap one then the next. When you get to the end, start over."

"I don't think I can break it."

"What is this break? You're not a going to break the stone. You're going to open the stone. The stone, it doesn't like to break. Now you can try."

I took a deep breath and hit the first wedge with all my might.

"No, not so hard, Jimmy," he said, taking the hammer. "The stone it doesn't like that. Let me tell you something. Sometimes we think it takes more muscles to do the hard work than we need to use. *Capire?*"

"Huh?"

"*Capire,*" he repeated. "Do you understand?"

Of course I didn't understand Italian so I simply answered *no* at which point Sal said a phrase I'd hear time and again: "*Dio mio.*" At the time, I didn't understand that either, but I let it go.

"Now, I want you to listen," he went on, almost singing the final word, which he pronounced *leesin*. It wasn't easy for me to understand him, especially on my first day in his shop. Sometimes he mixed Italian in with his English. When he was mad, a flood of Italian roared through the shop. Both curses and compliments flowed liberally from his lips, and I learned pretty quickly which was which.

"What you need to know is that the tool, it works for you, you don't work for it. You work together. You fight-a the tool you never win. So, first I want you to be nice to the hammer," he said, handing it back to me. "Lift it up and down. Find the balance where it is. Let the hammer know that you're willing to work together. Now we start over."

I hefted the hammer, feeling its heaviness, its willing to do my bidding. I struck the silvery top of the wedge, hearing a dull thud come from the stone.

"Ah, bravo, Jimmy Boy. Now you hit the next one and go to the end, then start over."

I did as I was told. With each blow, I felt the hammer

working with me like it was an extension of my arm. After going down the line of wedges a few times, Sal stopped me. He instructed me to look at the side of the stone. Pointing to a hairline crack, he said, "There you see, the stone, it's opening. Whatever we find in there, nobody ever seen it before. Millions of years, it's closed up. Back to the first day it was created. Before you and me. A few more hits and you've done it."

I went back and struck each wedge in turn until the stone split.

Iridescence filled the air—a shimmer of light that lasted for only the tiniest of moments before slipping away. Sal let out a long deep breath, as if he'd just said a prayer. After a brief silence, he said, "*Luce di Dio*. The light of God. Like beauty of a young woman. Like life. A rainbow." He turned to me, his face radiant. "You see it? You see it, Jimmy Boy?"

"Yes!" I said, joining in the excitement. "But it went away so fast! It just disappeared."

"The light, it's like youth to age. Age to death. Like you and me," he laughed, reaching out to shake my hand.

I was startled when Sal took my hand in his, and almost pulled away. It was the first time a man had held my hand like that, and it felt huge. By contrast, Mom's were cool and soft, a little bony, not heavy and rough like Sal's. I wondered if my father had hands like that.

That was my first lesson in stone carving. At the time, I was a bit confused about it all and I didn't have a clue about what Sal meant with light being like a young women or about life or a rainbow. But that didn't matter. What mattered to me was feeling like I was special. It was like Sal was always a part of me. Like we knew each other forever. When Sal invited me to come back the next day, I couldn't wait to run home and tell Mom.

On my second day with Sal, and every day for weeks after that, I practiced carving twenty-six blocks that Sal molded from plaster of Paris. Each one marked on one of its six sides with a penciled outline of a letter in one of six styles or *fonts*. Then he made ten more with the numbers zero through nine. Some, he'd tell me to carve in relief, others to engrave. He didn't push me or criticize. If I made a mistake, he'd show me how to fix it. "Everybody they make the mistakes," he'd say. "It's fools don't know how to fix them."

He could make me shrink to an inch high just by looking at me. Once, in anger at myself for not being able to get a number right, I tossed the chisel onto the bench. It rolled and landed on the floor. Sal was out back at the time, racking some stone with a forklift, so how he heard it I don't know—but he did. He didn't come running, just walked in deliberately, squinting his eyes at me like he was aiming a gun and I was the target. When he was just a couple inches from my face, he looked down at the chisel, then back at me. I bent over and picked it up. I put it into his outstretched hand.

"Go home," he said.

I wanted to cry, but managed to hold back the tears as I walked over to the door.

"Tomorrow," he said as I left.

I was so relieved, I let myself cry.

The next day, he told me that when he was an apprentice, if he'd dropped a chisel he would've been beaten senseless. He might even have been made to sleep outside and fed bread and water for a week. "Drop a chisel when you're sixty feet up the side of a building and somebody could get killed," he lectured.

I never dropped a chisel again.

He told me other things about his childhood, too, mostly about being hit or fighting with other boys, or having to work fifteen hours a day. His parents had given him a choice of becoming a priest or a carver. It hadn't been much of a decision, he told me.

Most of the time, Sal was patient. When I screwed up, he'd say, *Do it again*, or *That's-a no good*, and of course *Dio mio*. When I really messed up, I'd get a *Jesus, Mary, and Joseph* or *Jesu priest*. He praised me, too. When I did a particularly good job on something, he'd rub my head and say, *bellisimo* or *perfecto*, or my favorite, *bravo*.

Every day, Sal had a new problem for me to work on. It wasn't easy but it was fun. At the end of the summer, Sal put up a display of my work in the alley right outside his shop. It was just a couple of boards set on horses, lined with six alphabets and ten numbers in different styles. A sign read, *The Work of Jim Robertson*.

Workers from the other shops came by to admire my carvings and congratulate me. When Mom appeared, Sal went right over to her and told her all about how good my work was. She even gave him a hug and told him that he was a gift from God. He blushed and thanked her. By the end of the day, my head was as big as a tow truck.

When it was time to return to school, I missed the long days at Sal's shop. The first week or so, I'd run over there after school, but always found it locked up and empty. Clearly, Sal was sticking to his schedule of locking up around two; he had no intention of deviating from it for my sake.

One afternoon, about ten days into the school year, Sal

came to our place. "You want-a to work?" he asked me.

I flew down those eighteen concrete steps faster than water over a dam. It turned out he'd been away visiting his daughter. From then on, he kept the shop open until five during school months.

When I look back to those early days with Sal, I know that he had planned it as a test, to see if I had the soul of a carver. If I could see the *luce*. If I could come to appreciate the mysterious connection between a craftsman and his tools. He would tell me years later that he had been ready to quit carving then. He'd been at it more than sixty years and was very proud of his work, but he despaired for lack of an apprentice. "To pass on the craft," he told me once, "is to live forever."

Once I became a regular at his shop, he'd take me on jaunts around Milwaukee. He called it *frogging around*—hopping from one place to another. He showed me hundreds of his carvings all over the city. Most were gravestones, but he'd also created memorials for the DAR, Veterans of Foreign Wars, The Knights of Columbus. He even did storefront repairs. We went into quiet churches lit by candles and filled with statues. All of Sal's work was in marble or limestone. He hated granite, which he called *pietra del diavolo,* "devil stone." "No *luce*—no soul," he said. He'd also rant about what people wanted chiseled into his tombstones. "Born and die. Is that it? A person's life nothing but name and dates! *Dio mio.*"

Soon, I started spending every day with Sal. I learned that his wife, Maria, had died three years earlier. He had two grown children, a boy and a girl, but they had moved away. He never mentioned any grandchildren or other relatives.

Once in a while, somebody would stop by the shop. They'd

talk with Sal in Italian for a few minutes, and that would be that. Most days, around ten in the morning, Sal would take me to a diner about a mile south on Kinnickinnic Avenue. Everybody knew him there. Years later, whenever I saw the television show *Cheers*, I'd think of Sal and me walking into the Red Stripe Diner to a chorus of "Hi, boys." Sal didn't care that I was nine years old. If I wanted coffee, he'd buy me a cup, laced with cream and sugar. And we always shared a slice of banana cream pie.

Back at the shop, we'd work until noon, have lunch from Sal's battered old lunchbox, or I'd bring a mayonnaise sandwich, which Sal thought was *rifiuto di pano*—a waste of bread. After lunch, it was back to work until two or three, whenever he wanted to quit.

5

School didn't seem the same since my summer with Sal. Geography meant finding the world's great quarries—I became obsessed with *foraminifera*. I wrote a paper describing the difference between sedimentary rocks and igneous rocks and got an A. I went to the library and checked out any book I could find about stone. I studied different kinds of limestone, from the rough stuff to the illustrious Carrara. I had little interest in after-school activities with one exception. Her name was Ginger. She was my new art teacher. And that *activity,* which occurred during my senior year, came at a high cost.

But school was just an interruption in what I considered to be my "real" life. Every day, I rushed home, changed my clothes, and ran over to Sal's shop. I had few friends and—ever since Billy Parsons had broken out in some strange rash that his parents blamed on Westen's Chrome plating—none whose parents would let them come to the alley to play. For what it's worth, I'd been playing in Westen's since I was little kid and had never suffered more than a burning sensation in my nose.

Sometimes, Sal worked on Saturday, but never on Sunday. The alley was deserted on Sunday, so, to keep myself occupied on the loneliest day of the week, I made up a Sunday game. I called it Saving Dad. It was up to me to free him. I'd sneak around the empty alley as if it were a heavily guarded prison in Korea. I killed a lot of imaginary Chinese and North Koreans during those raids, finally freeing Dad and making Mom very proud and happy.

I used to hope that somehow my Sunday game would become real, so we could move to a house. I thought about dad a lot, and not just on Sundays. Maybe he was alive somewhere. If he was dead, where was his body? For Mom, each day was greeted with the hope that Dad would somehow come home and everything would be life as it should be. "Your Dad is always with us," she'd say. Of course for me as a child *life as it should be* was what I was living. I was pretty lonely and would like to have more friends my age to play with. As I grew older, I realized that my father was not coming home, though I never told Mom that I felt that way. Even so, I missed my father very much. I still do. *MIA* is cruel.

In time, my apprenticeship with Sal advanced to the rudi-ments of carving fleurs-de-lis, various vines, roses, and other flowers. I got really good at doing the finger nails on some of Sal's statues. When I had been carving for about three years, Sal told me about the hidden messages that he incorporated into his work. "Nobody live just years," he said. "They live life. They eat and cut the grass and have kids. They make the mistakes like everybody does. They pray to God to save them. They do things people remember. Maybe make good root beer, or grow the best peas, or become the best baker in the neighborhood. Everybody is remembered for something. The way they wear their clothes or makeup. Small things. Personal things," he told me. When Sal carved a memorial, he always put something into the carving that was specifically about that person. He hid these things.

I'd finish a fleur-de-lis and he'd come over and command, "Watch!" With a tiny chisel, he'd carve a message. The first time he showed me, he carved, "Your dandelion wine is the best." The stone was for the grave of one of the guys that went to the same barber shop that Sal did. He didn't know the guy all that well, only that whenever Sal got his hair cut, he'd get a glass of Dom's dandelion wine. He told me that to him, the wine was what made Dom Dom and not a father or a guy who worked the primary forge at Briggs & Stratton. Dom was the guy who made wine, and Sal thought he should be remembered for that.

"I get it," I said, "but…why hide it?"

Sal looked at me like I was crazy. "You want somebody who doesn't know the man to think something bad? If I do it right, only those who know him well get the message. They feel the words, they don't see them. They go to visit his grave and say something like, *Hey, Dom made the best wine, huh?* And they nudge each other and remember him. They don't got to see the words to get the feeling."

From that moment on I'd practice hiding things, too, trying to fool Sal. And I got him more often than not! I think I got better at hiding messages than he was. I wondered what I could hide in my father's gravestone—if there ever was one. What were the little things about my Dad that made him special?

6

Hans Biettermeir's Stein Works, across the alley from Sal's place, wasn't like Bumpy's or Westen's; it was more orderly and felt damp like it does after it rain. I didn't go there much. The workers were mostly women who did the designs with what they called *glazing*. Two men, Mexicans who didn't speak much English, mixed clay and fired the kilns. I never saw Hans at the other places in the alley, but he came over to Sal's a lot, maybe three or four times a week. He always asked about Mom and if we needed anything, and how I was doing at Lutheran School.

I was about ten years old when Hans built a new house on Lake Michigan. He invited me and Mom to the housewarming party, but Mom decided not to go. Instead, she made a tray of peanut-butter cookies for me to take and I went with Sal.

I'd never known such places existed. The house was huge, with big windows overlooking Lake Michigan. I was the only kid there, but I had a good time mainly because of Miss Gumpfrey, Hans's housekeeper. I helped her in the kitchen and did small tasks like dumping ash trays and keeping the ice bucket filled. I guess she took a liking to me because after that, Hans would take me home once a week or so for some of Miss Gumpfrey's potato pancakes.

I used to help grate the potatoes for her. She'd squeeze out the water with a piece of cheesecloth, mix in some onion, an egg or two, a little sugar, salt and nutmeg. I'd eat them with catsup or sometimes Miss Gumpfrey would sprinkle one of them with sugar. I could eat a hundred of her potato pancakes. She always sent me home with a container of soup or a plate of dumplings, or a hearty chunk of roast beef or pork—enough to last three or four days.

Like I said before, it wasn't unusual for Hans to come by Sal's shop at the end of the day, so I wasn't surprised when he showed up during Christmas break of my senior year. I was sprawled out on a beat-up overstuffed couch in Sal's office, which was just a walled-off corner of the shop. In addition to the couch, it had a desk and chair, a coal heater, and a wrecked La-Z-Boy that refused to recline more than a few inches.

"Where's Sal?" Hans asked me.

"He's taking a leak," I said, not even looking up from one of Sal's old copies of *Popular Mechanics.*

Sal came out, zipping his pants and kicking the door shut in one fluid motion. "Hey, *compagno!*" he said cheerfully to his friend.

Hans walked over to him and in a dead-serious tone, said, "We need to talk."

"So…talk," Sal said.

Hans looked at me then back to Sal. "Outside."

"*Mumma mia!*" Sal threw up his hands like he was annoyed,

but followed Hans to the door.

They were outside for maybe ten minutes, and when they came back, Sal looked like he'd swallowed vinegar. Hans sat down in the La-Z-Boy, but Sal came straight over and stood scowling down at me like he'd done that day years ago when I dropped the chisel.

I glanced over at Hans, who was looking at the floor. Turning back to Sal, I asked, "What's going on?"

Ignoring me, Sal went over to the stove and opened its cast-iron door. Bluish-orange flames danced on the clean grate. He tossed in a shovel full of coal chunks and the fire started crackling and spitting little stars out of the opening like miniature fireworks. He slammed the door with a clank that came at me like a gunshot, then jammed the shovel back into the scuttle and turned to face me.

"Hans tells me that the trustees at your school just had a meeting."

"And?" I said, sitting up.

"*Ginger.* You know that name?"

"I…yeah…ah…Miss Anderson. She's my art teacher."

I could feel myself getting red. It really was none of their business or anybody else's what went on between me and Ginger. For years I went to school then rushed home to work in Sal's shop. I helped Mom with keeping up the apartment and even cooked once in a while. I had few friends, didn't play sports or any of that stuff. Being with Ginger was the first time I experienced who I was, just me being me. Not as Sal's apprentice or helping Mom's caretaker. And I'd be damned if I had to explain myself.

"She's more than your art teacher from what Hans tells me.

And that's-a no good. *Dio mio*, Jimmy Boy." Shaking his head and mumbling to himself, Sal turned and walked away from me. I turned to look at Hans.

"I….I don't understand. What does my private life have to do with the Board of Trustees? It's none of their damn business."

Sal went over to his desk. He rummaged through the top drawer and got a Perodi cigar. Perodis look like little dried dog turds and smell worse. He lit the thing and puffed on it until a blue haze layered itself close to the ceiling. Then he went back over to the door and stood like he was guarding it. Pointing the cigar at Hans he asked, "So, what do we need to do?"

Hans slid forward on the La-Z-Boy. He rested his elbows on his thighs, looked over at me, and said, "Jim, the trustees are asking you to leave school."

"What! Me?" I turned to look at Hans. "I'm being expelled?" I sputtered. "Why?"

"Jesus, Mary and Joseph," Sal butted in, jabbing his Perodi into the air. "That's-a not right. That teacher, she's the one should be tossed out, not Jimmy. He needs to graduate. Dio mio!"

"Dammit, Sal," Hans shot back, "Calm down, and while you're at it the smell of that thing is killing us."

Murmuring curses I knew to be some of the worst in his vast repertoire, Sal marched over to the stove, opened the door, and tossed the cigar inside. *"Fanculo!"* he declared.

"Miss Anderson's already gone," Hans told me. "She left yesterday. To where, who knows. But let's not get off track here. At this point, it's your future we need to be concerned about."

"Ginger was fired? This is pure bullshit!"

"I'm not finished, Jim, so just listen: You're not being expelled. They're not throwing you out. They're asking you to leave early, right away, diploma included. It's a good offer but it's up to you. We can talk more about this tomorrow." Hans turned to Sal. "I think maybe you two best talk things over." And with that, Hans left.

I stared at Sal for a long time before murmuring, "I...I don't know what to say." Sal didn't respond.

"She taught me a lot about art. We even went to the Art Institute in Chicago—she had me pick up an application to go there."

"Sounds like she taught you a lot more than just going to some art school," Sal said brusquely.

"So what? I'm eighteen! And since when is my private life anybody else's business? Don't my feelings count for anything? Screw this!" I got up and headed for the door. Sal raised his hands like he was surrendering.

"Sit back down, Jimmy Boy. We can figure this out. C'mon Sit down. What d'ya say?"

Reluctantly, I returned to the couch.

Sal grabbed a wire-backed chair he kept near the stove, plopped it down in front of me and straddled it. "Now I tell you something," he said leaning forward like he didn't want anyone to hear what he had to say. "I'll tell you something that I never tell anybody and now I'm telling you. Sometime before I married Maria, I did it with a girl named Angela. We were only seventeen so it wasn't with a teacher, I'll tell you that, or I'd be sitting here like *il eunuco*. We sinned, and I pray to God that we wouldn't be too long in *purgatorio* for that." Sal sat back and raised his right index finger, which he used to punctuate his talk. "You know...on one side you got the love. On the other side not far away, you got the lust. Angela and me, we had the lust. Maria and me, we had the love. So, you Jimmy Boy, you had the lust?"

"I was in love, Sal. I still am." Sal glared at me.

"So, you never told old Sal about this?"

"It was private, Sal. Maybe the first time I had something all to myself. Do you understand?"

"Yeah, I do. So when did all this start?"

"In the fall. She was our new art teacher. Really pretty. I mean, really. Everything she did drove me crazy. The way she talked and walked. Everything Sal. Even—"

"Jesu priest! Enough! So, how long were you getting in this teacher's pants?"

"Geez Sal, it wasn't like that." I got up and paced about. "We stopped seeing each other in early November. November 2nd, to be exact. We were together for only two months. And for the record, I miss her."

"Do you love this girl?"

"Yeh. I think so."

"Think? You think so? You don't-a know?"

"I know how she made me feel."

"Uh-huh. That's what old Sal thought. It's the lust. That's what it is. We all feel the lust, Jimmy Boy. Even an old man like me," he chuckled. "But the love. When you feel the love, everything it changes. And the love, it never goes away. You remember when you first saw the *Luce di Dio*."

"Yeah, and?"

"The light in the stone. That's-a like the love. You see the light that's inside the person. You don't see that, the love it's not there. And I tell you one more thing, to get to the *Luce*, it takes the trust and the courage to find it. You know, like opening the stone. You must be gentle, not to hit the hammer too hard. *Capire?*"

I really was not in the mood for a sermon. I wanted outta there.

He got up from his chair and came over to me. "*Il fulmine,*" he said. "That's the beginning. Do you know what that means?" I shook my head. "*Il fulmine.* Go ahead, Jimmy. You say that."

I stood and said half-heartedly, "*Il fulmine.*"

"*Mama mia,* this is the thunderbolt. You say it like this…" With fists punching high in the air, Sal shouted, "*Fulmine!*" Eyeballing me he said, "We do it together."

Reluctantly, I joined Sal and fell into a chant, repeating over and over, "*Fulmine! Fulmine! Fulmine!*"

"Bravo, Jimmy Boy. Now you know. The teacher, she was the lust. When you find the one true love, you feel the *fulmine.* You will see the *Luce di Dio.* You got that, Jimmy Boy?"

"I got it Sal, I got it."

"*Bene, bene.* Now, go home to bed."

I left and took a slow walk home. *Miss Anderson's already gone. She left yesterday.* Han's words were like knife blades. She could've called or dropped by or whatever. But to just leave me without saying a word hurt like hell.

Jingling bells from a wreath Mom had hung on the door announced my arrival.

"Is that you?" she called out cheerfully.

"Yeah," I said. "Who else?" I took off my coat and hung it on the usual hook just inside the door.

"Tea or hot chocolate?"

"I don't want anything right now." I skulked over to my

favorite chair and flopped down. Mom came in from the kitchen.

"Is there something wrong?"

"I've got a bit of a problem."

"Oh, dear," she said, perching on the arm of the chair. "What kind of problem, James?" Mom got formal like that when she wanted answers.

"I was just over at Sal's when Hans came by and told me that the school wants me to graduate early, diploma and all. They want me out now. Hans said it was up to me."

"What's up to you?"

"Whether or not I leave now or try and stay until graduation."

"Why do they want you to leave school now?"

"Because...well, because...because I had an affair with my art teacher," I blurted out.

"You what!" Mom said then fell silent, stood and walked over to the front window. Staring down on the alley below she asked quietly, "What do you mean that you were having an affair?" A very long minute or so passed. When I didn't answer, Mom turned, looked at me and said "Well?"

"It just happened, Mom,"

Taking her time, she walked over to me and asked, "She isn't pregnant, is she?"

"No, Mom! Jesus!"

"Well, *that's* a blessing, anyway. When did this all happen?"

Reluctantly, I told Mom, "It was with our new art teacher. Just out of college. Anyway, it all started when we she took me to the art museum to see the sculpture garden. I guess she liked the way I carved stone and all that. And well, like I just said, it just happened."

I abruptly stopped, got out of the chair and paced around

the room. "Dammit Mom, don't I deserve a little privacy? This is something I really don't want to talk about right now. Let me just say that we broke up. I mean it didn't last very long. They fired her. She's gone."

Mom came over to me, put her hand on my shoulder and said. "I understand, Jim. I may not be so good at this sort of thing, but I'm the only parent you've got and I love you. We'll get through this." She kissed me on the forehead and said, "If you want something to eat, just let me know."

7

When morning came, I didn't feel much like getting out of bed. I had tossed and turned all night, thinking about what I might do next. I wondered if anybody at school would miss me...if they'd even care that I was gone.

This thing with Ginger meant a lot more to me than I was willing to share with Mom, Sal, or Hans, or anybody else for that matter. Having sex for the first time, I mean, nobody forgets that. And I was damn sure that it was nobody's business but mine. But our relationship went far beyond jumping into bed; she was only four years older than me, but way beyond me in terms of experience. She made me realize that my world was really small. Basically, I spent my life with Mom, Hans, and Sal. I felt safe and loved and all that, but there was little opportunity for me to figure out who I was. Being with Ginger, a part of me came alive, even if she left without saying good-bye. Maybe it was time for me to open my own block of stone. Find my own light. *Luce di* Jimmy Boy.

I dozed off and on, and it was almost noon when I finally

got dressed and went into the kitchen, Hans was seated at the table, a cup of coffee in hand. Looking my direction, Mom asked. "Coffee?"

I nodded, said hi to Hans and sat down. Mom brought me a cup of coffee, and asked me if I'd slept well. She made no mention of our talk the previous night.

"I can't say I did, Mom," I answered.

"Hans and I were talking about what you might do now that you're graduating early," she said. "Have you given it any thought, Jim?"

"That's all I've been thinking about," I said, looking from one of them to the other. "That's what was keeping me awake. I… should probably get a job…maybe take some college classes, too. I was thinking about asking Sal if he'd hire me. I don't know."

"There's so much to think about. Why don't I let you two have a nice man-to-man talk. I'll be in my room if you need anything." She kissed me on the cheek and left the kitchen.

Hans broke the silence. "I saw Sal this morning before coming over here. I want you to know that we're not judging you for what went on and I know this whole thing doesn't seem fair. But let's put your time with Miss Anderson aside for now and focus on your future."

"She meant a lot to me, Hans. It wasn't all about sex. I want you to know that."

"I do, Jim. Trust me, I do. But it's time to move forward. You're old enough to understand that life can be tough. You've experienced loss. You know what it feels like to be good at something, and what it feels like to screw up and pay the price. The thing is, as you get older, it's all about choice. Making decisions. And you're facing some of those right now…like, what are you going to do with the next phase of your life?"

I got up from the table, walked over to the kitchen sink, and looked out the window into the backyard. I thought about the application for the Art Institute sitting on my dresser. I'd promised myself most every day that I'd fill it out when I got home from school, but something was holding me back; I just couldn't do it. I'd escape the thought by going over to Sal's to carve. When it came down to it, that's pretty much what I'd been doing since I was a kid; escaping to Sal's.

I turned around and looked at Hans. "Anyway, I have to think about Mom."

Hans stood and came over to me.

"Your mom is a lot tougher than you know. Trust me. That's something we can talk about later." Clearing his throat to change the subject, Hans said, "Has Sal ever invited you to his house?"

"No."

"Do you ever wonder why?"

"Sure…I've thought about it."

"I bring it up because I want you to understand something. When Sal's wife Maria died, he was devastated. Knowing Sal, he'd probably never given any real thought to living life without her. He was…well…kind of a ghost. And then good old fate stepped in and you appeared. Has Sal ever talked to you about his kids?"

"Not much," I answered. "All I know is he has a son and a daughter."

"You've been hanging around with Sal for—what is it? Around ten years? Do you think it's odd that you've never met his children?"

"I never really thought about it much," I said, but I was lying. I'd thought about it. If my dad was around, I'd want to be with him all the time. How could Sal's kids just disappear? As far as I was concerned, they were ingrates. But the truth is … maybe I really didn't *want* them to show up. Maybe I kind of wanted Sal to myself.

"When Sal's kids graduated," Hans continued, "they left town so fast you'd think they were escaping from prison. Sal never talked about it with me, but my guess is that he was one strict papa. So then he was alone. Jim…I'm not sure Sal would have made it if you hadn't shown up."

"I don't know if I'd have made it either. He…he's been like a father to me.

"Yes, I can see that. It's been an honest-to-god two-way street—good for both of you—but it's more than that, too. You became his apprentice, and good one, at that. It's not every day a craftsman like Sal gets a chance to pass on what he knows. You need to take some credit here, too, Jim. It's not just that Sal has taught you things. It's that you've learned. Being a good learner is what defines a good teacher. You can't have one without the other.

"I remember how proud he was about those plaster blocks you did in the beginning. He seemed as young as I've ever seen him. Passing on what he knows to someone younger is Sal's way of living forever. That said, Jim, this conversation—the decisions you're making about your future—this is all about you; not Sal or your mother, but you."

I turned back to look out the window and said, "You understand, don't you?

"Yes Jim, I think I do. Now there's no one on this green

earth that wouldn't praise you for all you've done for your mother—and for Sal, too. But there comes a time when you need to think about yourself. I would bet that both of them want you to move on with your life, build on who you are and see what you might become."

I turned back to look at Hans. "Even so…I'm all Mom has, Hans. I can't just walk away from her. I just couldn't do that. We both know that my dad isn't coming home."

"Excuse me, you two."

We both looked over to see Mom standing in the doorway. She was wearing a white sweater and a pleated blue knee-length skirt she hadn't worn in years.

She smiled at me then looked at Hans and said, "Why don't you tell Jim what you and I talked about before lazybones, here, got out of bed?"

"Well, Jim," Hans said, "this being Christmas Eve, I've invited you two over to my place for a celebration and your mom agreed to come. Miss Gumpfrey will have everything ready, including the guest rooms so you can stay overnight. That sound good, Mary?"

"Yes, it certainly does. That is, if Jim doesn't have other plans…"

"Sounds great."

"It's all set, then," Hans chimed in. He walked over to the front door and put on his overcoat. Before leaving, he turned to me and said, "Oh, Jim, Sal wants you to stop by. How about I come back here around four this afternoon and pick you two up? It's going to be a wonderful Christmas!"

After Hans left, I turned to Mom. "What brought all this on? I mean, it's nice of Hans and all, but you've barely stepped out of the house for—what? It's been years, Mom."

"Why don't we go into the living room and talk about it, Jim. Would that be okay?"

I nodded and followed her to the sofa. We sat in silence for a moment, then Mom said, "Jim…last night when you told me about this…this *thing* you had with that teacher, I really didn't know what to think. I still don't. What I do know is that you're lucky she didn't get pregnant and that you didn't get expelled. You know that, don't you?"

"Mom, yes. I…I'm really sorry if you're ashamed of me."

"It isn't about what I think, James. And no, I'm not ashamed of you. But this *fling,* or whatever you call it, could have really messed up your life. You got off easy, James. I hope you know that. Life doesn't always give us a chance like this."

"Yes, Mom, I know."

"I've thought about my own role in this, James. I guess I've been a little too lax with you over the years; letting you run around, do what you want. I know some of the blame here is mine."

"No, Mom, don't say that!"

Mom stood and walked over to front window She was quiet for a few moments before turning to look at me.

"Listen, James," she said. "I want to tell you something important. Are you ready to listen?"

I nodded.

She took a deep breath and held my gaze. "James…it seems like one day you were my sweet little boy, the next you were a young man with a life of your own and…*grown-up problems.* As much as I love our life here together, I've made up my mind. It's time for you to move on with things. And that means going to school or getting a job, or whatever you want to do—wherever you want to do it. It means getting on with your own life—not worrying about me all the time. And James…I know this is what your father would want, too. I…I heard what you said to Hans—about Dad not coming home."

"Mom, I—"

"Let me finish. I miss your father every day, James, and pray for his return—but I'm not living in a fantasy. I've come to accept that there's very little chance we'll get him back, but that tiny ray of hope keeps me going. I expect I'll hang on to that until I die. The thing you need to understand is that I'm stronger than you think. And one reason for it is that your father *is* alive in one very important way. He lives in *you.* That gives me the strength to do what I know I must, and it should do the same for you. It should help you move on with your life. And if that means leaving Milwaukee, then that is what you must do."

My mouth opened, but nothing came out. I guess I didn't know what to say—we'd never really talked like this.

"You asked me why I accepted Hans's invitation to spend Christmas at his house and you're right that I seldom leave our place." Mom said. "But it's time that I do. I need to get on with what life I have left. Now, why don't you run off to Sal's while I pack things for tonight?"

I got up from the sofa and walked over to Mom. "I love you Mom," I said, giving her a kiss on her cheek.

"I love you, too," she said. "Now go." Catching herself, she added, "I baked Sal a tin of cookies. They're in the kitchen. Let me go and get them."

I went to the door and grabbed my coat. Mom handed me the tin and I was on my way.

8

There was no smell to compare with that of Sal's office. Over the years, a mixture of Perodi cigar smoke and sulfur fumes from the coal stove had etched itself into every crevice, every pore, every bit of cloth, and finally into every neuron of my own olfactory memory. For me, the smell of that room represented peace and security. And so it was on that Christmas Eve morning, as I settled into the old couch. After putting the tin of cookies on his desk and making me swear that I'd give Mom a big thank-you hug, Sal parked himself in his wire-backed chair. He got right to the point.

"You have the talent. You have the feel for the stone. You see the *Luce di Dio*. You don't learn this in school. Nobody can teach it to you. But the talent goes no place without the learning. The sweat, the practice, knowing what tool to use and when, how hard or soft to strike the chisel, how to turn a thought into something real, that is the learning.

"I watch you work the stone. I hear the touch you bring to the chisel I hear your curses when you screw-up. I hear the soft murmurs when you talk to the talent inside of yourself. And all of that is what is rare. But, now here is the hard part, the rare of the rare: To do all that over a lifetime. Not as a hobby or something to do on a rainy day. But forever.

"The easy thing for you to do is come here and work, but that's no good for you. You need to fly, Jimmy, fly out like a bird that leaves the nest. You must or you will never learn who you are. And if you don't learn that, then the talent, it goes to waste. That's why you can't stay here."

"You sound like Mom," I said. Sal gave me a big grin.

"*Mamma sa meglio*, Jimmy Boy. Mamma, she knows best."

We both stood. I wondered if Sal was invited to Hans's for Christmas Eve. As I was trying to decide whether it would be right to ask him as much, he informed me that he had to leave, to go and help get his church ready for Christmas Mass. "Me and Maria, we always go to the church for the Christmas Eve," he said. "One last thing before you go. Wait here." Sal disappeared into the shop and was back in a few minutes. Handing me a small, heavy canvas bag, "For the Merry Christmas," he said. Inside were a set of prime chisels, the ones Sal kept to himself. The ones he never let me touch.

"But Sal…"

"It is time, Jimmy Boy. I'm closing up shop. It's time for old Sal to retire. Now go."

Hanging from the eaves and covering the shrubbery, twinkling lights greeted us as we pulled into Hans's driveway. Inside, a fully decorated spruce tree stood in front of the huge window overlooking Lake Michigan. Mom was clearly awestruck at the grandeur of the place. After settling into the lavish guest quarters,

Mom and I joined Hans and Miss Gumpfrey in the living room. Mom was in Wonderland. Drawn to the tree, she walked slowly toward it, her hand gently caressing the backs of upholstered chairs and sofas. Her eyes scanned the tree soaring upward into the lofty ceiling. A haloed angel dressed in shimmering white topped the tree. Miss Gumpfrey joined her. After a moment of softly talking to each other, Miss Gumpfrey asked Mom to join her in the kitchen. "We need to get the eggnog and some nice cookies," she said. "We're going to have such a good time."

A yule log crackled in the large stone fireplace. Raising our glasses of spiked eggnog, Hans gave a toast: "To friends" he declared. "To all those we love and to all those who love us."

And so began one of the best Christmases I ever had, before or since. Modest gift-giving, quiet talk, and an array of foods that ran the gamut from fruit-filled crepes for breakfast to a succulent stuffed turkey with all the trimmings for Christmas dinner filled the days. There was no mention of school or my future…just laughter and aimless chatter among genuine friends. I swear, Mom looked ten years younger by the time we'd packed up to leave.

On the way home late Christmas day, Hans took a slight detour about a mile from his place, into a driveway marked by a sign that said *Laurel Hill Village*. He explained that the village was a new place where older people mingle with younger people each sharing common spaces including an exercise room, a place to have parties, a reading room, and a small library. "They have a healthcare facility which includes assisted living and a nursing home." Turning to me, he said, "Jim, we both thought maybe you'd want to see this."

Not really knowing what to make of it, I just gaped out the

window at the snow-dusted lawns and handsome, low-slung brick buildings all hung with holiday lights. "Mom…is there something you want to tell me?" I asked.

"In due time," Mom said, making it clear the conversation was over.

In due time came just after the new year. One night after dinner, as Mom and I were clearing the table together, she said, "You know…I've been thinking about that Laurel Hill Village. It was lovely, don't you think? It's quite expensive to live there, but if we sold our place…and combined that with what I receive from the Army, we could afford it. Of course," she added, "you would need to find your own place."

"I think you're right," I said, feeling like Mom was giving me a clear signal that life as I knew it was about to change whether I liked it or not. I thought about what Hans had said about moving on with my life, Sal retiring and encouraging me to see the world, and now Mom tossing me from the nest. It was time for me to get going. To where, I had no idea.

As it turned out, the answer came in the form of a recruitment ad I received from the US Army.

I enlisted on January 3, 1968.

Beth

JUNE 19–20, 1993

9

I liked the idea of going on a mission, as Smithy Paulson called it. Mom's car would get me there. It's a thirteen-year-old powder-blue Plymouth Horizon with 53,000 miles on it. She didn't drive much—to church, mostly. She worked part-time as a clerk in Rhey's Pharmacy, but walked there most of the time. Mr. Gianelli, Heidi's dad, had me take the car to his mechanic for, as he put it, "a complete look over."

Dwayne, the mechanic, changed the oil and checked the brakes, tires, and cooling system before pronouncing it ready for the road. Before I left, he made sure that I knew how to check the oil and tire pressure, and cautioned me to keep an eye on the temperature gauge. "If it gets too near the red, stop someplace and have them check the coolant," he warned.

Heidi's dad mapped my trip out for me on one of those TripTiks from AAA, and I started wishing they'd taught us to read a road map in school. He said that I should avoid Chicago—that it's like a nuthouse up there—a yellow high-lighted line on the map took me around Indianapolis, then west into Illinois. To Bloomington of all places. "The yellow brick road," Heidi's mom called it.

The night before I left, I had dinner with Jake. Prior to my parents' accident and learning that I had a sister, Jake and I had already planned to have a going-away dinner for just the two of us. Jake had enlisted in the Navy, hoping to become a Navy Seal, and was leaving for basic training in the morning. As it turned out, he'd be on his way to join the Navy while I was on my way to Wisconsin. We ended the evening promising to stay in touch. I dropped a few tears. I think Jake Keck might mean more to me than I'm willing to admit. I'm going to miss him. I hope that we can stay in touch.

Going around Indianapolis was no big deal and I probably could have done the same with Chicago. I was a bit nervous because I'd never driven on an Interstate highway before. It took some getting used to but once I settled into the flow of traffic, I calmed down. I couldn't believe how much traffic there was, especially those big tractor-trailers that zoomed by me like I was standing still. I crossed over into Illinois around 10:30; another first for me, being out of Indiana. It wasn't even noon when I saw a sign for Bloomington. I'd gone from Bloomington, Indiana, to Bloomington, Illinois, which, for some reason made me laugh out loud even though nobody could hear me.

Heidi's dad had suggested I stay overnight there, and had even made me a reservation at the Best Western right off Exit 2A. The motel looked like one of the dorms at IU, only stuck in the middle of a parking lot. I stopped there, sat in the car, and ate one of the three ham sandwiches that Heidi's mom had packed. She always puts some kind of mayonnaise or salad dressing on her sandwiches, which isn't so bad, but she could keep the all-grain bread. It's like eating cardboard with bits of wood chips thrown in.

I decided I wanted to keep driving, and went inside to try and cancel the reservation. It turned out to be no problem; Mr. Gianelli won't be charged. He was even going to pay for the room and I never even knew it. The clerk said she'd make reservations for me someplace else if I wanted her to, but I told her that I didn't know where I'd be.

As I walked out of the motel, I took a good look at the Horizon. Mom had taken really good care of it, and there wasn't a dent or scratch anywhere; just shiny powder-blue, like a robin's egg. I guess it was the one thing that was truly hers—her getaway car. A monster SUV parked two spots over made Mom's car look like a pretty toy, or a little hussy messing with the big boys. I tapped her roof and declared, "I christen thee Hussy."

Before getting back on the road, I checked out the map that Heidi's dad gave me. He had written a note that said I should get on Interstate 39 and head north. Easily done with the entrance ramp just past the motel. I popped a cassette in the tape player, turned up the volume, and headed onto the highway heading north. Pete Paulson had been right when he said I was on a mission. Finding Anna was my search for the Holy Grail.

I wasn't expecting Anna to take me in or anything; I didn't even know if she knew I existed. But I did kind of hope she'd like me. I mean, what if she didn't want me around? I fought negative thoughts like that by saying "Aunt Beth" over and over.

I wondered what she looked like. Did she have long hair or short? Brown or blonde? Blue eyes or brown? Was she tall or short? I decided she must have blue eyes like mine, light brown hair like Mom's, and that she was five-foot-seven, which is two inches taller than me. I bet she didn't wear a stud in her nose though, and I doubted she had purple hair with streaks of blond.

Mr. Paulson had said that Jim was a stone carver. It made me think of those old *Dragnet* shows that opened with this big hand pounding the number VII into a piece of stone. That's how I pictured Jim: a guy with big, sweaty hands banging a chisel.

The drive north was boring: huge farms cleaved by this band of concrete. But it wasn't ugly given that everything was covered with every shade of green you could ask for. When Hussy and I crossed into Wisconsin, I let out a whoop and blew her horn. I'd never been in three states in one day before. It's really interesting how things seem to change abruptly from one state to the next: the trees, the landscape. It's like you could tell you were in a new place even if there were no signs. Maybe that's how they drew up the map borders in the first place—just waited for things to change and drew a line. I wondered if my geography teacher, Miss Altameir would like that idea.

I made it to Janesville before dark and thought about just driving, but decided it was a little too late. Besides, I was still around 200 miles from Clayton. There was no way that I could get there tonight; I still had to find a motel and everything. I was thinking what it would be like when I got into Clayton: what if I were to bump into Anna at a restaurant or while I was getting gas or something? That would be weird, and not the way I wanted it to happen. I had this picture of meeting her: *Hello, my name is Beth, I'm your sister.* And then she'd give me a big hug. We'd get all teary-eyed, then go and have a long lunch. I'd meet my nieces or maybe a niece and a nephew, and her husband Jim would be like a big brother to me. Anyway, I knew that however the meeting happened, I wanted to be rested up for it.

I pulled in at the first motel I came to, one of these one-level, strung out places. It wasn't a chain, though—it was called DanAnns. I could hear Smithy Paulson warning me about staying in a dump, but I was too tired to keep room-hunting. I parked between two pick-ups and Hussy started flirting the moment I turned her off. The lobby, with its fake-wood-paneled walls and plastic furniture, was overseen by a tired-looking clerk who gave me a shifty what-are-you-doing-here look.

"You need a room, or just directions?"

"A room."

"How many nights?"

"One."

"Okay, then, we can do that. How will ya be payin'?"

The day after the funeral, Father Jamison had introduced me to a lawyer who was willing to handle my parents' legal stuff for a small fee. He'd told me not to worry, that I'd probably clear my parents' debts and still have a small inheritance left over. In the meantime, he set me up with a $3,000 bank loan that his firm guaranteed and my first credit card, which I handed over to the clerk. Transaction number one.

After I stashed my stuff in dingy little Room 7, I locked it behind me and came back to ask the clerk where I might get something to eat. Turns out the motel was near a small strip mall with a McDonalds, KFC, IHOP, and some small shops. I headed for the tried-and-true and got a Big Mac, fries, and one of those gluey shakes—chocolate-colored. I sat in a booth next to a window overlooking the parking lot. I'd eaten at McDonalds plenty of times, but always with friends, never alone.

It struck me that I was chalking up a lot of firsts: driving on an Interstate, staying in a motel, eating alone. The weird part is, I kind of liked the aloneness—at least so far.

After I ate, I headed back to the motel. I was pretty tired but there was no way I could sleep, and not just because of the saggy mattress. It was because I'd been going sixty-five all day. I just couldn't dial down to zero so quickly. I wondered how truckers got to sleep.

I laid awake thinking about Anna: what she looked like, how she wore her hair, how she dressed. I'd know all the answers and lots more the next day—or hoped I would. I was a little concerned about the fact that Heidi's dad hadn't been able to find Anna's phone number. Was it that she didn't have a phone? Maybe she was some kind of leftover hippie and preferred to be left alone. I had to stop thinking before I drove myself nuts.

Alone and away from home. I kept thinking about it. I could hear the TV in the next room and thought I recognized an old rerun of *The Hulk*. I kept getting up to check out Hussy like somebody might steal her or bang into her.

I spent the night tossing and turning and awoke to the raspy buzzing of the alarm clock. It took me a few seconds to figure out where I was, and when I got my bearings, I got up and went to the window. Hussy was just as I'd left her, safe and snug.

I headed to the bathroom, but one look at the crummy shower convinced me take a birdbath at the sink. The towels were thin but clean. I got dressed, packed up, checked out, and drove the short distance to the IHOP where I had breakfast. It was a little scary to think that I was this close to finding my sister. I mean it wasn't a sure bet or anything. According to the map, Eau Claire was around 200 miles north, which I guessed would take around three hours, then another 30 minutes to make it to Clayton. I'd be there by noon. My god is this real or what!

Wisconsin is nothing like Indiana. Everything was in full bloom down there, like it was summer already. Up here, it was more like springtime. There were more trees than I was used to, too—forests, almost—and lots of small farms that weren't at all like the gargantuan fields I passed by in Illinois. The more north I drove, the more I felt a sense of being in a special place. Still on the Interstate, I didn't feel as close to the land like I'd like to be, but it still felt like I belonged there. Maybe it's because Anna lives here.

There were only a few cars on the road, so I didn't have any trouble passing the occasional farm tractors and slow-moving trucks. I drove through Cadot, a small town that had a cheese factory right on the main street. A sign on the way out of town informed me that I was crossing the 45 North latitude. If I remembered my geography right, that was like where the Ukraine was. Short growing seasons, long winters. A little further north, my eye caught a farmer plowing, just turning at the far end of the field. Curious, I pulled over to the side of the road to watch. The plow was cutting ribbons through the dirt in perfectly straight rows. I'd never thought much about farming before. It actually looked like fun.

I drove through a town called Ladysmith and came close to stopping at someplace called the Indianhead Cafe—my IHOP breakfast being long gone by that time—but I was too antsy to get to Clayton. My stomach would just have to wait.

"Good Morning, Mom," I said out loud at one point, as if she were sitting right next to me. "I don't know much about you."

"What do you want to know?" she said—except it was me, answering for her.

"More than just that your maiden name is Phillips and you were born in Kentucky. And that you go to church a lot and work at Rhey's and like to knit and sew."

I had to stop the conversation at that point, since that's all I really knew about my mom. Maybe Anna could fill me in.

About twenty miles further north, I finally saw a sign for Clayton: Muskie Café, Clayton's Best Eatery, Two Miles. The sign was green and orange, with this ugly fish jumping out of the water to catch a monstrous cheeseburger. Lunch at last.

The Muskie Café would have fit right in on the TV series *Northern Exposure,* with its rough board siding and silver tin roof. The sign attached to the roof was a neon version of the billboard I'd seen on my way into town: a flashing orange fish grabbing at a green cheeseburger.

My stomach felt like that fish, and I realized I was more nervous than hungry. I mean, I was actually *in* Clayton, and it wasn't a big city or anything. I figured everybody must know everybody else. Anna could be inside right now, having one of those cheeseburgers, and I wouldn't even recognize her. I got out of the car, stretched, took a few really deep breaths, and went on in.

Three bearded men sitting at the U-shaped counter stared at me like I just flew in from Mars as I made my way to a table by a window. It had salt and pepper shakers shaped like ballet dancers, and a hand-written note was propped up against the sugar dispenser: Place mats woven by residents of the Creekside Nursing Home. Available for $1.50 at the counter. I used the shiny chrome napkin holder as a mirror to check myself out.

"I like your hair. Passing through?"

I looked up and saw the waitress standing over me with a menu. "Well…" I stammered, "I'm not…well I'm not really sure. Maybe I am."

"Oh, I'm sorry," she said. "Sometimes I'm just too nosy. But it's always nice to see a fresh face. I've lived here all my life. Name's Jill. What can I get you, honey—cup of coffee to start?"

Maybe Jill knows Anna, I thought. She seemed about the right age. "Just a Coke and a cheeseburger," I said. "I'm Beth, by the way."

"Well, Beth, welcome to the North Woods. I'll put your order in." She turned to leave.

"Actually," I said, "Can I ask you something?"

She turned back and smiled. "Sure, honey. Shoot."

"I'm here looking for someone…her name is Anna Robertson. I guess I was wondering…since you've lived here so long and all—"

"Hmmm, let's see. Robertson, you say? I don't think I know any Robertsons." Turning toward the counter, she called out, "You boys know anybody around here named Robertson?"

I could feel my face getting red as the three men at the counter looked me over, then huddled up like they had some secret or something. I was getting pretty antsy when one of the guys finally answered the waitress's question: "Yup, you bet, Don't you remember those folks who used to live out to Double J?"

"Used to?" I broke in, my stomach churning.

"Well…this was a good while back. It's not like I was friends with 'em…but I knew of 'em."

"How far back do you mean? A year, five years…?" My voice came out sounding a little desperate, and I looked down at the table to hide my tears.

"I don't know for sure…maybe ten years?"

Stunned, I didn't say anything, but I must've looked like I was going to cry or something, because Jill put her hand on my shoulder and said, "You okay, honey?"

"No…" I said, my voice coming out all trembly, "I'm not… okay…"

Jill reached over and grabbed a napkin. "Here," she said, "let me get your order in. You'll feel better after you eat something. Then we'll try and get to the bottom of things."

"The restroom?" I asked, wiping my eyes.

"Just over there," she said, pointing toward the back.

My cheeseburger and Coke were on the table when I got back, and my stomach grumbled at the smell. I sat down, took sip of soda, then bit into the best cheeseburger I've ever eaten. Jill came over just as I finished wolfing it down, which took about five minutes.

"Feeling better?" she asked.

"Much, thank you."

"Now, Beth, how can I help you?"

I'd decided to keep the details of my story to myself until I could think it through. If Anna and Jim had moved away, maybe they had a reason. I'd just have to find out what I could and try to track them down. But first, I wanted to see where they'd lived.

"Um…the old Robertson place that guy mentioned…is it very far from here?"

Turning to the man who'd spoken up, she said, "Sam, can you come over here, please?"

Sam was at least six feet tall, with a full beard, neatly trimmed, and dark brown eyes. His cap read "Prentice Hydraulics." When he arrived at the table, Jill asked him if he could give me directions to what he'd called "Double J."

"Well, yougouphighwayeighttillyoucometodoubleJthentakealeftgoforaboutamile—"

"Sam," Jill cut in, "how's this nice girl supposed to understand a thing you're saying? Slow down and tell her right."

"Sorry," Sam said, then repeated the directions slowly, one step at a time. I nodded and repeated everything he said back to him, so I'd remember it. As soon as I thanked him, he scurried back to his buddies. I finished my lunch, paid the bill, and thanked Jill for everything.

"Honey, we're open twenty-four/seven, every day of the year but Christmas. You come back any time," she said, then handed me a napkin. "Sam and the boys drew you a map on this just in case you may need it."

I gave the boys a thumbs-up and left.

Jim

1968–1974

10

My small world shattered like a beer glass hitting a tile floor. Mom, Sal, Hans, school, any remaining memories of Ginger… all blown away by boot camp. The guys came from anywhere and everywhere: snot-noses, scholars, punks, and blockheads, all marching to the same beat. Teams and individuals randomly called "baby-assed motherfuckers" by a sergeant with a head like a honeydew. We were made to crawl through mud, climb slimy ropes, keep our heads down, kick ass. Luckily, there was always enough food to keep us going.

Basic training was basic, all right. In just eight weeks, we learned a hundred ways to kill or get killed: bullets or clap, grenades or drugs…it was about survival. Slowly, we turned into a team of proud bastards, ready to kill or be killed. Ready to serve.

News from back home came in the form of a few short notes from Hans and Mom. She seemed to be adjusting well in her new home at Laurel Hill; life went on without me. Then, two days before the end of basic training and heading home for a three-day leave, I received a shocking telegram:

Jim, Call me. Sal died, Hans

I was stunned into silence. I neatly folded the telegram and tucked it away in my shirt pocket close to my heart. I didn't want to believe that Sal was gone. I walked quietly back to my barracks and packed, then called Hans to have him pick me up at the airport. I was not going to miss Sal's funeral.

We drove directly to the funeral home, arriving just in time to join the procession. Led by a hearse and a car with Sal's kids, a long line of cars threaded its way through the streets of Milwaukee to St. Anthony's Cemetery. Hans and I stood in the background with a small grouping of mourners while Sal's family surrounded the grave site. I was surprised at the number of his relatives that showed up for the funeral. He never talked to me about having such a large family and I never saw any of them at Sal's shop. I wondered if they knew Sal as I knew him. As people departed, I approached Sal's grave. Looking down at the casket, I said quietly, "Thank you, Sal."

Off to the side, two women were looking at the crisp white marble stone adjacent to Sal's resting place. It marked the grave of Sal's beloved Maria. "I wish I could love or be loved like that," I heard one of women say. I moved closer to the stone. An angel with wings spreading edge to edge was centered midway across the stone. Hidden in each wing was the word *Luce di Dio*. Love radiated from that stone.

After the funeral, Hans drove me to his house where I settled into the guest quarters. Miss Gumpfrey gave me a big hug and told me that we were having a pork-roast with a side of potato pancakes. After eating mess for eight weeks, I'd have been happy with anything she put on the table, but this...my mouth literally watered.

Taking some time before dinner, I borrowed Hans's car and drove out to Laurel Hill to visit Mom. We talked a lot about how our lives have changed over the past eight weeks. At one point she told me how worried she was when I told her that I joined the army. "I didn't say anything then," she said. "I remember when Phillip was drafted. All that army stuff came flooding back. I just decided that you made your own decision and that was that. Just promise me that you'll not take extra risks." After I assured her that I wasn't out looking to be a hero, Mom insisted on giving me a tour of the facility, acting like she owned the place, and introduced me to everyone she could. "I met so many wonderful people," she said, "but I simply can't remember many names. But that's ok. Many of them can't remember mine either," she quipped. Our visit ended with "I'll see you tomorrow."

I returned to Hans's place to that scrumptious dinner. Exhausted, I was asleep before the sun went down.

The next morning, I headed for my old neighborhood. From what Hans told me, Sal died in a raging fire that consumed his shop. Speculation had it that Sal might have had a heart attack or stroke while he was stoking the old coal stove, resulting in a fire that leveled the place. I'd braced myself for the scene, but nothing could have prepared me; it was like a punch in the gut. The shop where I'd spent my entire childhood had been reduced to a scattering of charred ruins. Defiantly standing its ground, the beast of a compressor loomed over the rest, blackened and bent as if it had been brutally attacked. The heavy wooden carving blocks were now large chunks of ashy charcoal. Blocks of stone were tarnished but didn't seem to care one way or the other. I went to where the old coal stove had once sat so proudly and bowed my head.

"God bless you, Sal," I murmured over the blackened ruins. "I love you, old man. Give my best to Maria." I dried my eyes and left, taking the wonders of my childhood with me—good solid memories on which to build a life. What life? I wasn't sure. But, the US Army? They seemed to have it all figured out.

I'd wanted Corps of Engineering—building bridges, airfields, crappers, anything. Listing 'stone carver' as my occupation, though, had somehow implied 'gravestone,' which led to 'grave.' I was assigned to Graves Registration. The prevailing sentiment was that I was a lucky guy—that my assignment to GRREG meant I wouldn't have to face the enemy. After my exhausting three-day leave, I took off for eight weeks of Advanced Individual Training at Fort Lee in Virginia. I arrived for duty at Ton Son Nhut Air Force Base on March 14, 1969, where I was assigned to the mortuary. The place was spotless. Large overhead fans moved the warm moist acrid air that seeped into every pore of my body. People spoke quietly. Respect was everywhere.

We didn't do cosmetizing, dressing, or casketing; that was done back home. We just cleaned, identified, embalmed, pack-aged, and sent. It was meticulous work: name, date, rank, serial number. Dog Tags. Identifying was critical. I'd work my twelve hours, sleep, screw around in Saigon, then get back to the grind. The simple fact was that there was nothing that could erase what we saw day-after-day. Saigon visits or watching a movie or going to USO events helped some but not enough to still the endless, unbreakable cycle of dead soldiers. I did spend some of my free time writing to Mom, telling her that I was busy doing con-struction work. That I was safe and enjoying going to Saigon for R&R. I said nothing about what I really did or that I couldn't sleep at night, or that I preferred to be alone. She'd write back telling me about the exciting time she had playing BINGO or going to the dance parties that Laurel Hill had every Saturday night. Writing those letters and pretending everything was just great helped me take a breather from the truth.

To ward off restless nights, I started carrying on pretend conversations with my dad and Sal. I'd conjure them up sitting at a table opposite me. One night, I told my ghost counselors that I had a dream about how one huge block of limestone after another rolled off some monstrous engraving machine. Each one of them had the name, rank, and serial number of one of the guys I had prepared to send home to his family. I asked them what I should do about commemorating my soldiers' personal qualities. My advisors rubbed their chins, chattered back and forth, then disappeared. It took them about a week to get back to me. When they did reappear, they said it was my duty to see that these guys would be remembered for something other than being born and being killed. *Shortened lives are still lives*, they told me. *Make them your friends.*

A few nights later, I was working on a boy whose face was missing. Since I was in initial processing, I was first in line to see the bodies, whatever shape they were in. If they'd come from one of the medical facilities, they were clean; dirt- and blood-encrusted if they'd come direct. I'd open the body bag and go from there, first checking for tags or other identifiers and always being certain to establish beyond any doubt whatsoever the identity of the soldier. Then I'd assign a processing number. This one…the poor kid. His face was just *gone,* as if he'd been sliced from temple to temple by some monstrous cleaver. I focused on his perfectly intact ears, tracing one of them with my index finger. The lobe was bouncy and pliable. Once I'd gotten him ready for processing, I wrote on the bottom of his paperwork, 'You have beautiful ears.'

During that shift, at the bottom of each report I wrote something personal: 'You have the greatest freckles,' or 'You have nice teeth,' or 'Your hands are perfect.' Before my shift was over, I was standing at attention in front of one very pissed off Lieutenant Major John Jay Regels. He'd looked at my reports and wanted an explanation for my "weirdo comments." I told him that I wanted to get to know the soldiers that I worked on. "I don't want to forget them," The fact was I thought it was none of his damn business. He told me about the psycho ward and sent me to a shrink, all of which was noted on my service record.

The shrink, Major Dr. Tom Hadden, was all concerned about why I felt that I had to write these comments. I told him what Sal said about remembering people for the little things they did, like Dom and his dandelion wine. That feeling a personal connection with my soldiers made the work more tolerable. He seemed to accept the reason and sent me on my way. He didn't ask how I was getting along or anything else. And I wasn't about to tell him that I couldn't sleep, or that I sometimes really wanted to just be alone, or that I thought of my dead soldiers as friends. I learned that in the army the less said the better.

Instead of writing on the reports, I began keeping a diary. I spent my time off interviewing the buddies of the dead and I got a lot of stuff about who they were. I titled my diary *My Soldiers*, and became obsessed with it. When my enlistment ended, I signed up for another tour and then another, and over those years, my diary grew fat with well over a thousand names. The more I learned about my soldiers, the better I felt. And the better I could sleep.

11

I mustered out of the Army in January 1974 out in San Diego, California, with a few 'stay-in-touch' friends and a firsthand knowledge of the human cost of warfare. I donated my uniform to a local theatre company. Maybe they'll have use for it down the road.

Early on during my six years in the service, I had used my leaves to run back to Milwaukee. The few times I visited, I noticed that Mom was more and more distant. I was concerned enough to speak with the the Laurel Hill physician assigned to my mother. He informed me that he suspected that Mom had early-onset dementia. He recommended a move to assisted living, and possibly to their nursing home if the dementia progressed.

I returned to Milwaukee twice more, hoping against hope that Mom would show signs of improvement. But she just got worse. I found it difficult if not impossible to fully accept that she had trouble recognizing me.

"Mom," I said, "Do you know who I am?"

She looked at me quizzically. "Are you Phillip?" she asked.

"No, but you're close. Phillip was your husband. I'm your son James."

"Of course you are," she said. Her eyes looked vacant.

I tried to build on her memories of my father but Mom just stared silently at the far wall. Tearfully, I said, "I love you, Mom," and left her room.

After that visit, I made a tough decision. Rather than use my precious leave-time running back to Milwaukee, I decided to travel, visiting cities like London, my ancestral home of Swansea, Budapest, Amsterdam, Vienna, and many places in between. I even visited Sal's hometown of Molfetta. And once I got free of the Army, it was time to head back to Milwaukee and home. *Home?* Milwaukee felt more like where I was *from* rather than a place I could call *home*.

I was old enough to vote, had $8,435 in savings, and my heart was set on a Ford 250—three-quarter ton, like Sal used to have. But I bought a 1949 International instead because its curved fenders reminded me of a truck I had played with when I was a kid. I just couldn't resist it. It was a four-speed, with a windshield that cranked out to flood the driver and passenger with whatever their nostrils could bear. It screamed like a banshee above fifty. I thought about having it repainted, but decided that faded red was part of the deal—the patina of work. It'd carry a lot of stone, that I knew. I drove it home, avoiding the sterile interstate highways as much as I could, opting instead for two-laners with a view.

Driving cross-country, watching farmers tend their fields and people rushing from one place to another didn't make any sense. Here we were, tending to life as if it was normal. How could things be this normal when our country's at war? What could possibly be normal about thousands of our young men who would never get another chance to wipe their brow, flirt, put on a pair of shoes, cut the grass, or flush a toilet. All the things that we do as humans were gone from them like passing clouds. It pissed me off to think of it!

The first place I went when I hit town was Franklin Alley. After all I'd been through, I needed to make that pilgrimage—to bathe in the peace of nostalgia. Sal's place was a crab-grassed lot; Westen's was closed. I didn't recognize any of the guys standing around Bumpy's. Our old apartment had unfamiliar curtains in the windows and the garage underneath it was now a foreign-car repair shop.

Only Hans's Stein Works was just as I remembered it, but Hans wasn't around.

Lunch at the Red Stripe Diner felt the same as ever. I ordered a tuna sandwich and washed it down with a cup of coffee loaded with sugar and cream, trying to recapture the taste I remembered from my first visit there with Sal. I can't say the attempt was totally successful, but the banana cream pie was so good I wanted to cry.

Next on my list was a visit with Mom. I wasn't sure what to expect but knew I shouldn't expect Mom to be back to "normal." The only difference at Laurel Hill from my last visit was that the shrubs were taller. Mom's early-onset dementia had progressed. I guess I knew that it would, but it was still a shock when she didn't respond to me at all when I took her hands in mine. She just stared. My kiss to her forehead did bring out a soft and familiar smile. I took solace in the fact that she seemed at peace. I won't lie—this was really tough stuff. It was like her mind abandoned her to fend for herself. I wanted to believe that she heard me. That she knew who I was. That there was a flicker of remembrance of our life together. I had to believe that I was still a part of her memory. When I left, Mom was staring at the floor. I went to my truck and cried.

I drove to Hans's house, which had become my home away from home, and he welcomed me back with open arms. For my first meal back in Milwaukee as a civilian, Miss Gumpfrey turned out a lot of potato pancakes, which she served with sour cream and brats, and it felt like family. I avoided talking about Vietnam, and Hans was kind enough not to press me. But he did ask what I planned to do with the rest of my life.

A week earlier, I had been in Vietnam. How was I supposed to know what the hell I was going to do? For the moment, it seemed enough just to try to get used to waking up in a real bed, buying gas, taking a crap without rushing it. I told Hans that I was hoping to find a job carving, but I had no real plan for doing it. Again, he didn't press me.

I went to bed right after dessert—dead tired—but lay awake for a long time, listening to Lake Michigan slap its ice-laden water against the rocky shore. Where would I go from here? My mind flipped back to a time in Sal's shop when he'd gotten a delivery of Indiana limestone. Solidified foraminifera. *Large chunks of old dead sea creatures* is the way Sal described the rough-cut blocks. "Oolitic limestone. The best limestone in the world."

Oolitic, Indiana, it would be.

I got out of bed and dug out my diary from its safe place at the bottom of my bag. I leafed through it, catching one or another name and phrase: Jeremy T. Collins—*I remember the time you won the bass fishing contest*; Michael F. Ramsey—*You could beat anybody at eight-ball*; Frederick William Johns—*Teaching Walt*

Whitman was heaven for you; Bagley Tracy Petersdorf—*Highest yield for one acre of corn*; Jesse Mark Stevens—*Your collard greens won Best Tasting at the Rolands County Fair*. My friends. Sleep finally took over.

At breakfast the next morning, I told Hans that I was heading to Oolitic to find a job carving. He quipped that the name sounded like some far-off galaxy, asked me what made me choose such a place.

I chuckled, then told him that the town was named after a certain kind of limestone. "Sal said it was the best limestone in the world," I said. I didn't tell him anything about my diary, or that I was thinking about carving a memorial for "my soldiers." He didn't press me about it—just said that he was glad I was getting on with my life and that he'd always be ready to help if I needed anything. After breakfast, we went into Hans's garage where he had stored my tools, including the precious trove of chisels Sal had given to me.

On my way out, Miss Gumpfrey handed me a bag of sandwiches and gave me a peck on the cheek. I could see a tear glistening in her eye.

"Don't worry—either of you," I said. "I'll be back soon to see Mom. And you, too."

12

Oolitic was a neat little town, and struck me as the perfect place to a get a new start. There wasn't much in the way of housing so I checked out a tourist home—a kind of boarding house for transients. A list of handwritten rules was taped to the bathroom mirror and numero uno was, 'Be quiet at all times.' I got out of there.

I drove around and found one of the quarries, a huge pit with very few people working it. It wasn't abandoned or water-filled or anything like that, just not busy like I thought it'd be. When I couldn't find a decent rental in Oolitic, I headed south to Bedford, passing a sign that said Limestone Capital of the World.

I left my truck in a parking lot just north of the town square. The county courthouse that sat in the middle of the Bedford town square was a stone carver's dream; Sal would've loved it. I spent about a half hour walking around it, looking for carvers' personal touches. I studied their chisel marks—the stone carver's signature—and I could tell that at least five different guys had worked on it. When I'd admired it long enough, I meandered around the square, stopping in stores and window shopping. I bought a jacket, a pair of jeans, and some expensive shit-kicking boots. I finally ended up at a place at the far end of the square called Clay Rodell's Café.

I put my shopping bags down by the coat rack and took a seat. "Whattleuhav?"

"I beg your pardon?" I was still getting used to the dimly lit barroom. "Whattleitbe?"

"Oh—I'll have a beer. Miller, if you have it."

"You're new here," the bartender said, reaching for a cold one and flipping off the cap in one smooth practiced move. "It's on the house. Where ya from?"

"Milwaukee," I answered, raising my glass to him in thanks. The truth was, I didn't see myself being from anywhere at that moment.

"Good place to come from," he said, stroking the three-day growth on his chin. "At least you're not from back east." He said it as if 'back east' was enemy territory. "How long ya been in Bedford?"

I looked at my watch.

"About an hour and twenty minutes."

"Just enough time to have a beer, I guess. You planning on sticking around?"

"For now anyway."

"Can I ask your name?"

"Jim. Jim Robertson."

"I'm the owner of this place. Clay Rodell," he said, offering his hand for a shake across the bar. "Welcome to Bedford, Jim." He headed on down the bar.

I gazed around, looked up at the smoke-stained ceiling. The

place was worn and dark, but my eye was drawn to an intricately carved limestone slab that sat amidst the colorful liquor bottles lining the mirrored back of the bar. It read: Clay Rodell's Café, Softball Champs 1941.

"Where are you working?"

The voice startled me and I turned to my right to see a guy I hadn't noticed, two stools away. He was scrawny, with a beard that looked like it'd been caught in a buzz saw. I almost laughed. In Saigon, an opening question like that usually led to a quick pitch from the local pimp. I guess I waited too long to answer, because the guy repeated the question.

"I…I'm not working anywhere…yet," I said, "but I'm looking." I tried to make up for my tardy answer by offering a smile.

"What kinda work ya looking for?"

"I'm a stone carver. Been a while, though."

The guy turned away, and at first I thought I'd offended him. "Hey!" he yelled down the bar to three guys quietly sipping their beer. "This guy's a stone carver. Anybody know where he might find work?"

The trio erupted into backslapping and laughter, punctuated by bullshit.

"Shieeee…there's no damn work for nobody here, boy, let alone a newbie."

"Go home kid; there ain't much work since the war—and I mean the *real* war!"

I reddened up. "Real war!" I shouted at the men. Standing, I asked, "Who said that?"

The tallest of the three said. "I did," then added, "I didn't mean to offend. It's just that this Vietnam thing is not a war, not like fighting the Nazi's. It's a police action. That's what they call it, a police action."

"I don't give a shit what 'they' call it. Soldiers are dying just like they do in any damn war. It's 'real' enough for them." I emptied my glass and slammed it back on the bar and turned to leave.

"Hold on," the bartender said, coming over to me. "I own this place and I don't like seeing anyone leave mad, especially a newcomer. Let me give everybody a drink on the house and let things settle."

The tall man said, "Like I said, I didn't mean to offend. I'm sorry if I did."

I accepted his apology with indifference and sat back down.

"So, Jim…ah it's alright to call you that? I heard you tell Clay your name.

"It is my name, so go right ahead.

"Sorry for that fracus. Sometimes I just say the damndest things. Anyway, you can call me Al. Al Poncelli." He slid over to the stool next to mine and stuck out his hand, which I took in mine. Truth is, he looked the way I felt—in need of some-body to talk to.

"Matter of fact, Al, I'm looking for a place to settle in for a while. I'm thinking about that trailer over in the parking lot with the 'for rent' sign."

"*That* trailer?" Poncelli laughed a bit too hard and long for my comfort. "More people have screwed in that trailer than live in the whole county! This time of year, it's probably colder than a witch's tit in there."

"Yeah, I…kind of figured that." I didn't like jokes at my expense. *Real war* still echoed in my head. Maybe Bedford was not where I belonged after all.

Poncelli signaled the bartender, who brought us two free beers. "Here's to you kid," he said, then leaned toward me. "So, tell me, Jim…you don't look old enough to be a stone carver."

"I'm twenty-four," I said.

"When I was your age, I couldn't even piss my name in the snow."

"I can believe that," I said, and to my relief, he laughed.

"So…what does a young guy like you think of that shitstorm over in Vietnam?"

"One thing I think is that it's a *real war,*" I said, raising my voice so that the guy who'd made the wisecrack might hear me.

"Jesus, don't get so touchy," Al said, raising his palms. "That guy didn't mean nothin'. I guess I'm right in assuming you're a vet, then…"

For some reason, his tone calmed my nerves. I answer, "Yes, I served in Vietnam."

Al sat quiet for a moment then said, "Ah, Chist. I'm sorry kid."

"Don't worry about it, Al. I guess you had no way of knowing."

Changing the subject, I asked, "So, how come there's no work here?"

At that, the guy got real passionate. "Glass!" he said. He lifted his beer glass, peering through the rich amber then downed it. "See this?" he said, holding up the empty, foam-stained glass. "This is what everybody wants nowadays. Glass. Cold, flat sheets of nothing—skyscrapers of melted sand held together with glue, not worth a plugged nickel. Pure bullshit! That's what it is. Makes a stone man cry." Al put his beer back on the bar, grabbed a napkin and dramatically wiped tears that weren't there. Picking up his beer, he went on. "Back in the fifties, people started using mainly glass instead of stone for their buildings—thought it was 'modern' or some such. Did you know the guys from around here cut all the stone for the Empire State Building? And the Pentagon…the National Cathedral… even the Tribune Tower in Chicago. That building is one for the ages, I'm tellin' ya."

"Wow," I said, not really knowing quite how to respond. "But surely there's still a need for stone. On the level…do you think there's some work around here for me, if I'm…not too picky?"

"There's always work for good carvers," he said. "You might have to travel like a son-of-a-bitch to find it, though. There's some work right here in town, too, but it don't pay nothin'. Line work. The old quarry workers are having a time of it," he said sadly, gesturing toward the men sitting at the far end of the bar. "Used to be, a man could work his ass off; now he sits on it."

"I'll find something to do," I said. "The pay isn't important to me—at least not right now."

"So what is?" Al added, "that is, if you don't mind telling me."

"I came to look around, find some limestone for a project I have in mind."

"Ha! If stone's what you want, you came to the right place. Whatever else you wanna say about this area, we got the best limestone in the world."

"So I've been told."

"What kind of project you have in mind?"

"Oh…just something I want to do." The truth was I had no idea what to do about carving a memorial. Al knew not to push it.

"Well, if you're interested in line carving, I could talk to the boss. That's what I'm doing these days."

"Yes, I'm interested—thanks…Al." I was beginning to think my new friend was an okay guy.

We sat quietly for a few moments, then Al launched into his own story. I guess he figured it was his turn to cough up some personal details. He'd come to Indiana from New York. His father had been a master stone carver who worked on a cathedral there—St. John the Divine. I gathered from the way he talked about it that it was a pretty big deal. He'd learned carving from his dad, then came to the Midwest to work on a big project and ended up settling in Oolitic. His old man had immigrated from Italy and sounded a lot like Sal.

"It's not that there's no work out there," he went on, "but at this point, it's easier to just take line work so I can stay home with my Toni."

We drank another beer—my treat this time—and kept chatting, until finally Al said, "Tell you what, Jim. My sister's got a place over at Salt Creek, just on the edge of town. Oolitic, that is. It's small. Three rooms maybe, but it's nice. Used to be a toll shed for the road but that was back a-ways. She'd probably rent it to you if I put in a good word—for a lot less than you're paying for that tin can over there. Might need some fixin' up, but what the hell? You interested?"

I said I was, and we arranged to meet in Oolitic around seven.

The toll house turned out to be more shack than house, but it was clean and furnished, and had a gas space heater for warmth. The biggest of its three rooms was the kitchen, which ran all across the back. The front half was divided into a sitting room, bedroom, and a small bathroom. At fifteen dollars a month plus utilities, it was a steal—and it beat Army living. No more snores and farts all night. Nobody trudging past my bed to the latrine. I could turn the lights on and off as I pleased, put stuff in the refrigerator, cook my own food.

I spent the next three days cleaning up the place, getting groceries, drinking beer. Al stopped by with a loaf of crusty Italian bread his wife, Toni, had baked. "If you're looking for work, the boss said he'd give you a try. Just go over to Carving Shed Six at seven tomorrow morning."

"Al...thank you. I really—"

"Ah, don't worry about it," he said with a wave, then gave me directions. Before I could even offer him a beer, he was out the door.

I hadn't touched my tools since before going to Vietnam but they were in pretty good shape. I decided not to use Sal's chisels just yet. I'd have to practice with them before they worked for me. There are good chisels and there are not-so-good chisels. Mine were pretty good, but Sal's were great: hand-forged for perfect heft and feel. The crowns were slightly mushroomed over from many years of use. The scratches and nicks were a hieroglyphic record of Sal and his teacher before him.

Carving Shed Six—the only one currently in use, from what I could tell—was cavernous and mostly empty. A line of ten carvers, each busy with his own project, stretched single file down the middle. Heavy canvas sheets hung between each of them, like blinders between toilet stalls. The air was dusty and filled with the clinking music of chisels.

I was in stall number four chipping away at chunks of

limestone. I was told by the foreman that they were to become decorative lintels for the windows of a small chapel being built on the estate of some guy named Huxley Deavers, a wealthy industrialist from Clarion, Pennsylvania. His company made cans, so every carving had to have a can in it somewhere. My first assignment was to carve a stack of tuna cans on each lintel. Now and then—maybe three times a day—this kid would come by and ask, "Any chisels?"

Once I figured out what he meant, I'd just say, "nope." Periodically, I'd hear other carvers calling out, "Chisel Boy, Chisel Boy," and he'd come running, pick up some guy's chisels, and take them to be sharpened. There was no way in hell anybody was going to touch mine. Besides, if you know what you're doing, you don't dull your chisels all that much. I touched mine up at night with a file.

Al was right. It was boring and the pay was worse. Near the end of the week, Smithy Paulson, the on-site blacksmith, paid me a visit to ask why I never sent a chisel up for sharpening. I sensed disappointment in his voice, as if he thought I didn't like him or trust his work or something.

He eyeballed my chisels and gave a low whistle. "Those are mighty fine," he said. "If you need them touched up or anything, you got my word I'll be real careful. It'd be my pleasure."

I felt so bad, I put my number one in his hands. "Thanks," I said. "This one could use a little polish."

The next day, he personally brought it to my stall, the bezel glimmering like a diamond. I was beginning to like the people of Oolitic, if not the job.

13

They got a few months out of me before I'd had it up to my eyeballs with the endless repetition. I'd saved a good bit of money while I was in the Army, so I didn't need the pittance they were paying—and I'd gotten what I needed out of the job: contacts. I knew I could get the best limestone the world had to offer, if I could just come up with a plan for my memorial. Every night I'd run schemes through my mind that, by morning, seemed absurd. I had this one idea of carving all the names in one big block, but then what? It'd weigh tons. Another idea was to carve a whole lot of slabs, one for each state. I wrote a few letters to state governments telling them about my idea, but got no replies. My ghost counselors were silent and had been since I left Vietnam.

I was in no hurry. I was willing to wait for the right idea and a way to carry it out. I ate out most of the time, at diners or family restaurants, even though it made me feel pretty alone. I dated a few times but nothing ever came of it. No *fulmine*, that's for sure. I wonder sometimes if I would ever find a mate,

somebody to love who would love me back, A life partner.
Growing up without a father I never really experienced what
it's like to be married. What do couples do day in and day out?
How do they manage with kids and paying the bills and all that?
Every couple weeks or so, I was invited to Al and Toni's place
for dinner. I would leave with a full belly and a hopeful heart
that I would find my one and only.

Sometimes I ate at Rodell's, watched TV, talked with the
guys. The menu wasn't much, just hot dogs, hamburgers, and
heated-up frozen pizza, with or without pepperoni; beer nuts
as an appetizer, pickled eggs for dessert, and as much beer as
you could drink and still find your way home. For me, that was
six glasses, but rarely did I drink that much. When I did it was
usually when I was with a bunch of guys celebrating a win at the
dart board, or rallying behind the Green Bay Packers.

The day I quit line carving, I went over to Rodell's with
Al, listening to him complain all the way: "If I carve another
goddam mess of ivy, I'll puke. I'd rather stick it to a bag of ham-
mers than do this. Christ, if I was on the road, I'd be working
on masterpieces...but without Toni, I'd go nuts. So I stay here
and go nuts with the boredom! What am I supposed to do?
Tell me that!"

Maybe they could tell that Al was in a mood; the boys at
Rodell's kept their distance. When he finally took a break from
his bitching, I told him I'd quit my job, and that I was thinking
of moving on.

"Those jobs around the country you're always talking about...
are you just bullshitting or is that for real?" Al assured me he
was on the level.

"If you're interested, I'll make some calls to guys I know.

I'm jealous as hell, though—" I cut him off before he started ranting again.

"So, why don't you and I take a shot at it together, then? You could come back and see Toni between jobs…working together, we could probably make some good money and take breaks when we felt like it."

Al went blank for a second and I could tell he was thinking it over.

"Let me know what you decide," I said, and walked toward the back to take a leak. When I got back to the bar, Al had ordered a second round.

"I made a decision," he announced, like he'd just solved the national debt. "You and me is going to be partners. We'll find enough work for two, that's for sure." For the next half hour, he told me about all the memorials around the area that needed repair. "People are all hot about putting names of their dead on display, but then they just forget about the whole thing. Caring for soldiers' monuments ought to be right up there with the way they keep banks. It doesn't make sense. I myself never fought in any war but if it was up to me—"

"Jesus, Al," I cut in. "So when do we start?"

"How about, Monday? I'll spend the weekend breaking the news to Toni. She's going to be pissed. Reminds me of this time one Christmas when we were supposed to go see her family but the car wouldn't start. That goddamn Nash…"

I picked up my glass and headed for a game of darts. Going on the road with Al was not going to be easy.

Al wasn't one to spend money on comfort. Rules or no rules, it was boarding houses all the way, with their bowled beds and bad food. I did my best to ignore the discomfort, but Al's endless complaints made me crazy. He wasn't kidding about needing that wife of his: being away from his beloved Toni had turned him into a mess of blubbering self-pity. We took Al's truck, which was a touch above mine. I drove most of the time because Al's talking distracted him from paying attention to the road, not to mention letting go of the wheel to shake both hands in the air to make a point.

Al had a lot of contacts who brought us a lot of work. Renovating monuments was a lot better than line carving, even though seeing them in such crappy shape pissed me off. Some of them were practically falling over. I shared Al's disbelief: How could a community so quickly abandon its fallen? People volunteer to clean up roads and stuff. Why not watch over memorials? What the hell did they think those names stood for?

By week six—our last one before taking a break—I was bustin' to get back to my quiet little shack, away from Al.

We were in Columbus, Ohio, when it happened.

Al was thirty feet up on a scaffold, repairing a broken bayonet on a civil war soldier's gun when he stepped back into open air. His last words were, "Hand me number two, will ya Jim?" I peered over the edge of the scaffold and saw Al writhing on the ground like he was trying to shake off a hundred snakes. By the time I made it down to his side, he wasn't moving anymore. His eyes were wide open and blood trickled from the corner of his mouth and one ear.

"Hang in there, Al!" I shouted, "C'mon man, don't give up!" but I knew it was pointless—I'd seen this before. I watched his eyes gloss over like a gray veil dropped on them. As I held his head in my lap, my watery eyes turned to faucets.

I'd cried once or twice in 'Nam, but had never lost it like this. Maybe I was making up for all the death I'd seen there, and for my old friend Sal. The park was empty—nobody was around. I knew I should look for a phone and call an ambulance or something, but I just couldn't move; I sat there holding Al for I don't know how long. I thought about what I might carve as a hidden epitaph for him. Maybe something like: 'A loving, scraggly son-of-a-bitch.'

It would take me a few more minutes to find my legs, and while I was sitting there, somebody came by and offered to get help. I stayed with Al until the ambulance came, and I rode with him as far as the hospital. Toni was devastated.

It was mid-June when we buried Al. That night, the barflies at Rodell's—or should I say my fellow barflies, since I was fast becoming one of them—retired his barstool. Like retiring a great athlete's number, this was a great honor and called for all the pomp and circumstance the place could muster. For Rodell's, that meant the juke box playing Merle Haggard and a toast of free beer all around, while Clay hung Al's stool from a hook high up by the ceiling next to three others—two high school teachers who got killed in World War II and Clay Rodell's wife, Sissy.

14

With Al gone, I was feeling pretty down. Why wouldn't I be? Sleepless nights like those in 'Nam returned full bore. I stopped going to Clay Rodell's Bar, ate at home, if you can call canned soup eating. Life was not good. When July 4th came along, I decided it might help for me to join in the town's celebration. At least give it a try. I was surprised at how many folks said it was nice to see me. Red, white, and blue banners, flags, pennants even on some kids' painted faces. I found myself being treated like a townie and I was surprised how much I enjoyed the recognition. I guess it didn't hurt that I was an eligible bachelor. Since I'd moved to town, every couple of weeks, somebody's wife asked if she could set me up with a nice young lady she knew, and sometimes I said yes. Every now and then I thought about trying to find Ginger, wherever she was, but I never followed through on it. I knew it was just a fantasy.

I kept reminding myself that the reason I'd come to Oolitic was to carve a memorial for *my* soldiers, though I still hadn't talked to anybody other than Al about it. I'd drawn up a couple plans, even begun carving a few samples, but nothing stuck.

After the formal festivities, which included a parade and a rousing speech delivered by our mayor, beer ran freely and hot dogs and hamburgers served as preliminaries for the pig roast scheduled for six sharp. After dark, there'd be dancing and fireworks.

Like most everybody else, I ate to within inches of killing myself. At one point, I wandered into the Odd Fellows Hall and flopped down in a metal folding chair. Alice Meade, the leader of the Order of Rebekah, asked us all to bow our heads in memory of fallen soldiers. She read the names of six Oolitic kids who'd died in Vietnam. People sat quiet for a while, then Alice spoke up again. She asked me and two others to stand, introducing us as "some of the guys that made it." This was greeted by polite applause, and somebody yelled out, "God bless you guys," but that was about it. The band struck up a tune and in minutes, everybody was on their feet dancing and having a good time. A few guys I'd met at Rodell's came over to say hey, but I was basically on my own.

I watched the dust play around in the low sunlight that streamed through the tall windows lining the hall. It was dream-like…everybody dancing around…the music. There was a lightness to it all, a lightheartedness. I wanted to stand up and tell everybody to get out. Go home. I wanted to tell them about how GRREG was still up and running, its refrigerators packed tight. I wanted Al to come over to me with his god-awful beard and give me a big goddamn bear hug.

But that wasn't going to happen. And the mortuary in 'Nam wasn't going to shut down for lack of business. And I didn't have any idea where I was going in life and what I'd do when I got there.

I got up and turned toward to the door, and that's when I saw her.

It was like something out of the movies. I swear to god, things went into slow motion. The band music faded. Kids' voices receded into a murky distance. All I could see was this drop-dead beautiful girl, and she was looking right into my eyes. There was nothing else to do but go over to her—I couldn't have stopped myself if I tried.

We both moved toward each other, slowly, like there was no rush at all. Without saying anything, I took her hand in mine and led her to the dance floor. If I'd been thinking straight, I'd have remembered that I couldn't dance if my life depended on it. But nothing seemed to matter except getting that girl in my arms.

Lucky for me, a slow song was playing. As we started to sway to the music, she felt incredibly light. She put her cheek against mine, and—I don't know how to describe it without sounding Hollywood, but—it just felt...*right*. I hadn't shaved for a day or two and I'm sure she thought she was cuddled up to a porcupine, but she didn't seem to mind. I breathed her in like fresh air. All the stuff with Al and Vietnam just faded away and there was no place but right there, on that dance floor, with that girl.

When the music stopped, she stepped back and said, "My name's Anna."

I stammered like a fool.

"Ah...nice to meet you...I'm...Jim."

"I know," she said with a smile that could melt an iceberg. "I know who you are." Then she turned on her heel and walked away, leaving me dazed, rooted to the spot, just watching her go. I don't know how long I stood there, but I guess it was long enough to draw attention to myself. The next thing I knew, people were polka-dancing around me like I was a statue.

As I stood there amidst the chaos, the name Anna bounced around in my head like a ping-pong ball. An older lady by the name of Mabel, who I knew vaguely, came over and said quietly, "You just dance with me a bit. Ease yourself down."

Clearly, she'd seen the whole thing unfold—so I guessed I didn't dream it. I let her lead me through some moves, but she could tell I didn't know a polka from a jitterbug so she gave up pretty quick and led me off to the side of the dance floor. In a motherly tone, like she was talking to some kid who'd skinned his knee, she said, "There's one thing you need to know, Jim. That girl, Anna? She's no more than sixteen or so. I don't think her daddy would take kindly to any shenanigans."

"Sixteen?" I said, my jaw dropping. "What do you mean by 'or'?!"

"Well she's not of age that's for sure. Young enough to put you in jail, soldier boy. You listen up. Her father's as mean as nest of hornets. You do *not* want to tangle with him or any of his kin…word to the wise."

Mabel was making sense and I knew it. Still…all my senses were filled with Anna. I said her name out loud and that's when Mabel kicked me in the shin.

"You better get control of yourself, Jim, and that's the last word I'm going to say about it. Go find yourself a proper grown-up woman!"

"Yes, ma'am," I said, feeling like a third-grader caught smoking.

All I could think about was getting out of there. I bid my goodnights and lit out for my toll house, even though it was barcly dark. I had some thinking to do.

That night, I was lonelier than I could ever remember being, even when I was overseas. I sat on the back porch watching the fireworks. As star clusters boomed and crackled in the dark sky, I raised my fist and yelled, *Fulmine! Fulmine! Fulmine!* The thunderbolt. Unlike when Sal first introduced me to the term, this time I said it with gusto. I was in love. This time it was for real. I wished I could tell Sal.

Lying in bed that night, I did the math. I was twenty-four, Anna was sixteen. When I'm thirty, she'll be twenty-two. Forty, she'll be thirty-two. When I reach seventy-five, she'll be sixty-eight....That didn't seem so bad.

I thought about how foolish I'd been, standing out in the backyard howling *fulmine* into the moonlit sky. Is this what happens when you fall in love?

In love? I didn't even know the girl, not really. And the warning from Mable, that Anna was only sixteen or "not of age," as Mabel put it. Be patient, I said to myself. Tap lightly. Let the hammer do the work. *Wait for Luce di Dio. It will come.*

15

I awoke from a sound sleep to somebody rapping on my back door. I checked the clock. *Six-thirty.* This better be good, I thought. When I peered around my bedroom door to take a look, I got the shock of my life: It was Anna. I grabbed a pair of pants and a shirt. *No time to shave. Good Lord, what's she doing here?*

"Anna? I…good morning!"

She looked me over, top to bottom. No getting around it, I was a mess.

"Good morning," she said pleasantly.

"Good morning." I said again, for lack of anything else to say.

"I'm sorry…I'm sorry to have wakened you. I just needed to talk."

"Oh, that's okay…I was awake, anyway," I lied. My voice sounded like I'd swallowed a rasp. "How do you know where I live?"

"Oh, everybody knows everything in Oolitic. I really didn't mean to intrude."

"No, no, that's okay."

Anna was chewing on her lower lip like she was searching for something more to say, and looking over my shoulder like she wanted to be invited in, but I was rooted to the spot, just drinking her in. After a little bit, she blurted out, "I just wanted to tell you how much I enjoyed our dance last night."

"You mean you can still walk?" I joked. "How many times did I step on your toes?"

"Not too many," she laughed.

I stepped out onto the back porch and closed the door behind me. "Wanna sit down?" I asked Anna, gesturing at the stairs. I didn't exactly have porch furniture. We sat on the top step and rested our feet on the one below.

"You remembered my name," she said.

"Of course! How could I not?"

"I first saw you in the grocery store," she said. "By the dairy case." I just looked at her.

"You probably think I'm silly, but that's where I first met you. At the grocery store. You had your head in the milk case and I was standing there, waiting for you to make up your mind. When you noticed me, you excused yourself and handed me a quart. I had actually come in for some heavy cream, but I didn't say anything. I mean, I just took the milk. So...when I saw you at the dance, I thought it'd be nice if we met." She seemed nervous and giddy, and I could see it now: *Sixteen* was written all over her.

"Well, I certainly remember last night, Anna. Thanks for the dance." After a few seconds when we looked everywhere but into each other's eyes, she said, "Vietnam...it must have been terrible."

"Yeah…it still is."

"I'm sorry," she said, blushing. "I didn't mean to pry."

"It's all right. When I was growing up it was Korea. Nobody wanted to talk about that either."

Anna's giddiness disappeared like a puff of air and she grew more serious. It made her look older, somehow.

"I'm too young to know much about what happened in Korea," she said. "Maybe I'm…just too young."

"To young for what?"

"You know…my being with you. Here like this."

"We're just talking, There's nothing wrong with that."

"What I mean to say is…well, it's like Hollywood."

"What does that mean?"

"Oh, never mind, I'm just being foolish."

I didn't respond and we sat in silence for what felt like decades. Last night's *fulmine* display was a lovesick me playing the game of love. Today, I'm a twenty-four-year-old having a conversation with a *maybe* sixteen-year-old-girl.

Breaking the silence, Anna stood and said excitedly, "Oh, I almost forgot. I want to invite you to a concert. I play the viola in the summer youth orchestra up in Bloomington. We're playing in the city park at the gazebo. Can you come?"

"Well ah. I'm not sure. Maybe I can. What time is it?" I said getting up.

"3 pm. Hope to see you there," she said sauntering off before disappearing into the woods behind my place.

Viola? I wondered, isn't that like a violin or something?

16

I went to the concert. The program listed her as "Anna Adamski, Principal Violist. Senior." That's how I learned Anna's last name. But what really caught my eye was the word 'Senior.' Anna's not sixteen unless she's a whiz-kid. She's at least seventeen, maybe even eighteen, or close to it. That buoyed my spirit. I went to the reception where I caught Anna's eye as she stood near the snack table. My heart skipped a beat. She was talking with a short, graying woman who was wearing a blue dress with a large colorful flower sewn on the front. Anna greeted me with a smile and introduced me to the woman as her mother, who said that it was nice to meet me before excusing herself to get a refill of punch. Anna and I talked briefly about the concert until her mother reappeared. Ignoring me, she told Anna that they needed to head home. As Mrs, Adamski left, Anna held back, turned to me and said quietly, "Tomorrow at three. Your backyard."

I drove back to Oolitic wondering whether Anna and I could ever be a couple. It wasn't just about our age difference. It was that I had so much more life experience than she did. It crossed my mind that my feelings for her might be my way of escaping my solitude. I went on like this, creating a list of why I should just get Anna out of my mind. It didn't work.

The next day was all about our meeting. I was waiting for her, seated in a comfortable lawn chair, one of two that I bought in the morning along with a small metal table. I had made some lemonade and cleaned up the place. Almost on the dot, Anna appeared from the woods dressed in a plaid skirt and white blouse. She was wearing sunglasses. I stood and pointed to the empty chair. "For you."

"Nice," she said sitting.

"I thought since we are going to have talks, I'd try to make us comfortable."

"You succeeded. Well how did you like the concert?"

"I've gotta admit…I don't know much about classical music. Really, I don't know much about anything beyond stonework and war. But to answer your question, I was impressed. I watched you enjoying yourself. How long have you been playing the…viola?"

"I started when I was four. On a little violin, actually. I switched to the viola when I was twelve, so…five years ago come June. I go up to Bloomington every week for a lesson at IU. I'm in the orchestra up there, too. The orchestra that you heard yesterday is similar to the one we have in the fall and winter, only we let younger players join us to get experience."

While Anna was talking, I did some quick math. "So, you're *seventeen?*"

"Yes, I'm seventeen. Why?"

"I thought…well I thought, you know, that maybe…you might be sixteen?"

"What! Are you comparing me to Lolita? What kind of girl do you think I am?"

"Who?"

"Never mind. Where did you get that I was sixteen?"

"At the dance. This lady at the dance said you were sixteen."

"Well, whoever she is, she's wrong. Now, can we get beyond my age?"

"I'm sorry for the confusion. So it's okay if I ask you out on a date."

"Of course it is. But I'm not sure I can do that just yet."

"Why not."

"Because of my parents."

"What about your parents?"

"You met my mother yesterday. Remember how she was, cold and standoffish?" I nodded. "Well that was because she saw that we were attracted to each other. I'm not allowed to date or even hint that I'm interested in dating."

"I don't understand. You're only one birthday away from being eighteen. That's when you're free to make your own decisions. Right?"

"Right, but that's seven months away. My birthday's in February, February 15th to be exact. The day after Valentine's Day. As far as my parents go, I don't know why they're so strict. They just are. Must we talk about them?"

"No, sorry." I paused for a restart, keeping in mind that the subject was obviously painful territory for her. "Seven months? That's not so bad," I said.

Leaning toward me she smiled. "I can wait if you can?" Tilting her head to the side she added, "Or, we can see each other on the sly."

"We can do that, too."

"Then let's."

"Let's what?

"Be sly."

We laughed. I stood up, went to Anna, leaned over and kissed her gently on the lips.

We spent almost an hour together talking about when and where we could safely meet and things we wanted to see and do. After Anna left, I went back inside where the forgotten lemonade sat patiently on the kitchen counter. I was dancing on air. I was in love.

We saw each other almost every day throughout the summer without her parents or anyone else knowing. Swimming, horseback riding, hiking, and making out like lovers are wont to do. And "no" meant no. Over the summer, we had long talks and shared snippets of our childhoods. I told her about Sal mentoring me in stone carving, about my father being MIA, what it was like to go Lutheran school—sans any reference to my time with Ginger of course. Anna talked about learning to play the viola in the youth orchestra, how she loved reading and going to concerts. She didn't talk about family and I knew enough not to push it. When she asked me what brought me to Oolitic, I told her about my time in 'Nam, leaving out the gory details. That the reason I came to Oolitic was to find the right stone to use to build a memorial, even though I hadn't firmed up what form that would take. Anna's response to all that was an affirming, "That's another reason why I love you."

In late August, Toni Poncelli called. "It's been a while" she said.

"Yes it has. How are you doing?"

"Oh, I really miss him, Jim. Thirty-four years is a long time to live with somebody—even a guy who drives you crazy sometimes."

I could tell she was doing her best to avoid tears. "Al was one of the best," I said. "I know you don't need me to tell you that. You need anything?"

Toni paused for a moment, then said, "For myself, no. But maybe there is something I need for Al. I've gotten recent calls meant for him. There's one of his pieces that needs repair. It's at The Sacred Heart Cathedral in Newark, New Jersey. I think Al would be real proud to have you do the work."

"Of course. How much damage is there?"

"I don't know Jim, but from what they told me, it's pretty bad. It's in the Baptistry. That's all I know. Maybe you can give them a call. Ask for a Mr. Beyers." She gave me the phone number. The last thing I felt like doing at that moment was hitting the road again. On the other hand, there was nothing I wouldn't do for Al, who'd gotten me on my feet when I washed up in Oolitic. I told Toni that I would be honored. She said they hoped it could be done before Christmas.

"That's doable," I said. "I'll give them a call and let you know how it goes."

Mr. Beyers confirmed that they wanted the job done before Christmas. He said he was sorry to tell me that I couldn't start the work until after Thanksgiving because of what he called a scheduled Convocation of Catholic Leaders. Rather than getting into all the details, I asked if he could send some photos of the damage and I would get back to him if I thought I needed more time. He promised he'd mail some Polaroids by day's end.

After the phone call, I went to Rodell's for dinner. "Taking up Al's work, eh?" Clay Rodell said after I told him about my conversation with Toni. "I remember the day you came in here." He looked up at Al's retired barstool. "Al was preaching away like some evangelical."

"Yeah…I miss him, Clay. But," I laughed, "I don't think I'll miss being on the road with him. You know, Al had a way of finding the worst damn rooming houses in every town we went to. Bad food, bad smells. I swear that trailer that used to be out back was probably better."

"So, what are you going to do on this trip—eat up your profits staying in fancy hotels?"

"To tell you the truth Clay, I haven't really thought about it." Rodell moved down the bar, checking for empties, then returned.

"You know, if you're thinking of going on the road again I just have an idea you might like," he said, looking to his left. "You see that guy down there?" I peered through the dark at a heavyset fellow resting on bared elbows.

"That's Stan Peters. Runs the bus garage for the county schools. He's always telling me about the school wanting to get rid of old buses. Claims they're in good shape but don't meet state guidelines and all. Stan told me they go for around a thousand dollars. Anyway, maybe you should get yourself a bus. Fix it up. Put a shop in it, along with a place to sleep."

I sipped my beer. I had to admit, it wasn't a bad idea. Anything would beat rooming houses and cheap motels.

"How long do you suppose it'd take to fix something like that up?"

"With a little help, you could be on the road in a couple weeks, I bet. I can let him know you're interested. If you get the bus, how about sellin' me that old truck of yours?"

"I'll let you know once I get a look at the photos. Now, how about serving me up one of those famous frozen pizzas of yours?"

The photos arrived two days later. From what I could tell, two weeks or so would be enough to do the job. I called Mr. Beyers and we agreed that I would start the Monday after Thanksgiving. I called Toni and told her about setting a date. She was delighted and said Godspeed before hanging up.

I went over to Rodell's and sealed the deal. I was going to be the proud owner of a school bus.

When I told Anna all about going to Newark for the repair work, she was very supportive, telling me that it's great that I was getting to 'ply my trade.' When I told her I wasn't going to leave until after Thanksgiving, she said, "That's a good four months away."

I had already given that some thought. For sure, I didn't want to slip back into the depressive state I was in prior to going to the 4th of July celebration, before dancing with her.

"Yes, it is. Four months to get back to work doing what I do best, carving stone. I was thinking of going back to doing some line work to earn some money. And having more time to be with you."

"You know what I think? I think you're underestimating yourself. You didn't come to Oolitic to do line work. Why not get down to building that memorial you talked about?"

"Not ready to start yet and please don't ask why because I don't have an answer." Lightening things up, I told her about buying the bus and fixing it up. She laughed, shook her head and told me that I must be crazy. I couldn't disagree.

Thanks to my buddies at the bar, it was only nine days from

the time I picked up the bus until it was ready for the road. It cost me twelve hundred bucks, twenty cases of beer, a couple gallons of pickled eggs, and a ton of cold cuts to get the job done. I offered everybody who helped me a bus seat to take home. Most of them wound up on the guys' front or back porches.

We installed two bunk beds across the aisle from each other, left a few of the seats in place, added a sofa, made up a rough dinette near the front, and installed a two-burner alcohol stove. We put in a used propane heater we bought from a travel trailer dealer in Bedford. A port-o-potty found a niche behind one of the bunk beds. Toni Poncelli gave me Al's hard-rock maple carving block, which I bolted to the floor in the back and hung a heavy canvass curtain to separate the workspace from the living area. All that was left was to load it up with my tools, clothes, and some groceries. Calling the bus a 'Working Schoolie', we christened it in early November. At our last meeting before I left, Anna and I drove to Bloomington for Anna's "special viola lesson," which just happened to be dinner for two. She was getting pretty good at finding ways for us to meet. I borrowed a car from one of the guys at Rodell's with the pretext that I was going to a meeting and the bus wouldn't work out.

On our way back to Oolitic, Anna said, "'Oh what a tangled web we weave / When first we practice to deceive.'"

"Shakespeare?"

"No, Sir Walter Scott."

"Is that how you feel?"

"Sometimes. I just wish we didn't have to be so secretive. And I don't like lying."

"I feel much the same way, Anna. Maybe when I get back from Newark we should meet with your parents and clear things up. What do you think?"

"Maybe, it might work with my mother but never with my father. He'd become violent."

"Did he ever hit you?"

"Sometimes but never like he did my mother."

"The bastard. How did you survive in that house?"

"Miss Jones" she said. "Without her, I have no idea how I would have survived. When I was in the third grade, my music teacher was Miss Jones. She lived in a room above Jay's Clothing. It's out of business now. She's the one that got me started on the viola. I liked her right away. She was great, always smiling. She never criticized me. I had to learn to play the violin first, and believe me, the sounds I made could've scared the dead. My school had this deal with a local music store where we could rent an instrument for just a little bit of money. I asked Mom and Dad if they would let me do it and it turned into a huge argument. Dad was against it but Mom was on my side. I'd never seen her get so mad at him. That's when Dad hit her. And I don't mean he slapped her—that had happened plenty of times. But this time, he hit her in the face with his fist. I could hear the crunch…I can still hear it. Then he hit her again and she fell over. I was crying, trying to get to her, get between them, but Dad pushed me away and I fell backwards. I think I went into shock or something, because the next thing I remember, Mom was locked in the bathroom and I was outside, banging on the door for her to let me in. She wouldn't open it, and finally I just went to my room and cried. I didn't see either of them until the next morning, and they acted like nothing had happened. Mom was missing one of her front teeth and her face was bruised. She got her tooth fixed later that week and we never even talked about it. That was the worst time but there were others. And every time it was the same thing, never a word said. It was like it never happened."

"When I went to Bible school the following Sunday, I told Father Lucas that I'd sinned. That I'd hurt my mom by wanting to play the violin. I told him that it had made my dad get really mad. Father Lucas said that it wasn't my fault. That God would take care of things. I don't know if it was God or Father Lucas but the next week, my dad went to the music store and got me a violin. It was half-size, perfect for me. He said I could play it as long as he didn't have to listen. I wasn't allowed to play at home, just at school. I stayed late every day and practiced. Mom used to come over once in a while, just to listen. When I got old enough, I switched to the viola. Miss Jones retired last year and moved to be with her brother in Nevada. She used to take me up to Bloomington on Saturdays to play in the youth orchestra at IU. She even took me to concerts and now and then she took me to a fancy restaurant in Bloomington where she taught me table manners and all that. I tell you, Jim, I'm certain that Miss Jones knew I had a tough home life and made an extra effort to make sure I was all right. So, to answer your question, that's how I survived. It was because I had a teacher who really cared. I'll miss her for the rest of my life."

"God bless Miss Jones," I said quietly with my guts in a knot, wanting more than anything to beat the living hell out of Anna's father.

We drove in silence until we reached my place in Oolitic where Anna left her mom's car.

Before she left, I asked Anna, "Can I write to you or…you

know, give you a call once in a while? Can we…stay in touch?"

"Privacy doesn't exist in my house, Jim. I want to keep this just between us for now, OK? Don't worry…I'm not going anywhere." She leaned forward and kissed me softly. "The moon," she said. "We'll talk to the moon. That'll work, don't you think?"

"Would you mind if I howled once in a while?"

"Howl yourself silly," she said, giving me a farewell kiss.

Climbing into her car, she said, "Now for some Shakespeare: 'Parting is such sweet sorrow.' I love you Jim Robertson, don't you forget that."

Beth

JUNE 20, 1993

17

The three-mile drive to Double J felt longer than my whole trip from Bloomington. Double J turned out to be a dirt road, making it feel like maybe I had four flat tires. I checked the napkin-map that Jill gave me and sure enough the word *dirt* was written just under Double J. All I could see in Hussy's rearview mirror was dust. The road was as straight as an arrow, with electric poles running down one side. I figured that meant people really did live out there.

It was pretty wonderful, actually. I mean I don't remember ever being in woods like this. I'm used to places like the IU campus where everything is manicured, no weeds, something blooming all the time. But here, it's nature doing its own thing. About a mile in, I came to the place Sam had described, a narrow grassy turn-off into the woods. I pulled off to the shoulder, parked, and got out. I crossed Double J and stood there, looking down the road into the woods. An iron rail gate painted silver closed it off; it was locked with a big padlock.

My belly was full of butterflies. There was something about

the way that grass road looked and felt—like nobody had used it in a very long time. I could see where tires had made ruts, but they were covered with grass. I thought about trying to maneuver Hussy around the gate, but large boulders on each side killed that idea. If I was going to trespass, it would have to be on foot.

I squeezed past the boulders and walked down the road, looking back every once in a while to make sure I could high-tail it back to the car if I had to. After twenty yards or so, the road curved to the left then sloped gently down a little hill. Part way down and to my right, I could just make out the roof of a small house. Maybe a cabin would be a better word. The roof was painted green so it blended into the trees. From the main road, you'd never know it was there. At the bottom of the hill there was a pile of rocks, or—not rocks really, but small blocks of stone. *Like a stone carver would use*, I thought. They were piled high into a cone shape that was taller than me—like somebody took a lot of trouble to build the thing. I stood there for a good long minute just looking up at it. I noticed that some of the blocks had words carved into them. *Interesting*. At that moment, though, I was really eager to get to the cabin and figured I could come back and check them out later.

Beyond the cone thing was a grassy field and further to my right was the cabin, its windows hidden behind wooden shutters that were painted the same green as the roof. So was the door.

Nobody was around, as far as I could tell. Just to make sure, I rapped hard on the door. No answer. I twisted the handle and the door gave just a little, then stuck. I turned back toward the grassy field. "Anybody here?" I yelled. My voice sounded different. Like it had wings.

Nobody answered. I walked around to the left side of the cabin, where bushes grew up around the foundation. I saw that one of the shutters was partly opened. A streak of sunlight was echoing off the partly exposed window. I pushed through the bushes to get to the window and then stood up on tiptoes, cupped my hands against the glass, and peeked in. A ray of sun was hitting the edge of a porcelain sink. I could make out stairs off to the right that seemed to go up into a loft. To the left, I could just make out part of a fireplace. The place was neat as a pin and didn't look the least bit lived-in. At least not lately. I hoped I was in the right place.

I went around to the back of the cabin and the first thing I saw was an old water- pump. I could tell that it had been painted red at one time, but rust had pretty much taken over. I couldn't resist grasping the big handle and giving it a few tugs. At first, it felt like it was broken, just clanked away. Then it started to get harder to lift and I heard gurgling like the pump was clearing its throat. When the water finally came, it did it in a big gush, splattering all over my sneakers. It ran a little rusty at first, but soon it was as clear as the sky, smacking onto a flat rock under the spout. I stopped pumping, shoved my cupped hands under the spout, and managed to get a nice handful. It tasted a little like iron, but was really cold and satisfying. I felt like maybe I was in one of those pioneer movies, like some little kid filling up a bucket to wash the dishes or take a bath or something.

My sneakers were soaked, so I took them off and warmed my feet in the sun. I leaned against the door and watched the pump dripping. I heard chattering that sounded like the squirrels back home. But when I scanned the nearby trees, which were just leafing out, I couldn't see anything. Birds were singing, but I had no idea what kind. I never noticed them much back home, except for the crows. There was no traffic noise or sirens or people talking. Just the sound of a light breeze in the trees and birds chirping away. I bet there wasn't even an ice-cream truck within a hundred miles of this place.

I scanned the field in every direction and saw big trees, little trees, little white flowers scattered everywhere, and bushes with little pink buds just aching to bust open. I closed my eyes, remembering a very similar sensation back in Indiana—just closing my eyes and listening. I'd been on the IU campus that time. I don't think there were birds though. I remembered hearing a violin so I must have been near the music building. The music I'd heard stuck with me. Every now and then I still hear it.

The sun felt great on my face and my feet were warming up. I let my mind wander. I'd left Bloomington just the day before, but it felt like it had been a lot longer. My parents' funeral had been just a week earlier but felt more like a lifetime ago. I wished I could call Mom and tell her where I was. I wondered if she could've told me where to find Anna—if this was even her place. Maybe Anna's house was further down the road, or maybe I'd missed it somehow. Maybe Sam knew more than what he'd told me and he was holding back. *Why didn't I press him for more details?* I felt a little panicky all of a sudden, like what seemed so peaceful was really full of hidden secrets.

Right then, I needed to get out of there and find out more. Somebody must know where Anna and Jim had gone.

"Where the hell are you, Anna?" I yelled into the woods, but only the birds answered, and they weren't telling.

I put my shoes back on and went back around to the front of the cabin. The grassy field in front of me was a lot bigger than our yard. I walked across it and came to some rubble that used to be a shack or tool shed or maybe a playhouse.

Something in the woods to my right at the edge of the field caught my eye—an old school bus. I did a double take because it looked so out of place. I could have missed it with all the bushes, but it still had most of its yellow paint and that stuck out against the green. The school name on its side was painted over in black and a dead branch lay across the roof.

I pushed through some thorny brambles to get a closer look, but I couldn't see in any of the bus's windows. It looked like they had curtains on them. I went around back and made my first real discovery. The license plate was rusty but I could still read "Indiana 1972." *Now we're getting somewhere!* But why a bus stuck here in the woods? Or was it some kind of camper? I came here to find my sister and so far it just felt like I was caught in some kind of mystery show. Perry Mason maybe or better yet an Alfred Hitchcock movie. I knew that was a bit over the top, but here I was with a cabin that was empty but being cared for, a pile of stones, and now an old school bus. What next?

I checked the door in the front of the bus but it wouldn't budge. So I went to the emergency door in the back. I grabbed the handle and it turned a bit. I pulled harder and the door creaked open. A musty smell that came rolling out reminded me of how our cellar smelled back home. I crawled up onto the bumper and stepped inside. Rusting tools laid scattered around like somebody just up and left. A thick canvas curtain separated me from the rest of the bus. When I pushed it aside, fine chalky dust fell and covered me from head to toe. Damn! I sneezed, fluffed my hair, and used my hands to brush myself off. I hadn't packed my suitcase with the idea that I'd be sleuthing around—no explorer's clothes. Once the dust settled, I walked slowly down the aisle of the bus, feeling like I had just stepped into a different world. I had been right when I thought that maybe it was a camper. Bunk beds, a place to cook, a built-in table. I went on forward, imaging Jim and Anna traveling around to places in this converted bus.

I was able to open the front door, welcoming in some much needed fresh air. I made myself comfortable on a chair next to a really neat built-in dinette table right behind the exit door. With all the work somebody put into changing this school bus into a camper, I wondered why they didn't they take it with them when they left. In fact, why did they leave in the first place? Why is the cabin so neat? I wasn't getting any answers sitting there. I got off my butt, and left the bus, intending to go back to Clayton, hoping for some real facts. I was closing the door when I heard somebody call my name. It sounded like the voice was coming from somewhere near the cabin. "Beth, are you here?"

Whoever it was—it was definitely a man's voice—he knew my name alright. Could it be Jim? Who else would know my name? I called back excitedly, "I'm over by the bus."

"I'll be right there," the man called back.

I peeked out of the door and saw this Paul Bunyan-type guy coming my way. He looked too old to be Jim, at least the way I pictured Jim to be. The closer he got the more nervous I became. How did he know my name? What does he want? I was ready to run—to where, I had no idea. I backed up. He stopped.

"I didn't mean to scare you. I'm Oscar. Oscar Golden. I knew Jim and Anna."

Knew Jim and Anna. Past tense. He didn't move...just

started talking real quietly, like you'd talk a cat out from under a bed.

He told me that Jill, the waitress from the Muskie Café, had told him I was coming out here, and that he figured he could answer whatever questions I had. When I didn't say anything, he asked me if I was okay. I wiped some dust off my blouse. "Just a bit dusty." I said. Responding to his quizzical look, I explained that I was in the bus looking around.

"No harm done, I suppose," he said. I took that to mean I was trespassing and better watch myself. A subtle warning but a warning nonetheless.

"Mister Golden, would you mind if I go up to the pump a wash up a little?"

"No I don't mind. I noticed the ground was wet around there so you must know where it is."

Subtle warning number two.

While we walked silently up to the pump, I felt sure that Mr. Golden knew the answers to all my questions; from the way he talked I guessed that getting him to open up would not be easy.

Mr. Goldman pumped while I washed my face and rinsed the dust from my hair.

When I was done, he handed me a big black-and-red bandana to use as a towel.

"It's clean," he said. "The missus just washed it."

It felt a little weird. I mean using his bandana like we were friends or something. Still it was better than cold water dripping all over me. I dried my hair and wiped off my face. When I handed it back to him I said, "Thank you Mr. Golden."

"I'd rather you call me Oscar. No need to be formal," he said, tossing his bandada over the pump to dry.

"I'll do that. By the way, is there a bathroom nearby?"

"There," he said, pointing to an outhouse at the end of a short path that ran behind the cabin. "Paper's on a nail just next to the door. I'll be right here."

An outhouse! This was new. I kept thinking a thousand spiders must live just under the toilet seat. I finished and got back outside as fast as I could, but I didn't hurry back to the pump. I took a little time to be with myself. I walked over to a bunch of tall pines and stood there, breathing in their heavy, piney scent. Immediately, I thought about Christmas. The first grade. We came to school one day and Miss Greyson had a big tree set up. The whole room smelled like that tree. For some reason, I found comfort in that simple memory. A minute later, a screechy bird or something made me jump a mile. I guess I was still a little shaky.

"It's just a blue jay. It won't hurt you," Oscar said, coming up the path.

"So..." I started, but really didn't know what else to say.

Oscar didn't seem to be in a hurry to talk about Jim and Anna. In fact, he didn't seem to want to talk at all—just pointed at the ground a little ways in the distance. I followed his finger but had no idea what I was looking for. "Yellow Lady Slipper," he said, walking a few feet and kneeling down on one knee. I followed and crouched next to him, feeling like a little girl discovering a new pretty something. It wasn't a bad feeling, really.

"Looks like a slipper, doesn't it?" I didn't answer. The flower was beautiful. I touched a petal and it was so soft I could barely feel it. Oscar stood up and looked around like he was a king of it all. He told me that in spring, the woods were covered with white flowers called *trillium*. The pink blossoms were wild cherry and the really red ones, paintbrushes.

"Blossoms help people forget about winter," he said, almost like he was just saying it to himself. "If they remembered it, nobody would ever stick around for the next one."

He started walking back toward the cabin and I followed him, dying to ask him about Jim and Anna, and why he said that he *I knew* them instead of *I know* them. When we got to the cabin, Oscar said, "My truck's up on the road, and Trooper's probably busting to get out. You want to come meet him?"

I guessed Trooper was a dog and nodded, although I wasn't a dog freak, especially for big ones. We hiked up the grassy road to Double J. Behind Hussy was a shiny red pickup. It looked new except for a scratch in the back, near the bumper. Inside was a big black dog. When I saw it, I stopped dead in my tracks. If he let that dog out, I was going to jump into the car and take off.

Seeing me act like a scared rabbit, Oscar said, "He's a big boy, but he's friendly enough—don't you worry about old Trooper. He just wants to stretch his legs—that OK?"

Trooper just sat there looking out of the window like a kid being kept in at recess. Oscar was looking at me too, a half smile on his face "Beth," he said quietly, "you can trust me and you can trust the dog. He's big but his heart's even bigger."

I just rolled my eyes, like *I give up,* and Oscar opened up the car door. The second Trooper leapt out, Oscar said, "Sit, now," and Trooper did as he was told, his tail wagging a mile a minute, sweeping a small cloud of dust off the dry road. Tentatively, I reached out and scratched his head, which was soft as silk. Oscar was right. Trooper was kind of a sweetheart. I bent down to rub him under the chin and he tried to lick my face, but I got out of the way of that tongue just in time. *No way.* I'd had enough of a shower under the pump.

I was suddenly struck with a thought. Yesterday at this time, I wasn't even in Wisconsin yet. Time had sped past, like I was standing still. It seemed like Heidi and Jake were on a different planet—or maybe I was. I'd been through so much in just a day, but I still didn't know anything about Anna. My head was buzzing with questions. The bus? The locked-up cabin? And who was this guy Oscar?

Here goes nothing, I thought and stood to ask. "You did say you knew Anna and Jim, right? So, do you know where they are?"

He just stood there staring into the woods like he didn't hear me or just ignoring my question. I was starting to get pissed. He was acting just like my supervisor at Walmart. Every time I'd ask about taking a break, she'd say something dumb like, how hot it was out, or how many kids were in the store. *Christ, what does it take to get a straight answer to a simple question?*

"Jim and Anna…" I said again. "Did she just disappear, or what?"

Oscar put his hand on fender of his truck and sort of leaned on it. "I heard you the first time," he said. "Why don't you tell me who you are and what you're doing in these parts, and we can go from there."

"I'm Anna's sister, that's who!" It just came out, but I was relieved once it did. I was kind of hoping he'd do a double take like Smithy Paulson did, but Oscar just looked at me. *Stared* is more like it.

"I didn't know she had a sister," he said as if he didn't care one way or the other.

"Well, join the crowd. Practically nobody else did either. Me included. This is her place, isn't it? The bus and all? It better be!"

Oscar moved away from truck. "Let's go down below, where we can talk." He gave some kind of signal to Trooper, and the dog followed him back across Double J and over to the gate.

I followed him to the bottom of the hill where we stopped by that weird tower of stones I came by earlier. He took one of the stones and handed it to me, but I almost dropped it because it was a lot heavier than it looked. I looked closer at the carved writing and read the words: *Sgt. Robert Wilson. Killed in action, October 18, 1969.* Oscar told me to turn it over, and I saw more stuff: *Your wife wears your old red shirt every night.*

I looked at Oscar. "So, what does it mean?"

He just held out his hand so I could give him the stone back. He set it in place and handed me another one: *Pfc. Frederick T. Jonas. Killed in action, March 23, 1970. The boys still talk about the time you bagged the twelve-pointer.*

"What is all this?"

"It's a memorial. To some of the boys who died in Vietnam." He didn't offer anything more, though he must have known I was curious. I swear, Trooper talked more than this guy. I mean, what was so hard about explaining things? It felt like I'd been with him half the afternoon and I had more questions now than when I pulled up on Double J.

Oscar walked away from the stone pile, and once again, I had no choice but to follow. Well…I guess I could've just jumped in my car and driven back to Indiana. But I wasn't ready to do that. I watched Oscar walk across the field toward the broken-down shack. The grass was high enough that he left a trail behind him. *If it was mowed, it'd be a pretty nice backyard.*

Without looking back, Oscar walked over by the busted

shed and stood there looking down at it. "This was Jim's carving shed," he told me. It finally seemed the right time to talk, so I launched into the story of my visit to Oolitic, and meeting Smithy Paulson. "That's how I knew Jim was a stone carver," I said. He pretty much just listened and nodded, so I kept talking. I told him about my parents dying, finding the letter…I kept expecting a big reaction, like, *Wow, what a story,* but he just stared at me like he had when I first told him that Anna was my sister.

I won't lie; his reaction made me a little uncomfortable. He didn't smile or anything, just studied me like, well…a science experiment or something. I hate being stared at. How long can anybody stand being stared at?

From the way Oscar responded, it was like he already knew about everything I told him. Like not a single thing I said surprised him. Maybe the guys back at the Muskie Café knew, too. Maybe the whole damn world knew stuff about me and my family that *I* didn't know. The thought of that made me pissed off again, like I was left to go it alone. I turned away from Oscar. *Let him look at my backside awhile* I thought, and walked a few steps toward the cabin. But I couldn't give up. I turned back to face him. I had to get answers.

"She was pregnant when she wrote the letter," I said, with a little defiance in my voice. "She already had a daughter named Sarah." I decided it was my turn to stare, and Oscar didn't seem to like it any more than I did. He moved away from the shed toward the woods. He stopped at what looked like a path that I hadn't noticed before. It cut into the woods at an angle so it wasn't easy to see, but maybe it was more visible from the cabin. I was about to tell Silent Oscar to shove it when he finally started talking. He didn't turn toward me though…just kept looking in the woods.

"A storm came through," he started out, talking really slowly, like the words were so heavy they were hard to get out. "It caught Anna out here—up there a ways…" He pointed up the path.

"What kind of storm?"

"Heavy wind. Knocked a lot of trees down."

"Did she get hurt?"

"It was a bad time…."

"Oscar, what are you telling me?" I said in a voice that didn't even sound like mine. I felt tears coming. "Please tell me what happened to Anna!" Oscar could see I was really upset but he didn't take a single step toward me—just stood where he was, at the head of the path.

"Anna didn't make it, Beth. A tree caught her."

"A tree caught her? You mean she died?! Is that what you're saying? That Anna's dead?"

"I'm sorry, Beth. All afternoon, I've been trying to work out how to break it to you, but there's just no good way to do it. I'm really sorry you came all the way out here to hear more bad news. You've certainly had your share of it."

Sorry?! Everybody was sorry…Father Jamison and the ladies and everybody at the funeral told me they were sorry about a million times. But what does that mean? Sorry for what? It wasn't their fault that my parents were in an accident, and it wasn't Oscar's fault that Anna died. And it didn't help me one bit to hear how sorry they all were.

"Beth…let's go back to the cabin for a little while," Oscar said, and for once there was real feeling in his voice.

Jim

1974–1975

18

Anna's parting words "I love you Jim Robertson, don't you forget that" stuck with me the entire time I was away. There were lonely times to be sure. But it felt good to be back doing what I was meant to do.

It took two days driving the eight-hundred mile journey to Newark. I followed the directions I had written out earlier. I drove up Bloomfield Avenue, turned right onto Clifton, and parked in front of the Sacred Heart Cathedral. I'd been to lots of churches with Sal, but this one was different. It was magnificent—overwhelming, almost. Two-story, double-hung bronze doors welcomed visitors inside—or kept them out. Sal once said that carvings mean nothing until they're in the place they were designed for. "You see a statue all done, sitting on the carving floor, and it's one thing," he'd said. "You set it up in the church or courtyard or whatever, and you got something else. If you do your job right, it becomes *sacred*."

When I stepped through those big doors, Sal's words came to life. Everywhere I looked there were carvings: saints, angels, shepherds, popes, stations of the cross, Mary, Joseph, Jesus, the Disciples, balustrades, flying buttresses, arcs, lintels…the quantity and variety of the pieces were staggering.

When I'd first seen the place from the outside, I'd thought it would be dark as midnight in there, but it was sparkling. Light shot in from big stained-glass windows, coloring the air in a manner I'd never experienced. Long, low oak pews stretched to the far walls to my right and left. By the time I reached the altar, I felt smaller than a scared private on his first day of boot camp. Exposed. As if I'd done something bad. I stopped at the altar rail and gazed up at the vaulted ceiling soaring roughly 200 feet above me. A massive crucifix hung directly over my head. I almost fell over backwards looking up at it.

"Excuse me. Excuse me, young man. May I help you?" The voice came from everywhere and nowhere. I turned nearly in a circle before I saw a tall man dressed in a black, floor-length robe. It was like he had come out of nowhere.

"I'm Jim Robertson. Here to work on the stone," I blurted. "My bus is parked out front."

"I'm sorry…bus?" said the priest.

"My work bus. I have my shop in it, and—"

"Your shop?"

I took a deep breath and started over. I explained that I'd been sent to repair a carving of John the Baptist that had been damaged.

"I'm supposed to see a Mr. Byers."

"Oh…yes," said the priest, a light finally dawning. "It's in the baptistery. Superintendent Byers takes care of the edifice." He swept his arm around his head. "Isn't it grand?"

"It certainly is," I said earnestly. "It must have taken quite a while to complete it."

"Oh, it did, young man. We started it in 1898, but with the wars and all, work was halted and resumed numerous times. We didn't hold our first service here until 1954."

I waited politely for him to say more, but he simply turned away and said, "Please follow me, I'll help you find Mr. Byers." The priest crossed himself in front of the altar before slipping his hands under a flap that hung in front of his robe. I didn't know what to do, so I gave a little nod in that direction, and followed him through a small door to the right of the altar. A narrow corridor ran along the back of what I guess you'd call the *apse,* to a wide hallway paved in shiny terrazzo that seemed to go on forever. The walls were painted a soft cream color. The priest stopped by an office door, dark oak paneled with an arched frame.

"Please wait here," he said.

After a few awkward minutes of standing in the empty hallway, a man who introduced himself as Fred Byers appeared. Byers was short and stocky, dressed in a drab tan shirt with an emblem that read *Superintendent.* The first thing he said after we exchanged names was, "Where are you parked?"

"Out front," I said. "I'm driving my Working Schoolie," I said.

"A what?"

I repeated myself, adding, "It's where I work and sleep." I didn't tell him about this being the first time I had her on the road.

"Sleep? We had a room set aside for you in the rectory. I think that'd be a bit more comfortable." The idea of staying in a rectory wasn't my cup of tea so I thanked him for the offer and I told him I'd be happier staying in the bus. "Well, hmm… I guess there's room enough if you park at the far end of the lot."

"There is one more thing you might help me with. I need to rent a car, I mean I can't ride around driving a bus."

"No, I agree," he chuckled. We do have two cars at the rectory. Perhaps you can use one of those once in awhile. Will that work? If not, I can drive you to a car rental place."

"That'll do." I said.

"The borrow or the rental?"

"The rental."

"Later today after we get you settled."

I drove the bus around to the back of the church, as instructed. Byers was waiting and pointed out where he wanted me to park. Then with a mumbled "follow me," he led me to the baptistery. I spent the rest of the day studying Al's carving—a large piece framed in oak—from the top of a heavy ladder.

The scene was Christ baptizing John, who stood knee-deep in water. Two bowing, haloed angels looked on. Cherubs peeked from the corners. Above, a dove fluttered. Everything was carved in prime Indiana limestone. It had Al written all over it, his chisel marks as good as a signature. There was a lot more work in it than met the eye. That scaffolding, or whatever it was, had really done a number on it. Damage was everywhere. Chips and scratches. A gouge ran down John's forehead. Christ's little finger was missing. On our way to pick-up a rental, I told Mr. Byers that the job would take a couple weeks or more, which got me a "That'll work."

Getting the repair work finished by early December was a stretch. Services were held daily, and I couldn't work while they were going on, nor during weddings, funerals, choir practice, organ practice, confessions…you name it. After a week of constant interruptions, I decided to carve between nine at night and five in the morning, which I got to like. Trying to sleep during the day was rough, though. The parking lot was noisier than a bowling alley. I thought about parking someplace else during the day, but it would be easier to drive a personnel carrier into battle than a school bus around Newark.

To pass my free time, I decided to carve something for Anna. Something small that she could keep hidden. I sketched out a few designs and settled on a round piece of marble that would be the size of a pocket watch but thicker. Looking for the right piece of marble led me to a kitchen counter business and they sent me to a warehouse in the nearby community of Montclair. I picked out a piece of pink marble that was perfect except that it was a two ton block that cost more than a small house. The salesman offered me a scrap piece of pink marble left over from somebody's kitchen redo. It wasn't exactly what I was looking for, but it would work. Having no access to a stone-cutting saw, I had the company cut the piece to size. I paid the man and left.

Into the middle of one side, I carved the name *Anna* surrounded by mistletoe. I used my tiniest chisels and some rifflers to smooth the finish. On the other side of the stone, I carved the words, *I love you now and forever* around the edge, leaving the middle blank for a wedding date, hoping it would some day come to that. It took me around twenty hours of meticulous work to finish the job. I wrapped it up in some clean rags and it packed it deep in my duffle bag where it joined my Diary.

Late at night, the clink of my maul and chisel bounced all around the church. Every now and then, I'd get into a rhythm—a cha-cha or something—and then I'd hum along. I sang. I talked to Sal. I listened to Al's ghost complain about the stupid bastard who damaged one of his best pieces. Thoughts of Vietnam and my soldiers would flicker in and out of my imagination like looking at an old-time movie. But most of the time, I thought about Anna.

On Monday, December 18, 1975, I made my final tap against the stone. I spent an hour or so showing off my work to Byers and the priest. They were duly impressed, and more than sufficiently grateful—there was a nice bonus in my check. But my mind was already on getting back to Oolitic. To see Anna, and to sleep in a real bed—I kept the two separate. A certain kind of patience seemed to accompany the certainty I had about her, and I was willing to wait. I'd occupy myself working on my memorial.

An idea for the memorial came to me during one of my visits to an industrial town named Kearney, located just across the Passaic River from Newark. Visiting the city park one day, I noticed a little symmetrical pile of stones someone had set up. A local guy told me it was a *cairn*. He explained that in Scotland, when a soldier went off to war, he'd take a stone from his garden and place it on a pile with all the others, usually in the town square or other public place. Soldiers that came back picked up stones from the pile, took them home and put them back in their gardens. The stones that were left became a memorial. That touched me. It was such a simple idea, and such a human one. It was just what I was looking for.

I decided that day that my own memorial would take the form of a cairn. I'd use limestone blocks the size of cobbles. On each one I'd carve the name of one of my soldiers and something personal about them from my diary. I'd assemble them all into some sort of pile, then try to contact as many of my soldiers' families as I could and invite them to come and pay their respects. They could take their soldier's stone with them if they wanted it, or leave it as part of the memorial. Anyone who couldn't make it, I'd offer to send them their stone—or take care of it for them.

19

It was late when I got home to Oolitic, and my back yard was pitch black. I grabbed the flashlight from under the seat and headed for the door, which was wide open. My Army training took over. I pitied any son-of-a-bitch dumb enough to cross me that night.

I reached in the doorway and flicked the light switch. Nothing. I slipped inside and found a godawful mess. Furniture was tossed around, clothes and papers strewn, even the calendar was torn off the wall. Somebody had had a good old time trashing every inch of the place.

I was trembling with rage. *Whoever did this is going to pay a hell of a price.* Stepping over the debris I headed for the bathroom to take a leak. Above the toilet was a note: 'Come to Mabel's.' An address was scribbled below.

With the exception of noise spilling out of the shabby Quarrymen's Bar and Grill, Oolitic was closed down tighter than a vacuum-packed jar of pickles. The hardest part of my walk over to Mabel's was walking down streets that, until that moment, had always seemed as friendly and welcoming as any I'd known in Milwaukee. Now I kept looking around to make sure nobody was going to jump me.

I ducked behind Russel's Grocery, walked the edge of the Soo Line railroad bed, crossed 6th Street, and crept along Mabel's backyard fence. I slipped through her half-opened gate, climbed the three steps onto her back porch and lightly tapped on the door. The next-door neighbor's dog opened up like cannon fire and I jumped a mile. The door opened and there was Mabel.

"I've been worried about you. Get in here!"

We stood in her dimly lit kitchen and I stole a few glances around. I'd never been to Mabel's place before, and here she was, standing in front of me in a long flannel nightgown.

"Don't pay any mind to that damn-fool dog," she said. "Come over here by the table. We have work to do."

"What the hell's going on?"

"Come sit and have some tea so I can tell ya."

"Those Adamskis—so I hear—boarded Anna up in her bedroom. They aren't the nicest people, everybody knows that. But I'm sure she's not been hurt or nothing. I just don't know."

She stopped talking—maybe because she could see I was seething. What kind of people would board up their daughter? I felt like I was in the middle of a Li'l Abner comic strip. Except there was nothing funny about this. And what did this have to do with my trashed home?

Mabel prepared the tea and carried the steeping cups to the table. "There's some fresh poppy seed rolls in that tin next to you. Help yourself, if you're hungry—and I imagine you are. Here's some cream for your tea. The sugar's in the bowl there, by the napkins." Mabel sat down across from me.

We sat stirring our tea. I got a poppy seed roll from the tin. I didn't realize how hungry I was until I'd wolfed it down. Mabel said she had some ham in the icebox, but I asked her to sit a minute. I needed some answers. "What's this all about?" I said

Mabel straight-armed, putting her palms flat on the table. "Near as I can figure it, Anna told her girlfriend—that snitch Gloria Hughes—that she's in love with you and that you two have been sneaking off together since the dance and it went from there."

"What do you mean 'went on from there'?"

"The gossip train came rumbling through town, that's what happened."

"Don't people fall in love around here? What's the big deal?"

Mabel's explosive response startled me so that my mug of tea almost went flying, "A man—what's your age?—and a veteran at that, messing around with a sixteen-year-old girl? I don't know how it is where you're from, but that's a big deal around here!"

"Look, Mabel, thanks for your help, but I've about had it up to here with Oolitic and Bedford...the entire state of Indiana for that matter. I've never seen people so goddamn righteous. So, I'm twenty-four and Anna's seventeen—not sixteen like you told me, by the way. And she'll be eighteen in two months."

"Sorry about that, but seventeen is still illegal. Why don't you go over and explain that to Emil Adamski. I'm sure he'll give you his ever lovin' blessing." She paused for a moment and told me to think about things while she made me a sandwich.

There was no point in going on about what did or didn't happen. Obviously, that wasn't even the point, since I'd already been tried and convicted in the court of public opinion. I'd pretty much decided to put this place in my rearview mirror—but I wasn't planning to leave without Anna if she was willing to go.

I realized then and there that I certainly did need some help. "Look, Mabel," I said while she made the sandwich. "I've got to get Anna. You were right about us…crazy as it is, we're in love, and I don't intend to just walk away, no matter how many people threaten me or trash my house. If anybody harms that girl—including her father—I'll kill the son-of-a-bitch!" I started to get up.

"That'll be enough of that," Mabel wagged her finger at me.

I flopped back down. "Mabel, why are you getting involved in this? You hardly know me."

"I've asked myself the same question and best answer I can give you is because I know firsthand what it's like to have love torn apart and that's all I'm going to say about it. Besides I can use a good adventure once in a while. If you don't want my help just let me know."

"No, I appreciate everything you're doing, I'm just curious."

"Well you know what that did to the cat. Now let's get down to business. We gotta make a plan," she said busying herself with her own sandwich. "We're lucky those vultures didn't come for you already. We can't overpower 'em so we gotta outsmart 'em. Muscles they got, brains, not so much."

"If I don't get Anna tonight, who knows what'll happen?"

"That's why we gotta—" The phone rang. "You sit still while I get that," Mabel said, waddling quickly into a hallway off the kitchen.

I was still stewing. While I was in Newark, I had planned it all out. Get married. Settle in Oolitic. Work on my memorial. If that meant waiting for Anna, I would wait for a month of Sundays. But that plan was shot to hell. Mabel came back into the kitchen.

"That was Alma Stinson, busybody who lives next door. Thanks to that mutt of hers, she spotted you—knows you're here. Good news is, she's kind of a romantic at heart—says she feels bad for you. I guess she's willing to help too, if it comes to it."

"How about Smithy Paulson? He's always struck me as a guy with his head on straight, and I know he likes me. He sharpening his pitchfork like the others?"

"I haven't seen Pete, but I would be awful careful. If I was to say, I think he'd be on your side, but you never know. When Smithy gets mad—why once he nearly threw my Matthew over a fence. It was down at the picnic grove and—"

"Mabel, sorry to interrupt, but I have to go."

"Well, darn, I'm just beside myself about how two old widows can help you—'sides feeding you that is."

"Mabel, you've already helped me, by being straight with me and hearing me out. And feeding me, to boot—thanks for the sandwich. You know…maybe there is something you and Alma could do. It's a long shot but is there any chance one of you knows how to drive a school bus?"

Mabel lit up.

"Shoot, I drove a limestone truck during the war, when the men were away. Couldn't be that much different."

"You did?" I chuckled at the thought of that.

"Don't you be laughing at me, you snot nose. Lots of us did. What'd you think, that we sat on our backsides when our men were off fighting?"

"No, I'm just…surprised. Can you handle a two-speed rear-end?"

"A two-speed? Why didn't you say so? I can shift a rear-end with the best of them!" She laughed as she pretended to shift gears with her right hand.

"Why, it's like part of me. Those old Brockways.... So, tell me...just what do you have in mind?"

"I'm not completely sure, but if you can get to my bus while I'm getting Anna and park it someplace near her place, maybe we can get out of here before anybody comes after us."

"That'd be a neat trick," she said, "with half the town on the lookout for you and the girl being held by her daddy..."

"Well that's where your neighbor comes in. Maybe she could mislead them all—get them onto a wild goose chase."

"By gosh darn, you are a devil. Somewhere between slim and none, we might just have a chance. Alma don't know a whole heck of a lot, but she knows how to handle a bunch of nitwits. Since her man left for God knows where, they flit around her like flies to honey. She won the Queen of Oolitic Crown back in forty-five. Why, the soldiers just went crazy over her, still do, by golly. I remember one time when Alma—"

"Mabel!"

"Oh, listen to me goin' on! Where's that bus of yours?"

"Parked at my place, key's in the ignition."

It was just past nine-thirty. We worked out a plan: I'd go with Mabel to the bus and get some tools, in case I had to get in through Anna's window. I'd give Mabel a few pointers about the bus, we'd split up and meet back up at the Salt Creek bridge.

"How long do you think it'll take for Alma to get the men away from Anna's house?" I asked Mabel.

"Let me talk it over with her," she said, and disappeared back to the hallway and I could hear her murmuring on the phone. When she returned, she was smiling.

"That Alma, what a gal. She said it'd take no time at all for her to convince 'em to run off after you. She's planning to send 'em down by the quarry—she's gettin' all dolled up to distract 'em, too. Said give her fifteen minutes or so, which is just about how long it'll take us to get everything you need. You ready?"

"Ready as ever. There's only one thing. What if Anna won't come with me?"

Mabel gave me a look of disbelief and said, "Let's go."

The first part of the plan went like clockwork. I watched Mabel pull away down the road in my old bus, driving it like she was born behind the wheel. I'd never been to Anna's house, but Mabel's directions were right on target and I found it easily. From the other side of the road, I could see four guys out front, standing around a hot charcoal grill listening to Jim Nabors singing Christmas Carols. I fell back down the block, cut through a neighbor's yard, and slipped around back, thinking that my experiences in 'Nam were coming in handy in a new and unexpected way.

Lucky for me, the place was a one-story ranch. Two of the four windows facing the backyard were covered with sheets of plywood, so I figured those were Anna's bedroom windows. I tapped quietly on the plywood. Nothing. Again, this time louder. A tap came back. I whispered, "Anna?"

I heard her whisper my name back to me; sweetest sound ever.

Suddenly, there was a commotion coming from the front of the house, followed by shouts of, "Let's get the bastard!" I stood stock-still until I heard them all jump into their pickups and tear off toward the quarry. Thank you, Alma!

Working as quietly as I could, I pried the plywood off the

window one sheet at a time. It was thin stuff, one step above cardboard. I didn't even need the pry-bar I'd brought from the bus. The second I could see her, Anna put her index finger to her lips.

"My mom's in the living room," she whispered.

"And your dad?" I whispered back.

"He ran off with those men looking for you."

I watched as she grabbed her backpack, dumped her schoolbooks and papers onto the bed, then rushed about filling it with clothes and other little things.

"Got your coat?"

"I can't. It's in the hall." She grabbed a heavy sweater out of her closet. "Here," she said, passing it through the open window, followed by her backpack and viola case.

"What's going on in there, honey?" It was her mother. We both held our breaths for a second.

"Nothing, Mom" Anna called back. "Just listening to the radio." She pulled the blanket off her bed and passed it to me, grabbed her purse, and was out of the window in a flash. We took a quick second for a hug before scurrying away to meet Mabel at the bridge, about a quarter of a mile away through a stretch of woods that Anna knew like the back of her hand.

We waited under the bridge like trolls for what seemed like hours. To stave off the chill, we cuddled up under the blanket, and that got us warm real quick. Just as I was getting ready to go out and try to track Mabel down—figuring she'd put the old bus into a ditch or something—she rounded the corner like a house afire.

"Get in, quick," she said. "I don't know how long it'll be before the guys figure out they was had."

Once we'd scrambled aboard, Mabel told us that Sheriff Chipole had stopped her thinking it was me. When he threatened to blow the whole thing wide open, Mabel told him she'd have no qualms about telling his wife about his trips to Alma's house. *To get his fill of donuts, so to speak,* is how she put it.

"That stopped him cold as a fish in ice water. Now get this bus out of here and go hide yourselves before it's your hide they've got!"

"What about getting you back to your house?" I asked, realizing we hadn't nailed down that part of the plan.

"I've been walkin' for more years than you've been eatin'," she said. "I know I'm a plump old thing, but I'll get there, don't you worry. Lovers' wings ain't no good lest you use 'em. Now git goin' before you can't."

Mabel turned to Anna and gave her a hug.

"And you, dear, you take good care of yourself."

We both thanked her as she shooed us into the bus with a Merry Christmas and a couple of pats on the rear.

"We'll never forget you, Mabel," Anna said.

"Few people do, dear," she said. "Now git!"

I slipped behind the wheel. "Merry Christmas," Mabel called out as I pulled slowly onto Route 37 North.

20

I had never thought about how the bus smelled. Greasy. Maybe a little moldy, like an old garage. I hadn't thought much about how it rode, either. Like a troop carrier with a busted tread. With Anna on board, I noticed everything. I began to see it as a bachelor pad on wheels—a wreck, if I wanted to admit it. I wished it went faster. Floored, it moved alright, but it wasn't what you'd call limber.

From the driver's seat it was hard to see Anna, who was sitting across the aisle in the seat behind the steps. Every time the road straightened out, I'd twist my neck around to catch a glimpse of her. She was snuggled in her blanket like it was a cocoon, her viola safe in its case on the seat next to her.

We were just south of Indianapolis when the bus lurched. My eyes went straight to the gas gauge: half full, so that wasn't the problem. We lurched again, this time followed by a quick buck.

"Is something wrong?" Anna said, sounding a little panicky.

"Hmm…might be the fuel pump," I said, pulling out the choke. The air-starved engine sounded like a snorting bull.

"Is that bad?" she asked. The bus jerked and bobbed. I tightened my grip on the wheel, willing her forward.

"Bad enough," I said, steering the bus to the side of the road.

"Can I do something?" Anna asked.

"I don't think so."

I pulled on the parking brake and flicked off the ignition, cut the lights and flicked on the blinkers. I looked over to Anna. "We might be here for awhile," I said. "May I join you?"

"I'd like that," she said, putting her viola case under the seat to make room. She opened the blanket to me. I sat down as close to her as it was possible for a person to get. The heat she'd stored in the blanket went right to my core. "How long do you think we'll be stuck here?" she asked.

"Not long I hope. I'll try starting it after giving the engine time to cool down. If that doesn't work, I'll have to find a way to get a tow."

"And just how are you going to do that? I thought you said this bus was in good shape."

"It didn't give me any trouble on my trip to Newark."

I could feel Anna's body becoming tense. "And just where does one find a tow in the middle of nowhere?" Pulling away from me she continued, "I mean, why do we have to run away like this? It's just everything happened so fast Jim. I didn't even know that you were back. And then you show up at my house. It doesn't seem real, yet here we are together. I don't even know where we're going, do you?"

As I was about to answer, flashing red lights flew across the windows. Anna squeezed my hand. "Why are police here?" she asked.

"Probably to help," I said, hoping I was right.

Hurrying to get out of the blanket I tripped, landing face

down on the floor. Back on my feet, I reached over, grabbed the door handle and gave it a pull. Below stood a cop, solidly built like the first six feet of the Washington Monument. Anna pulled the blanket tightly around herself. Looking me over with a bright flashlight, he asked, "A breakdown?"

"The engine, sir. I think it's not getting fuel. Maybe the fuel pump."

"Could be," he said. "Would you mind stepping off the bus. I'll need your license and registration."

"There on the back of the sun visor, I'll need to get them."

Keeping the flashlight on me, he gave me the go-ahead.

I gave a quick glance to Anna, stepped out of the bus and handed both cards to the officer. "Is there anyone else on board?" he asked.

"Yes Sir, my girlfriend."

"Ask her to step out, please."

I did as I was told.

Anna appeared at the door, the blanket draped over her shoulders. She stepped off the bus and stood next to me.

"Where are you headed?"

"We're going to Milwaukee, sir," I answered directly. This was news to Anna, who thankfully didn't say a word. Looking at Anna, he asked, "And what about you, miss? If there's anything you want to tell me about why you're here, now's the time."

"I'm fine, sir. I mean…Officer, sir…"

"No need to be nervous, young lady. I'm here to help. You have some identification?"

"My driver's license. It's in my purse…right on the seat inside."

"You can go and get it miss."

Anna came back with her license, which the officer put with the two cards I had given to him.

"I need to call these in. It won't take long so feel free to go back inside."

We hurried back in, and I tried starting engine. It turned over all right, but didn't fire. I joined Anna back under the blanket. "Do you think we're in trouble?" she asked.

"I don't see why we would be."

"Milwaukee? I remember you telling me that you were born there. Right?"

"Right you are."

"That's all I really know about your childhood. When are you going to fill me in?"

"As soon as we can have more than a few stolen hours together."

It didn't take long before the officer came back. We stepped off the bus again.

"Everything checks out, except for one thing. Have either of you heard of the term *Age of Consent*?" He sounding very serious. My heart began pounding. Anna nestled closer. We looked at each other in panic, too scared to say anything. "I didn't think so," the officer said matter-of-factly. "Well here in Indiana, if you're under eighteen having sex with someone older, it's illegal. It's pretty much the same in Wisconsin. I'm not going to press the issue with Miss Adamski having only two months before becoming legal, except to say for you two to take this warning seriously." He handed us back our cards.

Relieved beyond words, we gushed forth with thank you's and promises to take his advice. True to character, he maintained the dignity of his office and said nothing more about it.

After a short pause, he changed the subject altogether and said, "I heard you trying start the engine."

"No go, Sir."

"Let me see if I can get somebody down here," he said and walked back to his car.

I suggested to Anna that she might be more comfortable getting back on the bus, that I'd wait until the officer returned. I got a kiss on the cheek and Anna disappeared back into the bus. Alone in the cold night air, I thought about what Anna was saying before we were interrupted by those flashing red lights. We had known each other for six months. We still needed to learn so much about each other. Not just names, dates, and places, but the emotional side of things. Like what brings out a smile or a laugh, or heartbreak and tears. How we each think about ourselves or our place in the world. I had no doubt that Anna and I were in love. But that was only the beginning, the starting point of getting to love each other for who we are and what we become as our lives moves forward.

I was about to get back in the bus when the officer pulled up to me. Rolling down his window he said, "Josh is on the way. His place is just down the road, over by Clark's Hill. If anybody can get you back on the road, it's Josh. Good man."

"Thank you, sir, thank you for everything."

"Division?" he asked, catching me off guard. "Vietnam," he said.

"Quartermaster Corp sir. Grave Registration."

"Tough duty. Remember, this consent business is serious stuff." He drove away.

I stepped back in the bus, thinking how close I had come to being arrested. I flopped down in the driver's seat. It had been a long day with a good serving of stress. I was getting very sleepy and that was when it hit me that unless we found a motel or something, Anna would have to sleep on the bus. I leaned down and put my head on the steering wheel and closed my eyes in frustration.

Shortly, a wrecker pulled up, flashing amber. I got out of the bus and got a good look at Josh. He was dressed in greasy coveralls pulled up over a thick sweater. Tufts of hair were sticking out from a well-worn watch cap pulled down low over his forehead. He was tall and lean as a string bean.

"Before I try to get you to my garage, I'll feed her some dry gas and we'll see," he said. "You go turn it over."

Within minutes, the old bus was purring like a contented cat.

"Just some ice in the gas line," he said. "Should be okay now." Palm up, he added, "Twelve bucks will do."

I paid him and asked, "Is there a place we can stay the night?"

"There's motels up the way near the interstate but they're usually filled-up this time a year. Snow-birds heading south. Bit late to keep going. You could park behind my shop for the night if you want. Ain't fancy or nothin', but it'll get you off the road. You got some place to sleep in that bus of yours?"

"Yeah, I do," I answered.

"Then follow me."

This whole time Anna was scrunched up in her blanket, looking like she might be sleeping. I left her be but once we started moving, she got up and stood next to me. "Have a nap?" I asked.

"No. I was thinking about us. But I don't want to talk about it until we find the time and a warm place for me to have a good night's sleep."

I didn't say anything, buying time to think about what to do about the sleeping arrangements. In less than ten minutes, I had the bus parked in back of a battered old corrugated steel Quonset hut with a worn, hand-lettered sign that read 'Josh's Repair Shop.' "Use the facilities if ya need to," Josh said, waving the back of his hand at a battered door with a sign that read, *Place of Rest*. (Junkyard humor, I guess.) "I'm goin' back ta bed," he added over his shoulder as he disappeared around the side of the rusting building.

Anna scurried off to the facility while I got the heater going.

I'd been sleeping in the same sleeping bag for a few months so I was hesitant to give her that. I remembered an old army blanket I'd stuck in the back and went off to get it.

Coming back down the aisle, I saw that Anna had returned. "Not the cleanest blanket in the world. Sorry about all this."

"No, it's...to be honest, I'm a little nervous, I guess," she confessed. "I mean, being out here...you know...alone. Together. Remember what the cop said about me being illegal?"

"Anna," I said, gently, "I think what we really need is a good night's sleep. I'll take the left side bunk, you can use the one on the right."

Looking a little relieved, she gave me a quick peck on the cheek and we walked toward the back of the bus. When I'd installed the beds with the boys from Rodell's, I could never have imagined Anna sleeping on one of them.

"A-1 prison issue," I joked, folding the grimy army blanket in half and laying it on the cot. "If you need anything else, you'll have to yell; I sleep like a log."

"I'll be fine," Anna said firmly. "Don't worry about me. Goodnight." She dismissed me with another peck on the cheek, then crawled into bed. I could feel her watching me as I slinked into mine, slipping into the sleeping bag. I was exhausted.

In the morning, Anna woke me up with a light tap to my leg. Seeing her was like glimpsing an apparition, or the tail-end of a dream. The bus's windows were covered with frost.

"Hello," I said. Anna laughed.

"Remember me? Anna?"

"How could I forget?" The words came out like slurry. I still wasn't in full command of much of anything.

"It's a beautiful day," she chirped, all bright and shiny.

I crawled out of bed. "Warm enough?"

"Perfect. I had a good night's sleep. How about you?"

"Same as you," I answered, rubbing frost off a side window for a view of Josh's Repair Shop. Two large, well-used farm tractors framed a battered garage door. A rough tangle of cars and trucks in various states of decay and disrepair were spread around the place concentrically from the garage, stopping at the edge of a cornfield. Beyond, the cornstalk stubble stretched as far as I could see.

"For my first official night away from home, I think I did all right," Anna said, giving the new day a positive slant.

I opened my arms to her. We hugged. She stopped me from giving her a kiss, "Toothbrush first."

"I guess we should clean up and get going," I said.

"Yes, we should. But first I have to ask, are we still heading to Milwaukee?"

"Yes. To Hans's place."

"Who's Hans?"

"Oh, of course. Sorry… Hans is a very good old friend of

mine—you'll love him. I'll give him a call before we leave."

"When you talk to him, please tell him about our age difference. Given what that officer said yesterday, I don't think we should take any risk."

"Good suggestion but I don't think he'll care one way or the other. Why don't you take the first turn at the *place of rest*," I laughed, "while I make the call."

Once Anna had scurried off, I went around behind the bus, took a leak and headed for the phone.

As I got ready to make the call, Josh came out of his shop. "Good Morning," he said. "Have a good sleep?" I nodded. "Well that's good. By the way, your bus, does it need some fixin' up? Oil change or anything. You know you're welcome to stay while I give it a good lookover." I told him no thanks, that everything was fine since he fed it some dry gas. "Well, I was thinkin' that's all."

I could tell by his tone of voice that he was disappointed with losing out on some business. I handed him a ten dollar bill and thanked him for letting us stay the night. He gave me a smile and disappeared into his shop. I made my call.

21

"Nice to hear from you. How's living down in Indiana?"

Afraid of running out of quarters, I gave Hans a quick summary of what I was up to, then asked if it was alright to come for a visit, bringing along my girlfriend, Anna. When I mentioned our age difference, Hans showed concern.

"How much of a difference?"

I didn't expect this. "Anna will be eighteen in February."

"That's still makes her underage. Have her parents given her their blessing?"

I tried not to sound desperate. "Not really... Hans, trust me on this. I know that I'm asking a lot."

"Jim, it's not a matter of trust. It's a matter of law." Hans paused a second, which felt like forever, then said, "I don't think we can talk about all this on a phone call. Why don't you and Anna come on ahead. We can talk more about this once you get here. Do you have a place to stay?"

I hemmed and hawed, too screwed up to answer. "Okay, you can use our two separate guest rooms, he said, emphasizing the word separate. "When will you be arriving?"

"In about six hours."

"Drive safely," he said, and hung up.

I took a slow walk back to the bus, head down, feeling like I'd been kicked in the belly. I sat in the driver's seat. Looking in the rearview mirror, I could see Anna, absorbed in wrapping a gold-edged purple scarf around her neck. "I got this from Josh's lost-and-found," she said happily. "Looks brand new doesn't it? I could use a few other things though, Jim. Like, a toothbrush would be nice." When I didn't answer, she turned to look at me. "You look like what the cat dragged in. What's happened?" she asked? "Why so glum?"

I rose, went over to the bench by the table and flopped down.

Anna joined me. "Is this because of your talk with Hans?"

"Not what I expected," I said and told her about Hans's response to our age difference. "I'm not sure going to Milwaukee is the right thing to do. What do you think?"

She gave me a love-tap on the shoulder and said, "I'm sorry you feel this way but from what you told me, I think he's being generous, Jim. For sure, having separate bedroom suits me just fine. I'm surprised he's even letting us stay in his house. I think we're just going to have to deal with it.

"Look Jim, I told you how I was feeling on the way here. I mean, I was confused and very uncertain that I was doing the right thing. Well last night before I fell asleep, I made the deci-sion to take control of my life. It might sound silly, but it was like that light-bulb that pops up in the comics when a cartoon has an ah-ha moment. I decided, why let my parents continue to lock me in my bedroom? Why not think about Miss Jones, and how she helped guide me through my childhood? And about all the others who really cared about me. And especially, I thought about how I had the courage to dance with you in front of God and county.

"It sounds like Hans is willing to talk about how things are with us. Let's at least listen to what he has to say. If it doesn't work, we'll just have to find some other place. One thing for certain is we're not going back to Oolitic."

Anna stood and gave me a whack on the shoulder. "Where's my knight in shining armor? My Prince Valiant? Put Mr. Glum aside and let's get the show on the road. I need a toothbrush and some breakfast."

22

Even with a pause at a truck-stop for gas, lunch, a few goodies, a duffle bag and a toothbrush, we made good time. We arrived at Hans's place at a little before three o'clock. I avoided blocking the driveway, and parked out front, as far off the shoulder as possible. Just as I turned off the engine, I saw Hans coming down the driveway, waving his arms and yelling, "You can't park there."

He approached the bus and I slid open my window to a rush of bitter cold air. "You didn't say anything about having a bus," his frustration delivered in puffs of white steam. "You're going to have to put it somewhere else. Take it over to my warehouse, the one on Kinnickinnic. Do you remember where it is?"

"Yes, I do."

"Well, put it in the parking lot over there and I'll come and get you." He shuffled off, back up the driveway.

"Not the warmest greeting I've ever had," I said to Anna who was all scrunched up in what had become her place of choice.

"No, it wasn't," came her muffed response.

We parked in the lot as instructed. After a few minutes, Hans pulled up, popped open his trunk and we tossed in our duffle bags. Anna kept her viola on her lap during the fifteen minute drive back to the house. On the ride, Hans was more like his old self, asking us about our trip, telling us that Wisconsin was having one of its winter's cold snaps with below zero temperatures, and other time fillers. Anna and I took in the heated, plush leather backseat of Hans's well-appointed Mercedes Benz.

At the house, we grabbed our duffle bags from the trunk. Hans noted Anna hugging her viola case and smiled. "I take it that you play the viola."

"Yes, sir, I do."

"Wonderful instrument. And please call me Hans."

He led us from the garage into the house via a tiled mud-room and asked us to leave our luggage there. "Miss Gumpfrey's eager to see you and to meet Anna. Now come on you two!" We followed Hans through an entryway and into the kitchen where Miss Gumpfrey was waiting. Gracious as always, she welcomed us with a hug for and a warm handshake for Anna. She suggested that we gather our things and get comfortable before joining them in the living room. "Jim knows where the guest rooms are. I'll make us some nice tea. You do drink tea?" She directed the question to Anna.

"That would be very nice, thank you," Anna responded gracefully.

We sat across from each other on two matching upholstered sofas, with a glass coffee table between us. We chatted through sips of tea until Hans told us it was time to talk about our visit. "First of all, we want to welcome both of you." *That's nice to hear.* "That said, I think we need to address the problem of your age difference and especially your being together without parental consent. I discussed this with my lawyer and the first thing he did was check to determine if your parents reported Anna as a missing person. Fortunately, there is no such report." *Phew!* "But considering the Age of Consent laws in Wisconsin, his advice is that it might be best if you weren't staying in the same house overnight, even though the likelihood of being discovered and arrested is practically zero at this point of time." *So what's the big deal?* "But that could change if Anna's parents file a report. I assume you're both willing to take the risk?"

Anna and I looked at each other. "I am," I said. *It feels like we're already on trial.*

After a moment's hesitation, Anna said, "Me too."

"That's good to know. Now that's what the law says. But I feel like I have a moral responsibility. I talked this over with Miss Gumpfrey and we want assurance that you'll not enter each other's bedrooms. Is that clear? Can you agree to that?"

"I can," Anna said.

"Me too," I said. *Who needs this shit?*

Following some more getting-to-know-you chatter, I excused myself, saying I'd like to take a shower.

"Of course, Jim. Make yourself at home."

I took my shower and laid down on the bed to think things through. Anna and I needed some alone time to plan our next move. We knew we couldn't just roam around the country in a wretched bus. There was not a chance in hell of returning to Oolitic and I wasn't planning to stay in Milwaukee. We'd have enough money once I cashed the three-thousand dollar check I got for my work in Newark. The big question was where to go from here. *Be patient, I told myself. We'll figure* it out. I closed my eyes for a little nap.

I was awakened by a knock on the door and heard Hans say: "Jim, are you awake?" I grunted something back. "We're going to have some cocktails. You're welcome to join us."

Anna and Hans were standing next to a tall, fully decorated Christmas tree looking out at a darkened Lake Michigan, each holding a wine glass. Anna must have changed while I was napping. She was wearing her purple scarf with the gold trim, a pink pullover and the same pair of jeans she wore on the bus. She looked absolutely beautiful. I helped myself at the bar while they talked.

"This view! I don't think I've ever seen such a night sky full of stars and enough moonlight to see the water. I've never seen so much water."

Pointing south, Hans said, "Chicago's only about seventy miles, as the crow flies. Up north is the Green Bay Peninsula, and straight across is Michigan." Anna's head was swiveling back and forth as she took in the geography lesson.

"Standing here looking out is like a scene in *Mutiny on the Bounty* when Captain Bligh stares out over the sea." She looked at Hans and continued, "I love Charles Laughton, don't you?"

Hans's chuckled. "I don't know if *love* is the word I'd use, but he was one of the great ones." I stood back, watching Anna and Hans knitting a friendship.

"Excuse me, everyone," said Miss Gumpfrey as she came into the room. "Dinner will be ready in about half an hour. Now would be a good time to refresh your drinks if you care to."

"Can I do anything to help?" Anna asked.

"Thank you but, no, I'm fine." Miss Gumpfrey headed back to the kitchen.

Twenty minutes later, the four of us were seated in Hans's generous dining room, platters of steaming food spread over the broad table. Hunger plus sherry equals ravenous, and it was all I could do to wait until everyone was served before plowing through what was on my plate. Table manners weren't my finest suit, but I did my best. By contrast, Anna was graceful and perfectly at ease. The three of them touched on a wide variety of subjects before settling on the pluses and minuses of performing Bach with period instruments. Having nothing to contribute, I was content to listen to Anna talk about things I'd never known existed.

While we enjoyed a dessert of flan served with vintage port, Anna mentioned that she needed to go shopping for "a few things" as she put it. "I'd be more than pleased to take you, if that would suit you. I do know where to get the best bargains," Miss Gumpfrey offered.

"That would be very helpful, thank you."

"Just let me know when you'd like to go. I have nothing planned."

Soon after dessert was over, a very tired Anna went off to her guest suite. I walked down the hall with her. Half in panic, she said, "I have only a few dollars, Jim. How am I supposed to pay for things? I didn't know what to say. It's embarrassing." I tried to give her a hug but she pulled back. "I need money, not a hug."

"Calm down, Anna, Don't worry, I'll give you what you need."

Anna let out a long sigh, "Okay, Jim, it's not about the money. It's more about me having some control over my life. I'm sorry for my outbreak, but we really need to find time to have a talk. For now, let's call it a loan. When you go back, please ask Miss Gumpfrey if it's okay to go shopping later tomorrow morning. I'll assume it's alright unless you come back and rap on my door." Opening her arms to me, she said "Now how about giving me that hug."

Miss Gumpfrey was fine with the shopping time so no door rapping was necessary. It was getting near nine-thirty. Hans asked me if I would join him for a nightcap. He ushered me into his den, a wood paneled room just off the living room. He was curious to know how it came about that Anna and I had to be *on the lam,* as he put it. I told him as much as I cared to, focusing on the abuse that Anna was subjected to at home, being locked in her room, and the escape. "Weren't you concerned about the consequences? Running off with a young girl is pretty risky."

This is not what I wanted to talk about. Of course it was risky. Did I give it enough thought? No. Was I acting on impulse? Yes. Was staying in Oolitic and waiting for Anna to become legal a possibility? Yes/No. Was I getting sick and god-damn fed up with people judging my motives? Yes! Did I need to sit here and be talked to like I don't have a fucking brain? Well I hate to admit it but yes, actually. I needed to buy time and time is never cheap.

"Yes it was Hans and I'm grateful for your understanding and help, letting us stay here."

"That's fine, Jim. I hope that you understand why I needed to separate you two. I know you don't like it."

"I didn't like it at first, but I understand." I paused. "Changing the subject, I need to get a check cashed. Could you help me with that?

"For how much?

"Three-thousand dollars from The Archdiocese of New

Jersey…for some stone work."

"We can take care of it in the morning," he said. "You're doing alright then?"

"Yes," I told him, "I am." I wasn't looking for a handout.

I woke up around ten o'clock to an empty house. A note was taped to my door. "Coffee's made, breakfast pastries on the counter. The Chase Bank on Wisconsin Avenue will cash your check. You can use the car parked in the garage, the keys are in it."

The car was an aging Chevy hatchback whose heater had a hard time keeping up with the cold weather. But who's complaining? After cashing the check, I went to visit Mom at Laurel Village. A nurse happened to be just leaving Mom's room when I arrived. I asked her how mother was doing. Looking at Mom and patting her lightly on her shoulder, she answered, "Oh, she's doing just fine, aren't you dear." Mom continued looking into some far off place. "She's been talking up a storm this past week."

Noticing the curious look on my face, she continued, "Most of our Alzheimer patients hallucinate. I wouldn't be too concerned, if I were you. If she gets scared, tell her that you won't let anyone hurt her. Be gentle and reassuring."

I told her that I was more pleased than concerned that Mom was actually talking and not just staring into space like she did on my last visit. I asked if Mom needed anything. "The best thing you can bring to your mother is a smile and lots of love and understanding."

After the nurse left, I sat for awhile, hoping that Mom would say something but there was only silence. I kissed her on the forehead and told her that I loved her. "The next time I'll bring my girlfriend Anna. I know you'll like her."

When I got back to the house, Anna showed me her new wardrobe. It was mostly casual clothes with some warm winter wear thrown in, including two beautiful hand-knitted woolen sweaters, a sturdy pair of waterproof hiking boots, slippers, and a pair of sneakers. I complimented her on her selections.

"You can wear some of them tomorrow if you'd like to join me so I can show you around where I grew up, and if you're willing, after lunch we'll stop by to visit my mother."

That brought me a hug and a kiss and a "You bet I'll join you."

Over dinner, we mentioned our plans for tomorrow. "As long as you're in the neighborhood, stop by and I'll give you a tour of my business," Hans said. We thanked him for the offer.

In the morning, Anna appeared in her new winter clothes. She looked great and I told her so. "You look like the Queen of the North." That got a smile.

Anna and I set out on our tour right after breakfast. I parked in front of the building I grew up in and we walked the short distance to the bare spot of ground where Sal's shop once stood. I let nostalgia do its thing, awakening memories so crisp that I felt like I was reliving them. I regaled Anna with stories about my trial and tribulations working with Sal, until I got the 'You've told that one before.' At that point, we linked arms and walked the few steps over to Hans's stein manufacturing company. The damp clean smells of wet clay triggered a return of Mr. Nostalgia. This time I kept my thoughts pleasantly to myself. Anna was impressed with the entire tour and asked a trove of questions, particularly about the glazing and firing process.

We had lunch and did a little shopping, including new

bedding for the bus, before heading to Laurel Village.

Mom was agitated when we entered her room. "Flowers and dancing" she was saying repeatedly. I asked Anna to get some help.

"Flowers and dancing. Flowers and dancing."

Mom became anxious, flailing her arms about. I knelt down to reassure her that I was here to protect her. "I won't let anyone hurt you."

She began quieting down just before Anna came into the room with a nurse aide. Anna and I stepped aside. The nurse aide rubbed Mom's hand and said soothing words. Mom became quiet and settled, like she just awoke after a bad dream. The nurse aide suggested that it might be best if we left Mom to rest, and came back tomorrow.

Back in the car, I said to Anna, "That wasn't easy." She reached over and touched my arm. "No it wasn't," she said. "I wonder what she meant by 'flowers and dancing.' Does that happen often?"

"No. That was a first for me but whatever it means, it sure sounded like she was upset. I'll try to find out at my next visit." I looked at my watch. "It's only early afternoon. Maybe we can find a place to have that talk you mentioned yesterday."

"Have somewhere in mind?"

"I'm thinking the library. I remember going there as a kid. It's huge and, by the way, built with Indiana limestone."

We found a small unoccupied sitting room on the second floor and made ourselves comfortable. I asked Anna, "How are you feeling?"

"To be honest, I'm not sure myself. The biggest problem

at the moment is wanting to decide where we're going. If you have some place in mind, I'd like to know about it. I mean, even asking that question is like I'm denying my own self. Like I'm some distressed princess in need of saving. That's how I felt when you offered me money. You understand?"

"I do understand. And yes, we need to find a place to land, sooner than later. As far as the saving a princess part goes, I want you to know that wasn't even on my radar screen. I'm still amazed that you crawled out of your bedroom window into the arms of an older man you were just getting to know. That took some courage."

"Thanks for the compliment but I don't see it as being courageous. Impulsive maybe. Looking at it metaphorically, it was more like allowing my spirit to fly from a dragon's cave. True as I told you, my bedroom was my refuge. But the rest of my life was controlled by a ruthless drunk! It's only been four days—four days Jim—since that spirit of mine has been on the loose. I'm happy to report that she's having a ball! Anna Adamski hasn't caught up with her yet, but she's getting there. Now moving forward, I want you to know I didn't fall into the arms of an older man whom I was just getting to know. I fell into the arms of the love of my life. And before we have to get going, let's talk about what's next."

I got up from the chair and walked a few steps into the room. The way she raised her voice when she described her father as 'a ruthless drunk' reminded me just how difficult it must have been for her to grow up with the son-of-a-bitch. I went over to stand behind her chair and gently rubbed her shoulders. "Anna," I said, "Let's work on finding a place to be."

"As far as I'm concerned," she said twisting around to catch my eye, "we can stay right here in Milwaukee. It's got everything we need. I could get my GED, take viola lessons, go to concerts. Visit your mother. And I'm sure you could find lots of work carving. Maybe even have your own shop. What do you think?"

I moved back to my chair, "That sounds good on the surface. But staying here doesn't work for me. There's truth in that saying 'you can't go home again.' I'd rather go to some place where we can be left to grow our own life together."

I was glad that Anna didn't push her suggestion to stay in Milwaukee.

"Do you have some other place in mind?"

"I've been thinking about a town called Rhinelander."

Anna laughed, "You want to move to Germany?"

"How did you guess?" I played along, before bringing us back to the subject at hand. "Actually it's right here in Wisconsin."

"Where pray tell in Wisconsin?"

"Up north."

"How far up north?"

"About two-hundred miles."

Anna frowned, "It sounds like you put some thought into this. Tell me more."

"There's not much more to tell," I said. "When I got out of the service I was looking for a place to go. I got the idea from a buddy of mine in 'Nam who said Rhinelander was paradise on earth. It sounded promising, but I never pursued it past finding out where it was located."

"Well, let's go find out more. We *are* in a library," Anna said cheerfully.

An hour later we were agreeing that Rhinelander just might work. We knew we'd have to take a look if we wanted the reality. We had our concerns, including the ability for Anna to continue studying viola, the stress of long winters, and the need to make friends. For me, the question was how to make a living. I seriously doubted there was a need for Gargoyles in Northern Wisconsin. But we accepted that if we didn't like it, we'd move on.

We felt energized by the discussion and decided to leave the day after Christmas. That was just two days away, enough time to buy new bedding, get groceries, and make sure the bus was ready. On Christmas eve, Anna performed for the three of us. "A viola transcription of Bach's Suite Number Five for Unaccompanied Cello," she announced standing in front of the Christmas Tree. Hans and Miss Gumpfrey smiled and looked at each other. They had a wonderful time. I simply reveled in this wonderful music that I'd never heard before. Incredible.

On Christmas morning we opened our gifts: a box of chocolates for Miss Gumpfrey and a bottle of scotch for Hans with our thank you for his gracious hospitality. Anna surprised me with a plaid woolen scarf. "I bought it when I went shopping with Miss Gumpfrey. I think you're going to need it." I wrapped it around my neck. "I think so, too."

I reached deep into my pocket, I took out the stone I carved for Anna while in Newark. I had wrapped it tightly in red paper. "It's pretty heavy" she said as she tore off the wrapping. There was silence, followed by tears.

"You carved this for me?" She clutched the stone to her heart. "I've never seen anything so beautiful." She kissed me softly. "I'll keep this with me all my life." When Hans and Miss Gumpfrey looked at the stone, Hans reflected that Sal would be proud. Miss Gumpfrey smiled at Anna and remarked how lovely it was.

Hans's and Miss Gumpfrey's gifts to each other were gloves for him and a gift certificate to The Kitchen Shoppe, a trendy store in downtown Milwaukee, for her.

In the afternoon, we all visited Mom, gifting her with a cheerful blue and yellow woolen throw. She petted it like it was a cat sitting on her lap. She was happy. Mom died three weeks later, leaving me with the pleasant memory of our final visit. I never found out what flowers and dancing meant.

We returned to the house, and just before Anna and I got underway, Miss Gumpfrey called me aside and handed me a small envelope. "I think that with the way people are, you might give this to Anna." In the envelope was a gold wedding band. "It might keep people from being too nosey. And if you don't mind, I'd like to keep this just between you and me."

"You mean to make people think we're married?" I asked.

I wasn't surprised when she answered, "That's exactly what I mean."

Beth

JUNE 20, 1993

23

My sister Anna was dead? How could that be? I had a sister for a little while and then—poof! She was gone. It was like a bad dream. I stood looking down the overgrown path, not sure of what to say or how to act or anything. I think Oscar could see how I felt. I took his advice and followed him to the cabin. He fumbled for some keys, unlocked the door and we went inside.

It was cool and dimly lit with only the broken shutter letting in a ray of light. I sat down on an overstuffed sofa which faced the stone fireplace. Trooper flopped down on an oval rag-rug nearby. Oscar opened the shutters, flooding the cabin with sunlight.

"How are you feeling?" he asked.

I said I was okay, but I didn't really mean it. I didn't know how I was feeling. Shattered, maybe. Angry. Confused, for sure.

"What happened to the baby?" I asked. "The letter said that Anna was pregnant."

Oscar walked a few steps over to the fireplace and stood next to Trooper.

"Are you sure you want to hear all this now? Maybe you should get some rest first…."

"No, Oscar. I'll feel a lot better when I know what happened. I need to know. And what about Sarah? And Anna's husband? You have to tell me the whole story. I can take it."

"All right…might as well put it all on the table, Beth. Anna was still pregnant when she died. The baby…died with her."

"Oh, my God! I can't—it never ends! It's like right out of Shakespeare or something." I could hear my voice getting screechy so I stopped talking for a second to get a grip. Attempting a more normal voice, I said, "So…what about Sarah and Jim? What happened to them?"

"Before we get to that, I'm afraid I need to go out and use the facilities. Why don't you look around a bit?" he said, heading to the back door. "I'll be back in a minute." Trooper followed him outside, leaving me alone in the cabin.

Actually, Oscar was beginning to piss me off, using lame excuses to put off whatever it was keeping him from telling me. What else could it be? Maybe he's scared to tell me. I guessed I'd have to wait him out. But it was not easy!

I got up and walked over to the counter. I looked out of the window and saw Oscar and Trooper disappear into the woods. Maybe he knew I needed a little time to let everything sink in. Or maybe he was dreading what he had to tell me next.

In spite of myself, I got fascinated with the place immediately. Stairs leading to a loft caught my eye. How could I not go up there? The treads were made from logs cut in half and the railing, from small trees; there were little bumps where the branches used to be. At the top of the steps was a room with a little balcony that hung over the living room. Sun was pouring in through a skylight. Standing at the railing I could take in the whole place. *I could definitely see living like this.* I bet the house was around the same size as the one in Bloomington, but instead of being chopped up into tiny rooms, it was all open and airy.

The loft had two doors, one open and one closed. I could see through the open door that the room was furnished with stuff that seemed handmade, not bought from any store. I stepped inside. The bed had four short posts and a curved headboard, and was covered by a brightly colored, hand-made quilt. I picked up the edge of the quilt to see if the bed was made up and found that it wasn't. Just a bare mattress. The dresser was a plain chest of drawers with a mirror behind it. I pulled open a few of the drawers: empty.

When I caught sight of myself in the mirror, oh my god! My hair was all crazy, and nothing I did was going to fix it. Maybe I should have spent more time getting ready this morning, but I couldn't wait to get out of that sleazy motel. Thinking back to it, it seemed like a year ago, at least. And putting my head under the water pump sure didn't help...I guess I was lucky to look as good as I did.

The only thing on top of the dresser was a small, leather-covered box, real expensive looking, green with gold trim. I lifted the lid and inside was a round pink stone. In the center of it, in real pretty script, the name *ANNA* was carved. It was beautiful. I took it out of the box and found that it fit neatly in the palm of my hand. Tiny leaves were carved around the name. On the back was an inscription that read: *You live in my soul. I love you completely and forever.* The stone felt warm. I could have held it all day. This was the closest I'd come to touching Anna. I gave the stone a light kiss and—I swear to god—I felt like my sister's soul was melting into mine; like she and I were one person. "Oh Anna," I whispered, clutching the stone against my heart.

"I'm back!" Oscar's voice from below burst the bubble. I carefully put the pink stone back into the box. Lightly patting the lid, I said, "I'll be back. I promise."

From the top of the steps I could see Oscar looking out a window to the left of the fireplace. Trooper was back to his place on the oval rug. I lean against the railing and looked down. "It's really nice up here" I said,

"Yup," Oscar said, still staring out of the window. "I keep it up." I was halfway down the steps when he spoke again. "You mind me asking how old you are?"

"Eighteen," I said. "I just graduated."

"Well, congratulations. Going to college?"

"Indiana University. I'm not sure what to major in…maybe psychology."

Oscar sat down in a high-backed wooden chair across from the sofa.

"Take your time deciding. Eighteen is pretty young to decide about what to do with the rest of your life." I walked over to the sofa and sat down. After a moment, he added, "That's about how old Sarah would be, you know. Eighteen."

"*Would* be? Don't tell me she's dead, too?"

"No, she's not dead. Least as far as I know."

"So…you don't know where Sarah is?"

"I'm just not sure."

"Well, where's Jim, then?"

"I don't know that either."

I honestly didn't know what to ask next. Was this whole

thing going to be one big, sad dead end?

"But…this is—was—Jim and Anna's cabin, right? Or am I in Wonderland?"

"Oh, it's their cabin all right," he said. He paused for a moment, then said, "When you found the letter, did you find anything else?"

"Like what?"

"Oh…I don't know…maybe papers or some pictures? You know, stuff that people keep."

"Nope. Just insurance papers, the mortgage…regular stuff."

"Did your folks ever tell you they came up here?"

I was getting a little sick of Oscar and his riddles.

"No, they didn't. They never told me anything, Oscar, and now they *can't* tell me anything. That's why I came up here in the first place. Do you think maybe you could stop asking me questions and answer a few?"

"Look Beth, I'm trying my best here. You have to let me do this in my own way, though. Did you have a sister growing up? I don't mean Anna, but another one?"

"Dammit, Oscar, no!" I said, jumping up from the sofa. "I did not have a sister. I did not find any papers. I had a regular family—or thought I did—and now they're… gone and I'm here, and—" I sunk back into the sofa, my voice cracking, and put my hands over my eyes.

Oscar waited for me to calm down and look up at him again, then started speaking in that low, calm voice he had.

"Beth…here's what I know, in a nutshell. About a month after the accident, the Adamskis—your parents—came up here to take the baby away from Jim, claiming he wasn't a fit father. At the time, he probably wasn't, and we all knew it. He was having a pretty hard time after Anna…but what your parents didn't understand was that we were all pitching in, helping Jim out. In time, things would have worked out…Jim would have gotten himself back on his feet for the sake of his daughter. But the judge, he thought differently. And, as hard as we all fought the whole thing, your parents took Sarah away. Just like that."

My mind was reeling just trying to follow what he was saying. My parents would never do such a cruel thing. And if they did, what happened to Sarah?

"So let me get this straight, Oscar. Sarah was taken by my parents."

"Yup."

"And she was my age?"

"Thereabouts."

"And I was too young to remember anything about her."

"Probably right."

"So what the hell happened to her?"

"Beth. I think Sarah Robertson's sitting right here in front of me."

"What? I don't—Wait! Are you saying…you think *I'm Sarah*?"

Jim

1975–1978

24

Northern Wisconsin was a new world to us. Two lane roads cut through drifts of snow, some of the higher banks blocking our view of fields and forests. Small towns bustled with street life. Traffic lights were few and far between. It was dark when we reached Clayton, and I immediately began searching for some place we could park until morning. With its wide parking lot, Oscar Golden's Scrap Yard was an inviting, and as it turned out, fateful place to spend the night. We drove to the lot and had no trouble finding a good spot to park. We agreed to role play being married. "I never would have thought Miss Gumpfrey could be such a conniver," Anna said, showing off the shiny gold band.

We settled into our beds. I was restless but managed to fall asleep. Sometime past midnight, I awoke to a soft tapping on my shoulder.

I bolted upright. "Is there something wrong?"

"No, not really," Anna said quietly, clutching a bed sheet tightly around her.

I was wide awake by then—unless I was dreaming, which seemed a distinct possibility.

She let the bed sheet slide to the floor. I was immediately aroused. Our eyes met. We both smiled. I reached out and stroked her soft, warm belly. She laid her hand on mine and together we moved my hands slowly to her breasts. Anna leaned over me and we kissed. I pulled back the covers and she squeezed in next to me. The suppressed desire and longing we so carefully denied each other disappeared in a wave of love making. We cuddled, making a soft utterances. We explored each other's bodies. We tickled and we laughed. We became one. We spooned together like the lovers we were, and fell into a deep sleep.

I awoke to the smell of brewing coffee. "Good morning," I said, "anybody here?"

"Just me," Anna said coming over to me with mug in hand. She gave me a kiss. "That was some night," she said smiling. "It must have been the ring," she quipped.

"Whatever it was, I hope it happens again."

"We'll see," she said, returning to the stove. "Cereal or oatmeal?"

"Oatmeal," I answered, crawling out of bed.

New bed, new linens, new blankets, new pillows, new love. The bus was our honeymoon suite at the Ritz.

Just after breakfast, a fellow tapped on the door.

"You folks be wantin' gas?"

He was an ancient fellow with a curved back, a wary eye, craggy face, and the disposition of an alley cat.

"I hope it was okay for us to park here last night?" I said.

"Well, if it wasn't, it wouldn't matter none now, would it? Gas or not?"

"Yes, sir…thank you. I'll pull around to the pumps and you can fill 'er up. Any charge for staying the night?"

"You'll have to ask the boss about that, Mister. He's inside. If it was up to me, you'd pay plenty."

While the cranky old bastard filled the near-empty tank, Anna joined me outside. The building was a large wood-framed affair, covered with peeling gray paint. Above the door, nailed willy-nilly over the entire triangular eave were hundreds of deer antlers. I remembered my army buddy talking about the famous North Country bucks, and I gathered these were the remnants of same. I held the door for Anna.

It took our eyes a minute to adjust to the dimly lit interior. Coming into view were tiers of shelves laden with new and used tools, hoses, copper tubing, nuts, bolts, scraps of barbed wire, and literally hundreds of objects unrecognizable to anyone but those familiar with the ways of scrap yards. The air was heavy with odors of old grease and rancid gasoline. I liked the place, though I was pretty sure Anna could've done without it. Hanging from pipes that ran across the high ceiling were old garden tools mixed in with picture frames, some empty and others filled with faces of long forgotten families or primitive pastoral scenes.

A group of raggedly dressed old men sat sunken into a circle of over-stuffed chairs in the far corner of the room. They stared at us through deeply furrowed brows, their eyes almost hidden under shaggy untrimmed eyebrows. A middle-aged fellow dressed in jeans and a bright red flannel shirt appeared from behind a counter. "What is it you young folks are looking for?" he inquired affably.

"Well sir, we stayed in your parking lot last night, and I'd like to settle up. What do we owe you for the privilege?"

"Yeah, I saw you parked here when I came to work this morning. No charge."

"We came in last night around ten. Saw you were closed and didn't want to bother anybody."

The man looked out a dirty front window toward the bus. "King pins go bad pretty quick in those buses. Ever have them checked?"

"We just had it all gone over," I said. *What is it with mechanics? First Josh, now this guy.*

"Where's home?" the man asked.

I looked at Anna, paused, then answered, "Milwaukee."

"With Indiana plates?"

"Guess I should have said our last stop was Milwaukee. We're...moving on."

"Didn't mean to pry," the man said. "Where you headed then, if you don't mind me asking?"

Anna took over.

"Actually, sir, we're looking for a place that's quiet and peaceful. Thinking about Rhinelander. Do you know it?"

"Sure I do. It's just down the road. Nice enough place, but you might want to look around these parts first. We've got lots of quiet, that's for sure."

Anna looked my way and said, "I guess we could check out the area."

"Well, welcome to the North Woods," he said, brightening up. "My name's Oscar Golden, I own this place."

"Jim Robertson," I said, shaking Oscar's hand. He squeezed and I squeezed back in a friendly competition between a stone carver and a junk man. "This is my wife, Anna."

Damn, it felt good saying that!

"What'd they say?" I heard one of the old men yell to another.

"Young'uns lookin' fer land."

"Fur! They got themselves a license?"

"Why don't we step outside," suggested Oscar, shooting a glare at the old men. "They couldn't hear a volcano erupt, but they'll be sharing your business before you know it."

On our way out, we bumped into the guy that had pumped the gas. "Forty-six gallons," he said. "That comes to twenty-five dollars and thirty-five cents."

I paid the man and continued my chat with Oscar. As we neared the bus, he observed, "You got 'er fixed up pretty good. You two living in it?"

"For now," I replied. "It'll get us through until summer, until we figure out our next move. You want to see inside?" I was proud of the bus, of Anna, of being coupled, of everything in the whole wide world. I'd have invited a king or a bum to show off my new life.

"Love to," Oscar said. "We can talk about what's available around here."

I wasn't sure how he'd profit from this bit of neighborliness, but I was pretty sure he saw an angle in it.

Anna was first on board.

"Would you like some coffee, Oscar?" she asked. "You're our first guest."

"Can't turn it down then," Oscar said, giving the interior a once over. "You do this yourself?" he inquired.

"With some help," I answered, offering him a seat behind the built in booth.

Looking at Anna's shiny new wedding band, Oscar asked, "Just married?"

"In Milwaukee," Anna piped up.

"Well congratulations to both of you," Oscar said. "It'd be nice to have a coupla newlyweds up this way."

Anna brought the coffee pot and three cups to the table. "Cream and sugar?" she asked.

"Black's fine with me," Oscar said. Anna squeezed in close to me.

"Just so you know, even if you do end up in Rhinelander, I have whatever you might need to keep this bus going. And I have some good used trucks and cars out back, too. I can give you a good deal."

I nodded my appreciation as I sipped my coffee.

"Like I was saying before, we don't get a lot of young folks moving here, but believe it or not, some older folks show up to retire. Like the old men in the corner," he said, looking back to the building. "From the steel mills down south. Had enough of heat'd be my guess. I call them my turtles, the way they hug the ground," he laughed. "Every day they get more stooped over—but I love 'em. They're great men, every last one of them. Frank Toilsen, the fellow that gassed up your bus, why he's in his late seventies. If I can make it a little easier for him and the other men that made all the steel I deal in, well then that's what I'll do."

He paused, then continued, "Clayton's a good place to put down roots. My father came over from Minneapolis and opened this yard. Everybody thought he was crazy, but he built a pretty good business. The lumbering business is big here and I'll tell you, they use up a lot of steel to get the trees cut and sawed. What is it you do?"

"I carve stone," I said. "That's one of the reasons we came up here."

"Carve stone!" Oscar didn't hide his skepticism. "You'd be the one and only, that's for sure. No competition. But, maybe no business either."

"Oh, I'll find some business," I said confidently. "But, truth is, right now I'm working on some projects of my own."

"You mean you're an artist? Sculptor...?"

"I wouldn't call myself an artist, exactly. I just want to set up shop and go from there. My biggest problem will be to get stone shipped up here."

"I could help you with that," Oscar leapt in. "We get shipments of steel all the time. No reason why we couldn't get you some stone."

"Thanks, I'll keep that in mind," I said quietly.

Oscar popped off his worn hat and scratched his head like he was about to confess something. "You know...I've got some land I could sell. A good woodlot. Dry mostly. Would two forties do?"

"Forties?" Anna asked.

"Two forty-acre plots."

Wide-eyed, Anna looked at me. "Eighty acres!"

I sipped some coffee, trying to act nonchalant. *Am I dealing with a huckster? Tread lightly.* "I wasn't thinking about that much land," I said.

"You weren't?" Oscar scratched his head again. "You know, up here, that's not really so much. But if you want to live in town, why then, I think we need to get you over to the real-estate office."

"Oscar, I think that might be jumpin' the gun. We really

ought to just look around first…then maybe run over to Rhinelander. But…just out of curiosity, how much does two forties go for?"

Oscar slowly put his hat back on his head, taking his turn to be nonchalant.

"Well…it's good land…some real nice stands of oak in there. Like I said, it's mostly dry…higher than a lot of places around."

I nodded, let him keep talking.

"I guess I'd have to get somewhere around a hundred-twenty-five an acre."

I did the math over a few more sips of coffee. I thought about Sal's advice that when you're dealing, open your ears and shut your mouth. "Ten thousand?" I said in a level voice.

"That sounds about right," Oscar said.

"I guess it wouldn't hurt to take a look at it…but that's a bit out of our range."

Turning to Anna, I said, "What do you think?"

"Like you said, I guess it wouldn't hurt to look."

"I could drive you on up there," Oscar offered. "The snow's still pretty deep so we won't be able to get into the woods too far, but you'll get a good idea."

We crammed into Oscar's pickup and headed off the highway just north of town onto a neatly plowed dirt road. The sign read "JJ."

"WPA planted all these firs back during the Depression," Oscar said, commenting on the tall trees that lined the dirt road. "The land borders the Chequamegon National Forest, and you won't find any better for sale around here."

He parked and we hopped out. The air was impossibly fresh—cleaner than Milwaukee or dusty old Oolitic. Far sweeter than the mortuary in Nam. I knew right then and there that this was the place to be. But I wasn't sure how Anna felt.

With Oscar in the lead, we pushed through snow along an old lumbering road that cut into the woods and then before sloped down to a large clearing. Second-growth forest lined the road, though lots of trees were plenty big.

"There's a clearing just down the hill," Oscar said. "Used to be a small lumbering operation. You could build right there. Did I tell you the Thornapple River runs right through the property?"

I could only imagine what this place must look like in the spring and fall. My heart was pounding a little, and when I took Anna's hand, she gave mine a little squeeze, which told me that she was thinking the same thing. I worked hard to keep my mouth shut as we walked around, but Oscar knew we were hooked. He drove us back to his place with nary a word to interrupt our pondering what it might be like to live on eighty acres.

Back on the bus and alone, Anna and I shared our enthusiasm for the property, though she had some concerns that we might feel isolated out there. She had lots of other questions. Where could she continue studying the viola? Or go to concerts? And what about playing in an orchestra? Then there's finishing high school. And how about me finding work?

"Are we buying a fairy tale, or what?" she asked. "It's a little scary making such a big decision. Maybe we should think about renting first. What do you think?"

"I think we should go with the fairy tale."

I took Anna's hand and led her to the sofa, which felt really good after our chilly walk around the woods. "Jim," she asked quietly, "Can we really afford this? I mean…I'm planning to get a job and all, but—"

"Anna," I said, reaching over, taking her hand in mine, "when I was in Vietnam if anyone had told me I'd be in a position to buy eighty acres of prime forest land, I'd have thought he was nuts. Add to that dream having you in my life and, well my darling, I just can't see passing it up. As for the money, I have enough to get us settled. I've been making good money without too many expenses. With the money from Newark, I have a good nest egg in the bank in Bedford. I can do a bank transfer anytime."

"But there's something else on my mind. Outside of babysitting and stuff like that, I've never really had a job. Do you think anybody would hire me? To do a real job?"

"Of course I do, Anna. You're smart and well-spoken… organized…all the things people want. Anyway, we're a team, so I don't want you to worry. Let's get ourselves settled and go from there. If we buy this land, we'll both be working like crazy just to turn it into a home. And don't worry about your viola playing. We'll make it happen. I promise."

Anna responded, "You know you don't have to try and sell me on it. And you don't need to make promises. Let's agree that we'll give it a try for a couple years with no promises except that if things don't work out, we move on."

I agreed.

By evening, we were well on the way to owning "two of the best forties anywhere around these parts," as Oscar put it. I didn't know much about real estate, but I knew that at $9,255 it was a steal. Plus, Oscar agreed to have one of his workers plow away the snow and clear the place for building. He found an out-of-the-way spot for me to park the bus until spring, when we'd be able to move it to our land. I bought one of Oscar's used pick-ups to get around.

With Oscar's help and connections, we lined up people to clean up the old lumber road, run the utilities, drill a well, install a septic system and build a modest cabin, I was able to get a home loan from the VA for my Vietnam service to help fund the project.

On a cold day in late February, Anna and I had just returned to the bus after checking out the progress being made on our cabin. The cold temperature had stopped most of the work. Anna made some hot chocolate and we curled up on the sofa.

"Do you think our cabin will be ready by September?" Anna asked me.

"I don't see why not. Once it warms up things should move along."

"Well I hope so," she said.

"Are you worried about something? I guess living in a bus parked next to a scrap yard in the dead of winter is not the best way to spend our time. We could get an apartment until spring. Would you like that?"

Taking my hand and placing it on her belly, she said, "I think that the three of us would like that."

"The three...?"

"I went to see a doctor today and guess what? We're going to have a baby. I'm due in mid-September."

I gave Anna a big hug. I was overjoyed. Me, about to be a father! I thought of how I missed having a Dad when I was a kid and how I might make-up for that by having a child of my own. Anna and I spent the evening going through all the things we needed to get done before the baby was due. The first thing on the list was moving out of Work Schoolie and moving into the cabin.

When we told Oscar that Anna was pregnant, he promised us we'd be settled in time for the baby, no matter what it took—and we believed him. He helped us find an apartment to live in till the cabin was ready and went out of his way to make sure that we were comfortable. He may have been motivated by doing business, but he sure made our lives a lot easier. Once the temperature warmed up, we left the apartment and moved the bus to our woods. Things went into high gear.

On February 15, 1975, Anna's eighteenth birthday, we drove to Minneapolis and took our marriage vows before a kindly Notary Public. The man's wife and daughter served as witnesses. No one in Clayton was the wiser.

We moved into our cabin in early August and threw a big party to celebrate. Since coming to Clayton, Anna was quick to make friends. Book club at the library, pre-natal support group at the local Congregational Church, and even getting to know the local grocer. They all came. My friends from the junk yard showed up, too. Anna's friends took over with no ifs, ands or buts, relegating her to a comfortable lounger while they went around refilling people's punch cups and passing trays of food. The baby was due in mid-September.

A midwife locally known as Lady Linda delivered Sarah Anna Robertson on September 12, 1975. I helped Anna through labor, marveling at how strong she was. She'd grimace, then smile, then grimace again, the pattern repeating itself through each powerful contraction. Linking us together, she gripped my hand and held onto it right through the last push that brought Sarah into the world.

I'll never forget the image: my Anna, wet with perspiration, her hair clinging to her forehead in thick wet strands, contentment spreading across her face like light in the sky after a storm. The room was quiet; then came a sputtering cry that increased in volume and clarity.

"It's a girl," Lady Linda announced proudly. She laid our baby on Anna's bare chest, umbilical cord still attached. We'd decided to name her Sarah because we liked the sound of it. We'd gone into the woods and yelled out all the names we could think of, as if we were calling somebody home to dinner. 'Sarah' had the best echo.

25

Life was good. We'd never known such quiet. The woods would sing us to sleep. We had a favorite raccoon that came begging at the door every night. The creature was a genius at getting into our garbage can, making a mess in the process. The chipmunks became so friendly, they'd eat out of our hands. Deer were plentiful, and our neighbors Bill and Debbie Anslert two miles down the road told us they'd had a regular visit from a black bear, though we never saw it. We lived in our own little world and loved every minute of it.

Sarah was eighteen months old when Anna became pregnant for a second time. We probably conceived on Wolf Hill. We named it that because it was the highest ground on our property and the wolves were naturally drawn to it. They didn't bother us and we didn't bother them. We had a favorite spot under some towering pine trees. We'd play with Sarah until she fell asleep—which sometimes felt like forever—then make love into the late afternoon.

Living in northern Wisconsin meant learning to adjust

from warm summer days like those on Wolf Hill to brutally cold winters, when the temperature could plummet to twenty below zero for a week or more. Trees would scream and crack, emitting sounds like sharp gunshots. Our fireplace and wood stove burned night and day. We bought a snowmobile to get around and some sturdy cross-country skis, and I made a sled so we could pull Sarah behind us. I spent days in my carving shed, heated by an old cast-iron wood burner courtesy of Oscar. I called that stove Molly, and thanked her every night for keeping me warm.

The shed was primitive but sturdy. In time, I planned to side it in rough cedar, but for the time being, I let it go with tarpaper and lath. I had enough work, thanks to Toni Poncelli, who sent me lists of Al's contacts. That paid the bills. Oscar helped me with shipping and—always true to his word—found a steel hauler out of Gary willing to go to Bedford to pick up my order for fifteen-hundred blocks, each the size of a brick. I had them all stacked up outside the shed, and once a week or so, I set some time aside to carve them. I'd get through maybe a dozen or so in a good week. I didn't want to rush building the cairn. Each man deserved my best.

Pregnancy agreed with Anna, and she blossomed into a healthy twenty-year-old Madonna. She suffered less with nausea this time around; her biggest complaint was that her hair had seemed to morph into straw. Jamie Lynn, her hairdresser, gave her a cute little pixie cut. I switched from stroking her hair to ruffling it.

Her liveliness and confidence won Anna a wide circle of friends. Rarely a day passed without one or another of them coming for a visit or inviting her into town. After completing her GED, she enrolled in the local community college, harboring thoughts of one day getting a degree in music.

Late one night as we lay in bed, Anna asked, "What should I do about my parents?"

"What do you mean?" I asked, sitting-up, resting on my elbow.

"Well, I've been thinking a lot about it."

"You have!?"

"Yes, Jim. Now hear me out," she paused. "Sometimes I look at Sarah and wonder how nice it would be for her to have grandparents. She's going to be three soon…and with number two on the way…you know…having family is important. I know what I said back when we left Oolitic, that I'd never go back. I still feel that way. But maybe we could invite them here. I know my mom would love that."

Sometimes I'd look at Sarah and Mom would pop into my mind. I searched for Dad in her features, too. But with only an old photo to go by, I couldn't recognize anything of him in Sarah. I wished I could. Anna never said so, but she must have had similar thoughts.

Besides meeting her mother briefly at Anna's concert, I'd never actually met Anna's parents. I only knew what she'd told me about them, and it still made me angry to think about. But, if this was what Anna wanted, why not give it a chance? I propped myself up with a pillow and said, "I think you should follow your heart, Anna. Do what you think is best. I'll support you, no matter what."

She pulled herself close. "Jim, I know I might be disappointed. Sometimes I think I miss what I wished I had growing up, not what I really did have. I think about Mom, mostly.

How terribly abused she was. I used to think that she was weak, unwilling to stand up for herself, but now I think she was actually courageous. That the only way she had to survive was to not fight back. I don't know if that makes any sense, but that's how I feel. She was a good mother, protecting me by sacrificing herself. I never got to say goodbye to her; to tell her that I didn't hold anything against her—not even her silence." She paused, then asked me, "Do you think knowing that he has a granddaughter would change my father?"

"Your father? No," I said, "not if he's still drinking. But I know he's your father…and I promise he's never going to hurt you again. So however this turns out, we'll deal with it. Together."

Anna kissed me on the cheek. "Let's take it one step at a time. I'll write them tomorrow. We'll see what happens."

Two weeks later, the letter came back, "Address Unknown" stamped on the envelope in red. It took Lillian Adams, the reference librarian, less than a day to find their new address in Bloomington, Indiana. Anna put the unopened letter into a new envelope and mailed it again. We didn't speak of it after, but I noticed that Anna was more eager than usual to get the mail. One day after a few weeks had passed without a word, that eagerness turned into anger. Coming back from the mailbox, she threw a packet of mail onto the kitchen counter. "How could anybody not want to see their grandkids?" Teary eyed she ranted, "I give up. At least Mom could've sent a note. What's wrong with these people?" Going to the door, she declared, "I need to take for a walk." She returned a short time later, gave me a hug and said, "Well that's that."

Except for the interminable heat, which was unusual for

northern Wisconsin, the summer of 1977 was blissful. I had all the work I could handle, most of it restoring pieces sent to me from around the country. In late afternoons or early mornings, whichever suited me, I'd take my small tractor and groom the many trails we'd carved through our land. I gathered wood for the coming winter. Anna tended her gardens, keeping them watered from a pipe that ran down an embankment to nearby Thornapple River. In July, we took a week's vacation in the Apostle Islands in Lake Superior. Every month, we drove to Minneapolis so Anna could take a viola lesson at the MacPhail Center, and I finally got to hear her play that Reger piece. Before the recital, I think I was more nervous than she was. She wore a black skirt and white blouse, and looked so professional…I want to say that I was proud, but that sounds too paternal. It was more like I was intoxicated. I admit that the nuances of the music probably went over my head, but I found that the echoes of it stayed with me long after it was over.

The storm that changed everything hit in mid-August. The weather bureau said later it had been a downdraft storm, wind smashing down at 150 miles an hour, sweeping like a scythe through wheat.

The morning of the storm, I drove to Oscar's place to help him and a few guys install a new shear designed to cut through thick steel like it was butter. It took the better part of the afternoon to set up. Anna, three months pregnant, had cancelled her volunteer hours at the library to be with Sarah.

I was still working on the shear when the sky darkened and got greenish, like it does before a tornado. I dropped my tools and headed for my truck. Toilsen came running from the office.

"I tried calling Anna to see if she's okay and nobody answered. The operator said the lines were all working," he hollered.

"I'm on my way, Frank," I yelled back."

I took off with Oscar yelling that he'd be right behind me.

By the time I reached Double J, the wind was ripping off tree tops and sending them sailing into the darkened sky like frenzied birds. The noise was deafening. I fought my way to the cabin and went inside. I called for Anna and Sarah. When there was no answer, I went back out pulling the door shut behind me. I pushed my way into a wind filled with bits of everything it could get its fiendish hands on, heading for the carving shed. It was empty. The walls began to shudder and the wind screamed at a fever pitch. Bile was rising in my throat. I couldn't do a thing other than hunker down. The roof was starting to let go, lifting a little, then dropping back down. I thought it might hold, but in the next instant it was gone, ripped clean off. I just made it under my carving bench before the shed walls collapsed around me.

The wind passed through like a steam train, then everything went quiet. It took some doing to push my way through the twisted rubble, and when I looked up, I couldn't believe my eyes. The sky was turning blue. It struck me as a sign…a promise that Anna and Sarah were safe. I looked around. A huge branch had hit the roof of the bus, denting it inward. Miraculously, the cabin looked unharmed.

"Anna!" I called. "Sarah!"

At first I wasn't sure but then I heard it again. A soft whimper coming from Shadow Trail, named for the big trees that lined each side and kept it in darkness. I ran toward the sound, stopped, called out again, "Sarah!"

A tired little voice said one word: "Daddy."

My heart racing full bore, I zigzagged around branches and small trees. I tripped and fell and resumed running before I'd stood all the way up. I was a madman.

I spotted Sarah caught up in some branches from a thick oak limb, and tore my way through to get her out. As I hoisted her in my arms, I looked her over. She had a few scratches, but seemed blessedly okay.

Now, where are you, Anna?

I saw her shoe first, lying under a large limb like somebody had just tossed it there. I set Sarah down and said, "Stay right here, sweetheart," then squeezed my way under some branches. I found Anna in the thick of it. I touched her hand but it remained still. I couldn't see the rest of her. I tried to move the oak limb but it was too heavy. "Anna," I whispered, "don't give up, sweetheart!"

Behind me, I heard Oscar yelling for me.

"Over here," I called back. He rushed up the path with a couple of his boys, and in no time, they'd lifted the debris off of Anna. Her body seemed unnatural—twisted in an odd way. I'd seen bodies like this before. In 'Nam.

I knew she was dead. I could tell. I could always tell.

One of the boys ran to get the truck and go for an ambulance. I didn't stop him. I picked Anna up. Her body still warm. Limp. All broken to hell. I remember carrying her back to the cabin and laying her on the couch. I brushed my hands through her stubby hair. I kissed her forehead. I kissed her belly. The baby.

From then on, it's more haze than anything else.

A week later, I spread Anna's ashes around the gardens she loved. I did the best I could with Sarah, which wasn't much, considering the shape I was in. Thank God for friends, who came over day in and day out to take care of things. I tried to stay in the cabin, but I couldn't. Anna's essence was everywhere. I moved back into the bus with Sarah, who asked for Mommy too many times to count. I didn't know what to tell her. That the angels took Mommy away? That God needed Mommy in heaven? That our unborn child was too good to come to earth? *Bullshit!* I wanted to tell her that if God wanted little children and their mommies in heaven so bad, he shouldn't send them here the first place. That is, if there even was a God. After all I'd seen, I had to wonder. Was being born some kind of test you passed and then went to heaven? Did my dad pass the test? Did my soldiers pass?

Anna's death and, with it, the death of our promised child was almost too much to bear. Regular visits from friends saved me from going over the edge, especially when they brought their kids along. Watching three-year-old Sarah laughing and playing was just what I needed to carry on. I carved a thin slab of marble as a memorial to Anna. *Anna Robertson. Wife, Lover, Mother, Friend.* I set it up on Wolf Hill in a small open area between some hemlocks and a stand of white birch.

Oscar came by almost every day, often bring along some goodies for Sarah. On one particular day, Oscar said a woman by the name of Adamski had called him asking for Anna. How she got his number, he didn't say. That got my attention. He said that he told her the sad news that Anna had died in an accident.

"Do you know her?" he asked me.

"Yes. Anna's mother," I said, wondering what was going on. I didn't trust any contact from Anna's folks.

A week later I go my answer in the form of a registered letter: The Adamskis wanted custody of Sarah.

"Over my dead body," I said to the fireplace, the walls, the sink, the loft, trees. To Raccoon. To every creature for miles around.

Oscar's lawyer, Tom Crowley, did what he could for me. One witness after another assured the judge that I was, indeed, a fit and loving father. Oscar attested to my love for Anna and how I was able to move on with my life after her untimely and tragic death. Frank Toilsen and some of the turtles got a night in jail for bringing their shotguns onto the courthouse grounds to protest. Being so stooped over was a blessing in disguise. The best they could do was shoot up the shrubbery. I know they thought they were supporting me, and I loved them for it.

I could've killed Emil Adamski, the scrawny, ferret-faced bastard. Anna's mother looked beaten down. She didn't make eye contact with me or anybody else. Their lawyer extolled their virtues: God-fearing church-goers...hard-working Christians who lost their one and only daughter to a grown man who took advantage of her innocence. To a man whose service record showed mental instability. Who never once showed his daughter the inside of a church. A man who pretended to be married to Anna and had a child out-of-wedlock. That this man, pointing to me, ignored the Age of Consent laws in both Indiana and Wisconsin.

When their lawyer said I was unfit to be Sarah's father, I called him a goddamn liar. A few whacks of the judge's gavel and I was over the table. Two burly deputies held me back or I would have throttled the cowering Adamskis. I was hit with a contempt charge.

I never saw Sarah again.

After the hearing, I couldn't sleep. Every noise, every stir of the dried leaves pulled me further away, thickening the grayness of my life as if I was slowly going blind to what was or would ever be again. I don't remember deciding to take off. I do remember tossing my tools into the back of my truck like worthless chunks of iron. Just before I left, I put any food that might spoil in a pile by the back door for the raccoon. I wasn't sure where I'd go or if I'd ever return. I drove west skirting Minneapolis/St. Paul, and crossed into North Dakota before pulling over to get some sleep. The next morning, I stopped at a diner for breakfast. It was there that I read a newspaper article describing the work being done on Thunderhead Mountain. It read, "The great monument to Chief Crazy Horse continues to emerge after removing more than three million tons of granite."

"Where is this place?" I asked the waitress, pointing to the article.

"That way," she said, pointing westward. "Out near Rapid City."

Beth

JUNE 20–22, 1993

26

So. I'm not who I thought I was. The sister I longed to find was really my mother, and she's dead along with her unborn child. Sarah, whom I took as my niece, is really me. The parents I grew up with, also dead, were really my grandparents.

Then there's Jim. So much for having a brother-in-law. Jim's really my father. His whereabouts unknown. Maybe dead. What circle of hell did I buy into?

I sat stunned to silence as Oscar went on with the story about my mother's death during a vicious storm. How the Adamskis came to Clayton and got parental rights over me. And how Jim went into a deep depression and took off to heaven-knows-where.

While he rattled on, I was captive of my own swirling thoughts, swinging between sorrow and seething. Seething was winning the battle. I mean, what a deception! How many times did my mother—who's really grandmother—have the opportunity to tell me the truth about my past? Oscar knew where I was. Jim did, too. Why didn't they come and get me?

Or maybe send a birthday card? One big goddamn lie. At least I now know why Emil wouldn't let me call him Dad. God, to think that that man was my grandfather! Aren't grandfathers supposed to be kind and nice and somebody to feel good about? None of the above, Emil!

Oscar was saying something about my mother playing a viola when I butted in. "So where's Jim?" I asked, getting up from the sofa. Oscar stopped jabbering and told me he didn't know.

I stared down at Oscar and said, "Let me get this straight. The Adamskis came and got me. Jim knew where I was. You knew. The whole damn world knew. And all of you just let life run on as if I never existed. What the hell were you all thinking? That maybe I wouldn't care to know who I was? That me not knowing was the best way to go? I mean why keep this cabin so prim and proper? Are you hoping by some miracle, that everything will somehow work out? Well it hasn't, has it? I came up here to find a family and what did I get? Death all around and no good news anywhere!"

Oscar stood. "Hold on," he said. "I understand what you're saying. I agree that life hasn't been fair to you and things might have worked out differently. But that was then and this is now. Can't we just take it from here?"

"Take what from here? My family? What family? All dead except maybe Jim. And if he is alive, well the truth is he might as well be dead. It's been what, fifteen years or so and not a damn word from the man? Do I want to even try and find him? I don't think so. Look, Oscar, if I add things up I'm glad I made the trip. At least I know who I am. That's something. And I couldn't have known without this trip."

"Are you saying that you're done here?"

"That's what I'm thinking. I mean, why stay? I came looking for my sister and I found her. Isn't that enough?"

"What about your father?"

"Oscar, how many more times must I say that everybody knew where I was and didn't lift a finger, Huh? What about that?"

Oscar took a few steps toward the fireplace, turned to me and said, "Sarah, let me give you something to think about."

I interrupted. "For now how about calling me Beth or Beth Sarah. I don't think I'm quite ready for a new name just yet."

"I'll use Beth Sarah then," he said, acting like he was eager to get back to what he was saying. "What good would it have done if I showed up in Indiana to tell a youngster that her parents were really her grandparents? Those Adamskis had legal rights over you. All I would have done was cause you confusion and hurt. Don't believe for one minute that I didn't think about you. I'll tell you this, when Jill told me that a young woman was up here looking for the Robertsons, you popped right into my head. Then when I first saw you stepping off that bus earlier, I was near certain. That's why I was so darn off-putting when you were hitting me with one question after another. I was trying to figure it all out. I'm sorry about treating you that way, but I needed to be sure. If you can spare the time and don't have to rush back to Indiana, we could work together and try to find Jim. We need to know what happened to him. Where he is. When he took off without a word or leaving a note or whatever, why I just took it as something he had to do. That he'd come back on his own time. After about a month or so, I began to get worried so I tried to find him. Had the sheriff and all helping but nothing ever came of it. He just disappeared."

He paused. "What do you say?"

It was a lot to take in.

I needed some space. I walked over to the stairs leading up to the loft. "I have to think about this. Mind if I go upstairs?"

"You go right ahead. No hurry."

I took step by step trying to conjure up my parents using this same staircase. My hand slipped along the smooth knotty handrail. I reached the landing, went to the closed door I saw earlier, and opened it. Pink. A small bed with a chair next to it. A dresser painted white. Sunlight streaming in through a lacey curtain. A throw rug with the ABC's printed around its edge. A shelf of children's books. *Did my parents read to me?* This was my room. I tried to remember being here but nothing came back. I had no real memory of being here. But there was a familiarity about it. It was the same feeling I had at the water pump, only stronger.

I sat down in the chair and thought "I bet this is where my mother read to me." Knowing that I belonged here had shed a different light on things. Knowing my real name was a big deal, too. I mean, everybody knows me as Beth Adamski. My school records, driver's license, just everything. Changing stuff was going to be like taking an eraser to the last fifteen years. Is that even possible?

I left my bedroom, gently closed the door, and went into my parents' room. I opened the leather box and took out the stone I saw earlier. My mother's stone. I clutched it to my heart and uttered the word *Mom*. I sat down on the edge of the bed and closed my eyes. I wanted more than anything to just lay back on the bed and cuddle up to what might have been. What would it have been like to live with Mom and Dad? Growing up in a loving family. I admitted the truth to myself; living in

Oolitic was a little slice of hell, especially when Emil was drunk.

I opened my eyes and stared at the stone, reading aloud the words I read earlier: *You live in my soul. I love you completely and forever.* I flipped the stone back over and gently traced the tiny mistletoe leaves with my little finger. "He really loved you, Mom," I murmured then added, "You loved him, too, didn't you?" I sat quietly for a little bit, not being sure what to do or where to go. Smithy Paulson came to mind. *You've got spunk. You're on a mission.* "Maybe I should go and find Jim; that is, if he's still alive," I said aloud, as if Smithy Paulson and I were sitting on that big front porch of his. I mean, it's like if Dad didn't come searching for me, then I'm going to search for him.

I got up from the bed, put the stone in my pocket, walked to the top of the stairs, and looked down. Oscar was still sitting on the wooden chair across from the sofa, his head cupped in his hands looking at the floor. Trooper was still curled up on the oval rug.

"Oscar," I said getting his attention. "Do you think that Jim is still alive?"

Oscar looked up at me, took a moment to give himself a chin rub, then said, "I really wish I could say yes to that. But after all these years not hearing hide nor hair from him, I have to wonder."

"Are you still thinking that we could work together to find him?"

Oscar stood and said, "Yes, I sure am."

I came down the steps and asked, "How do we get started?"

"By you following me back to town and coming over to my place," he answered. "I know the missus would love to see you."

"Before we go, can I ask you a question?" He answered with

a nod of his head. "Why are you so interested in all this, I mean keeping the cabin up and everything?"

Oscar gave it some thought before answering. "Well for one thing, I have quite an investment in keeping the place in good shape. I can't just let it go to some auction house. I know that might sound too much like its all business with me but there's more to it. Simply put, your parents were like family to me and the missus. They were very special to have in our lives and to see you here today, why I'll tell you it's like having a gift from heaven. Does that answer your question?"

"Yes, thank you."

Oscar led me and Hussy back through town to a quiet road. About a mile later, he turned into a paved driveway. A sign said *Welcome! The Goldens.* We parked at the end of the driveway. Oscar grabbed my suitcase and together we followed Trooper into the house.

"Guess who I found," Oscar said to the *missus* who was busy in the kitchen. "Sarah Robertson."

The missus, whose name was Ethel, turned from her place at the stove, wiped her hands on her apron and grew a smile a mile wide. "Well, I never," she said, coming over to me. "Let me look at you." Our eyes met. A moment passed. We embraced. "Let's get you settled, then we'll have diner."

The guest room was actually a suite fit for a princess. There was a four-poster bed, a rocker, quilts and shams piled up like clouds. It looked like a picture from one of those *Good Housekeeping* magazines at the dentist's office. The bathroom was super-nice too, with a sparkling-clean shower stall separate from the big tub.

For dinner, we had roast beef, green beans and little potatoes. Oscar ate quietly, lost in his thoughts I guess. I was too tired to eat very much. Ethel could see that I was exhausted and didn't push me to fill in all that happened in my life. That could wait until morning.

After a long shower I climbed into bed. Before I drifted off, I thought about the letter. Anna was missing *her* mom when she wrote it. The fact that it said *Dear Mom and Dad* had thrown me a little at first—you know, because Emil never let me call him *Dad*. But now I know I'm Sarah and that Anna was his real daughter. So he let her call him *Dad,* and for me, it was Emil. Cruel, but it made a weird kind of sense. He was always distant from me. He couldn't have cared less about my getting A's on my report cards, or about anything having to do with school. My friends were never welcomed into the house. But he's gone now. Out of my life for good. I wonder what my real father is like.

But no matter how I thought about it, it didn't make much sense that Jim just disappeared and left everything behind, including me. The pink stone…and that big pile of stones with the soldiers' names and stuff…those were like his treasures. I mean, here was a guy who had white-knighted his true love right out through her window, even though he could've gotten arrested or shot or something. Somebody who would do that wouldn't just run away—would he?

Whatever the case, I was determined to find him.

In the morning over a big breakfast, Ethel told me that Oscar had filled her in on how I found my way to Clayton, and the stuff that went on yesterday. Ethel didn't go on about it. Instead she turned to telling me about my early childhood days, avoiding any reference to mother's death or my father leaving. "Jim and Anna and you came here every Sunday afternoon," she said, and went on to describe picnics, the gardens we planted, and how much fun we had going to the county fair. I gave my imagination a twirl, picturing how it must have been.

As we finished our coffee, Ethel said. "I like the stud in your nose. Maybe I should get one myself, but I don't think Oscar would like that."

"Well it might be fun to find out," I offered. "Where is Oscar anyway?"

"He's over at the yard looking for something that may help you to find your father.'"

"Yard?"

"Oscar owns a scrap yard. You'd almost think he lived there."

Right on cue, a yap from Trooper signaled that Oscar was back. As he came into the kitchen, Ethel asked him, "Did you find anything?"

"Sure did. A junkman keeps things." He was a junkman?

"Frank Toilson, an old guy that works for me—he was in his seventies when Jim and Anna came up here. Anyway, thanks to Frank, I have a lead on your dad. It might not go anywhere, but I was thinking last night about when Jim and Anna first arrived. They had just gotten married—in Milwaukee, they said. This morning I was looking through my stuff at the yard, and Frank handed me a dirty old index card that Jim gave him. Then I remembered: There was a fellow down in Milwaukee named Hans. Jim used my phone to call him from time to time. Once or twice, Hans called back when Jim wasn't around. I'd take a message…and wouldn't you know it, I still had the number. Last time I used it was after your mother's accident when Jim was in such a bad way. I thought maybe Hans could help him somehow, but it turned out Hans was sick at the time. I can't promise you'll find Jim, or even that Hans is still alive, but it's a place to start, don't you think?"

He handed me the card and I looked at the name—Hans Biettermeir—and a number scribbled in faded pencil.

"What do you think?" I asked Ethel, who had been listening quietly to the whole thing.

"I think you better get up off the chair and use the phone. The one in your room would be the most private."

I sat on the bed turning the card over and over in my hands, then took a deep breath and dialed the phone number. An old-lady voice answered—witchy, like her throat was full of gravel.

"Hello, this is Evelyn Gumpfrey."

"Um...hello, this is Beth—er, *Sarah* calling. I have some... questions that maybe you can answer...?"

"Well, I suppose I can try, my dear. But if you're from the Girl Scouts, I must tell you that I just ordered my cookies."

"No, I'm....not. I'm actually looking for someone named Hans Biettermeir?" I pronounced it as best I could.

"Oh dear...well...this is still his number, but I'm afraid Mr. Biettermeir passed away a few years back. It's just me here now. Maybe there's something I can help you with?"

"Actually," I said, "I'm trying to find a man named Jim Robertson."

There were a few seconds of silence. Then she said, "Yes, dear, go on..."

"He's..." I reached into my pocket and held the pink stone. "He's my father." I wondered if she could tell over the phone that I was getting a little bit teary just saying that.

"Oh, my dear. My dear, my dear, MY DEAR." She kept repeating it, each time at a higher pitch, like she was singing up a scale. "For heaven's sake. My goodness, after all these years. How is he? I've known him since he was just a boy!"

"No! I mean…that's why I'm calling. I don't know how he is, or…where he is, or even if he's still…alive. I never knew him. I didn't even know he existed until just recently."

"Why, child, I'm so sorry…but I'm having trouble understanding you. How could you not have known him?"

I told her the basic story, without going into all the details.

"You poor child. I did know about your mother's accident, bless her soul. But, oh my, I had no idea about any adoption."

"Miss…Gumpfrey," I said nervously, "about my father…. do you have any idea where he might be?"

"It's been so many years," she said quietly.

"I know. But I really want to find my father, Miss Gumpfrey. And I'd appreciate any help you can give me." It felt like she was holding something back—just like Oscar had done the day before.

"I heard your question, dear, and I am trying to think. My memory, you know…"

That made me feel bad for being impatient, so I apologized and just sat there, waiting for her to speak.

"You know, dear…I'm just not sure. I do have some letters and things put away. I could look for them."

"That would be great," I said. "Really—so nice of you. I can't tell you how much it would mean to me to find him…or find out more about him, at least." I felt a little like Judy Garland in *The Wizard of Oz*, asking strangers to help her get home.

"Of course, my dear, I'll do all I can to help. Do you live in

Milwaukee? Are you close by?"

I had no idea how far away Milwaukee was. I asked her to hold the line for a minute and excused myself to go ask Oscar.

"I'll wait, dear—but it is long distance." I set the phone on the nightstand, went to the kitchen, asked Oscar how far was it to Milwaukee, and was back on the phone in less than a minute,

"Oscar says we're about 200 miles from you." Before Miss Gumpfrey could say anything, I continued, "You said that you had some letters. Maybe you could…just read some of them to me over the phone?"

"Well I could, I suppose, but I have to find them first. I think I know where they might be. Is 200 miles too far to pay me a visit? I'm eighty-six, you know, so I try never to put things off. Perhaps you could even come tomorrow. I can have lunch ready…something nice for the two of us."

"Tomorrow? Well…I guess I could. But I don't want to put you out."

"Now, now, I don't have much occasion to use my good china. I'll make some nice sandwiches."

"I'll need directions."

Miss Gumpfrey gave me the address but had no idea how to get there. I said I'd figure it out and try to be there by noon.

"That's just as nice as it can be. I'll be waiting."

We said our good-byes and I sat on the edge of the bed to gather my thoughts. Who would ever think a mission could be so exhausting? I mean, I left home just three days ago—which feels more like three lifetimes ago—and now I'm off to meet a lady in Milwaukee who just might lead me to finding my real father.

Oscar and Ethyl were excited to hear about my talk with Miss Gumpfrey and that I would be off to Milwaukee in the morning. I explained that Hans had passed away, that Miss Gumpfrey was his housekeeper, and that she knew my father.

"Please give the guy over at your office a big thank-you for finding the card with the phone number," I said to Oscar.

Oscar looked at his watch said "We have lots of the day left How about coming with me over to the yard and you can tell Frank yourself? Besides, I'd like to show you my place. Then if you want we can stop over at the Muskie for a bit of lunch."

"Sounds like a plan to me," I said.

On the short drive to Oscar's place, he told me that Frank Toilson knew my parents. He said "Frank's ninety years old, but he had a memory to beat the band. He's the only guy left of a group of old men I called my Turtles."

I didn't ask.

The thing I noticed when we arrived at the junkyard was that the front of the building was covered with deer antlers. Not like one or two that you might find in somebody's den or maybe a men's club, but hundreds of them. Northern Wisconsin was not a place for Bambi, that's for sure. Inside were shelves full of metal parts, none of which I recognized. Hanging from the ceiling were all sorts of things from picture frames to a big wooden rake. Oscar led me to a darkened corner where an old man sat scrunched-up in a grey overstuffed chair.

"Wake up, Frank. Sarah's here to say hello," he said. As he left, he added, "I'll be at my desk while you two have a chat.

Frank twisted and turned, willing himself to stand. "Bejesus, why you're the prettiest girl to come into this place since your mother walked in here back in the dead of winter of 1975. Drove up here in a bus with Jim. I remember her coming in here like it was yesterday. You standing here is like Anna's come down from heaven to pay a visit. I'm just happy to be alive to see it."

I wasn't sure how to respond. "Me, too," I said. I thanked Frank for finding the phone number and told him that Miss Gumpfrey might give me a lead to finding my father.

"Oh, you'll find him, I'll tell you that. Jim went down where there's no light, no light at all, and here you are shining like the sun. Oscar told me what went on yesterday with you coming all the way up here to learn about who you are and all that. Damn hard to swallow, I'll tell you. Well, you never do know what's around the corner till you look. And you're lookin'. That takes some guts, let me tell you. More people run from the truth than to it. Like those ugly birds that hide in the sand. Truth, it can be so bright that people shut their eyes to it. But not you. You go find it and don't let no blockhead tell you not to. You bring some of that light to Jim."

Of course, I thought about Smithy Paulson saying about the same thing—having courage and spunk and all that. After Frank settled himself back down, I sat in chair nearby. And for the next hour or so, I quietly listened while he told me all about my parents, the building of the cabin, helping to keep the garden, Mom playing her viola, and how wonderful it all was before the storm that took my mother.

"That's the past and I tell you I've got lots of that. But that's not what's important; you can't drive a car looking in the rearview mirror. Now you go and find that father of yours and bring him home."

I promised Frank that I'd do just that.

After a tour of the yard, I said good-bye to Frank, and asked Oscar if it was okay if we skipped lunch. Even after a good-night's sleep, I was still feeling very tired. Going to the Muskie

Café sounded like just too much. Oscar agreed and we headed back to his place.

I laid down for a nap, awoke for an early supper, then headed straight to the shower and back to bed. I gave some thought to how I might feel when I found my father. I didn't get too far into it before falling fast asleep.

27

Before I left Clayton the next morning, Oscar gave me a *Gazetteer of Wisconsin,* a book of maps that showed every road, dirt or paved in the entire state. I took Highway 8 to Route 141, then South past Green Bay. It was familiar since I had to go by there for Jake: He worshipped the Green Bay Packers like it was his religion. His bedroom was all done up in green and gold. If he'd known I was that close to Green Bay, he'd have exploded. I blew him a kiss as I passed the sign. The more I wasn't able to see him, the more I missed him.

I rolled down the car windows for a breeze. The air seemed sweeter than I remembered it on my way up from Bloomington. Everything looked better, too. Maybe that was because I was part of it all now—*me.*

Exit 82 was easy enough to find. My next task was to get to the Schlitz Audubon Center, then turn on Fox Point Road. That was Miss Gumpfrey's road. She said to look for a stone arch marking her driveway. When I saw it, I cheered for myself.

As I made my way up the long white-gravel driveway, I

thought maybe I'd made a mistake and turned in to a lavish resort. The house wasn't a house so much as a mansion, and the grounds were lush and covered in tall trees. I could see blue water in the distance, stretching out behind the house. I liked the way the gravel crunched under Hussy's tires, like its purpose was to make you slow down and enjoy the private view. I felt a little nervous as I parked next to a stone sidewalk that led to the front door. I mean…I hadn't thought about what to expect, but this was a lot to take in.

The front door was really two front doors, and there was polished brass everywhere. I got out of the car and looked up. I swear, the trees surrounding the house went a hundred feet in the air. They were swaying like dancers. Before I even got up to the front door, a tall thin lady came out onto the big wraparound porch. The minute she said something, I knew it was Miss Gumpfrey. She reminded me of Grandma in Willa Cather's *My Antonia*—tall, a little stooped, with a high voice that commanded attention. The word 'regal' popped into my head. Her hair was done up in spiral braids that were pulled up along the sides of her head.

"My, oh my! You're all grown up," she declared. "Do come in, my dear, and make yourself comfortable."

Stepping into the stone floor entryway, I said, "You have a beautiful place."

"Oh, yes, that was Mr. Biettermeir's doing. He was very fussy when it came to doing things right."

I paused for a moment then followed Miss Gumpfrey down two steps into the most amazing living room I'd ever seen. A brass chandelier hung high overhead with bulbs like candle flames. One entire wall was taken up by a stone fireplace. I swear, you could burn whole trees in the thing. Everything was pretty but too formal for me.

Miss Gumpfrey came up behind me, startling me back to reality. "Would Prince of Wales be okay, dear? It's my favorite." When I just looked at her, she went on, "You do like tea, don't you?"

All I could think of was Lipton and its little bags of orange pekoe. "Yeah, sure," I answered, then corrected myself. "Yes, ma'am." I promised myself to mind my manners, especially since the place and this lady seemed so grand. Miss Gumpfrey told me to make myself comfortable while she got our tea.

I was feeling really out of place, even nervous that I might do something wrong or say something stupid. The rug was so thick it was like I sank in up to my ankles. I was just about to sit down when Miss Gumpfrey came back carrying a silver tray with a teapot, two cups and saucers, a creamer, sugar bowl, and dainty little spoons. She invited me to sit facing the big windows.

"Good and strong, lots of body," she said, pouring out two cups. "Knowing one's tea is like what Mr. Biettermeir said about knowing one's scotch. You have to pay attention to its character. Help yourself to cream and sugar."

"Thank you," I said. I'd never been served tea before, certainly not in cups so thin you could almost see through them. They had neat little flowers painted on them and tiny handles that even a pinky finger couldn't fit through. I was used to drinking from mugs.

"Mr. Biettermeir was a fine man," Miss Gumpfrey went on.

I listened as best I could, while trying to manipulate the little tweezers, or whatever they're called, for picking up the sugar cubes. They kept slipping out of my hand until I just gave up.

"When he died, he made sure that I'd be comfortable. I don't have to worry about a thing. He was that way." She reached for the sugar and I watched how she made her tea just right. She didn't even look. Two sugar lumps, a dash of cream, a swirl or two with a little spoon. Her thumb and forefinger pinched the teacup handle, little finger up. Then she took such a tiny sip that it hardly seemed worth all the work. I did my best to imitate her and she watched me with a gentle smile. I thought *this is how grandmas are.* Rich ones, anyway.

"Mine's blue," she said.

"I beg your pardon?"

"My hair. Yours is, hmm... so fresh. Don't we make a pair?" Miss Gumpfrey laughed. "Blue and...what color is that, dear?"

"Um...kind of purple, I guess."

"Well, it's just as pretty as a bunny rabbit!" She took another dainty sip and said, "I gave them a wedding ring so they could pretend to be married."

"Huh?"

"You see, your mother and father weren't of age. So I told them to pretend, to keep them safe.

I decided to just leave it alone. I'd never had a conversation with anyone like Mrs. Gumpfrey. Maybe it was her age or something, but I was not good at this.

She got a sad look on her face. "A few weeks before your mother died, Mr. Biettermeir fell ill. His heart, wouldn't beat right, you know. It became so weak he could barely move around. He'd always wanted to travel up to see your parents' place...still talked about it, weak as he was. When he heard that your mother died, well...I think it was all too much for him. He passed on soon after that. I felt bad that I didn't get up there myself, to see your father and pay my respects. But with all I had to do to settle things…." Her voice faded.

I told her I understood completely—as if it were me she was talking about visiting. She gave me a nice smile. I figured it was my turn to talk, so I started telling her what I'd learned since I'd been in Wisconsin—how my father went to pieces after my mother died. I told her about being taken by my grandparents and how I didn't know anything about it til after they died.

I could tell Miss Gumpfrey was genuinely shocked when I got to that part. "Taken by your grandparents? Oh, dear, I had no idea! You can be sure that if Mr. Biettermeir had been around to intervene, why, that just wouldn't have happened! And then your other grandparents died. How dreadful!"

I let it go without correcting her.

We didn't say anything for a while, just sat there sipping tea. Miss Gumpfrey broke the silence.

"After you called, I checked around and found something that might help you in your quest. I'll go and get it if you like?"

Yes, yes, yes!

"That would be great, thanks."

Once Miss Gumpfrey had excused herself, I stood up and walked over to the giant fireplace. There were a lot of pictures on the mantel, and I was looking at them when she came back into the room. She smiled and set the envelope she was carrying on a table by the big couch in front of the fireplace.

I was dying to see what she had found. But first I had a question about one of the photos. She seemed to guess what I was thinking and came to my side.

"Oh, you dear child," she said, laying the flat of her hand against my back as if to hold me up. "Why in heaven's name didn't I think about this picture! Mr. Biettermeir took it when your parents first came to us." She picked it up from the mantel and handed it to me. "I think this should be yours now, dear."

My mother looked so young and beautiful! My father was gazing at her like he'd been hit over the head. I saw it right away—my nose was just like his. There was no doubt about it. I couldn't help tearing up a little, though I managed not to cry full out. Miss Gumpfrey didn't run away when she saw my eyes spilling over, like Smithy Paulson did when I visited him in Oolitic. She put her arm around my shoulders and led me over to the big couch.

I sank so far into that sofa, I felt like the only thing showing was my head. Miss Gumpfrey sat down just to my right. "Do you really think I'll find him?" I asked her. "Yes, I do," she said firmly. She reached and picked up the envelope and handed it to me.

The second I started to open that envelope, my mind jumped back to the letter that started this whole trip: *Your Loving Daughter, Anna.* This time the note wasn't torn up.

Dear Miss Gumpfrey,
I am so sorry about Hans. Oscar told me about it. He meant very much to me. I'll always remember him. And you, too.
I hope that you are okay.
Sincerely, Jim

Scribbled on the bottom was, "I just found this so I'm sending it now."

There was no date on it, no return address. Just the note. When I asked Miss Gumpfrey if she remembered when she got it, she said, "It was after Mr. Biettermeir died. Oh," she giggled a little, "of course it was. What I mean is, it was quite a time after."

"I wonder what he means by just finding the note. I mean that's weird, don't you think?"

"Well dear, I just can't say."

Still…it was from *him*. In his own handwriting. I smiled— what else could I do? I mean the note didn't give me anything to go on. I thought about leaving, heading back to Clayton but gave it one last shot.

"Miss Gumpfrey, do you remember how you found out about my mother's death?"

"Oh, yes! Mr. Biettermeir got a call from a fellow who lived near your parents' home."

"That was probably Oscar."

"I wouldn't know his name, but that's how we found out."

"Hmm…that doesn't help much. I just have to ask again… what else can you tell me about him? Is there anything at all that might help me track him down?"

"Oh, child…well…I told you that I've known Jimmy ever since he was a little boy. He was special then, just as he was when he grew up. Now and then, Hans would bring little Jimmy home with him. I'd make potato pancakes, his favorite. He'd eat a stack of them as high as the moon." She laughed like she was watching some old home movie. "I swear, that boy acted as if he hadn't eaten in a week when I brought those out. And, of course there was his stone carving. You know about that, do you?"

I reached into my pocket for the pink stone but changed my mind.

"Some," I answered.

"Ever since he was very little, your father carved stone like his world depended on it. His teacher was as gruff a man as I ever met—no manners, mind you—but he was downright tender with little Jimmy."

Miss Gumpfrey fell silent. I assumed she was lost in her thoughts. I liked hearing her stories, and it was a nice visit and all, but I had a mission and this wasn't getting me any closer to it. Not really.

"Thanks for telling me all that, Miss Gumpfrey," I said, "but…maybe I should think about heading back to Clayton before it gets dark."

She just stared off into the distance and looked a little sad. I could tell she wanted me to stay longer.

"I've enjoyed your company, child," she said. "It took me back to some lovely times. But I guess you know everything that I do. I'm sorry I couldn't be of more help."

"Oh, no, Miss Gumpfrey. I really appreciate all that you've told me—and seeing your beautiful house." We got up from the sofa.

"You know…if you'd like to stay here for a night or two, it would be no problem at all. Why, I opened up the guest suite this morning to give it a—good airing out."

I gave the idea a quick thought, but, no. I just couldn't imagine hanging out with Miss Gumpfrey overnight—even though I was getting a little tired. My spunk was getting close to zero. I made my excuses, and she said she hoped that I'd find my father, adding, "You must know how hurt he was after Anna's death, dear. My grandfather used to say that a wounded bird can't fly back to the nest. Be grateful for the truth you have. Patience is a virtue, my dear."

I picked up the envelope that held my father's sympathy

note. I walked toward the middle of the room, still gripping the envelope, contemplating tearing it to bits and tossing the pieces into the big fireplace. I looked at the envelope again. That's when I noticed the postmark.

"Did you know that he was in Rapid City, South Dakota?"

"No, I didn't. Let me see what you've found."

I showed Miss Gumpfrey the postmark.

"Agatha Christie," she said, staring at me. "A clue. That's what Agatha Christie would call it," she said slyly. "What we need to do is figure out what he was doing in such a place."

"I'm not really sure how we do that," I said.

"Follow me," she said, taking charge like a five-star general. "The phone's in the kitchen."

I stood by as Miss Gumpfrey phoned long-distance information. She called me over to listen in. There were two listings for the name *Jim Robertson* listed in South Dakota. One turned out to be deceased. The other was born, raised and living on the family farm. The operator told her that there were some listings in the yellow pages under *Stone carving*, but again, his name wasn't listed. The Chamber of Commerce was no help either, but they gave Miss Gumpfrey the rundown on local happenings. "Mount Rushmore is the big attraction," a lady told her. "Then there's always the Crazy Horse Memorial. They're still working on it but it's fun to visit. I'm sure if you're looking for a stone carver, they could help you find one." Miss Gumpfrey wrote down a number, thanked the woman and cut the connection.

"I believe you have a call to make," she said, handing me the phone.

28

Miss Gumpfrey busied herself at the sink while I called. The lady that answered the phone had a North Country accent times ten. "Hello," she said. "Crazy Horse Memorial. My name's Marge. What can I do for you today?"

"Hello…Marge…my name's Sarah," I said nervously. "I'm calling to see if a James Robertson works there?"

"Well now, as a matter of fact he does. He's been here for years." I nearly jumped out of my pants. I looked over at Miss Gumpfrey and gave her a thumbs-up. She actually clapped. I was stunned and tongue-tied. "Um, I…no, I was just—"

"Are you coming to the ceremony then?" she cut in. The lady was almost singing, acting like she knew me. Like, here I was, dead serious about finding my father, and this stranger was acting like she's my aunt or something. They taught us to act like that at Walmart—act like a neighbor just walked in the door. At first, I had a real hard time doing it. I'd fake it pretty badly, like I was a cartoon character, but people actually liked it. They'd answer me all chirpy, like I really was their neighbor.

People are weird. Like if you smile and tell them they look perfectly ugly today, they'll thank you.

When I didn't answer Miss South Dakota, she said, "Why, Jim's one of the fellows helping with the opening."

"What opening?" I asked.

"The *opening*, for heaven's sakes. They're going to be opening Crazy Horse's eyes. It's pretty exciting, don't you think?"

I had no idea what she was talking about.

"When is it?"

"This Friday, in just two days at five-thirty in the morning. Just as the sun's coming up. I'd be pleased to make a reservation for you."

"Ma'am, I'm from Clayton, Wisconsin. I don't think I'll be able to make your...*eye-opening!*" I looked over at Miss Gumpfrey, who was frowning.

"Well, alrighty then. May I take a message for Jim?"

"Yeah. Tell him his daughter Sarah called." I hung up and told Miss Gumpfrey what I'd found out, and she could barely contain herself.

"Mr. Biettermeir would be so happy for you, my dear!" she said. "We have to get you out there."

"I don't think so, Miss Gumpfrey. Why should I race out there when he had years to find me and didn't even bother? Maybe it would have been better to find out he was dead."

"My word, child, bite your tongue!"

Miss Gumpfrey was trying so hard, and here I was, acting like a spoiled kid. I forced myself to calm down.

"It's just...I can't help feeling like some dog that was taken to the pound...and I'm supposed to go looking for my daddy!"

"Sarah, child, this is no time for you to give up. You came

all this way for a reason." Miss Gumpfrey moved into my space, her eyes biting into me like drills. "Now you listen to me, young lady. It is your choice of course. You can go back to where you came from, or you can finish what you set out to do—get out to South Dakota and get some answers." She paused. "So, what is it going to be?"

I swallowed hard. "I need to work things out. I'm not sure what to do."

"Maybe a walk would do you good," she said quietly.

"Yes," I said. "That's a good idea."

She led me to a door off of the kitchen. "The back steps lead down to the lake. It's a nice place for a walk."

From the living room window, I had spotted a path running through the scruffy pines. I found it easily and followed it down to the lake.

My father is a jerk! Just like Emil!

I ran along the beach until I couldn't run anymore. Catching my breath, I looked out over the lake. The setting sun cast my shadow onto the small waves lapping at the shore.

I started walking. I couldn't believe how much stuff had washed up here…cups, plastic bottles, plastic rope…. There were some neat things, too. Chunks of wood from trees. Pieces of glass that had been polished smooth by the lake waters. I walked for so long it started getting dark. The sun rays on the water looked like they were surfing, jumping from one little wave to the next. The colors made the lake look like it was on fire.

It took a long time to get back to the house. I figured Miss Gumpfrey would be pretty mad that I had stayed out so long, and I wouldn't blame her. She was nice, really. What she said about loving Mr. Biettermeir? God, it must be hard to love someone like that your whole life and then lose him. That kind of love…I wondered if I'll ever feel that…or if I even want to. Look what that kind of love did to my father!

I stood on a pebbled beach below the house. The living room window was like a big yellow wall far away—but seeming close, like a full moon. I found the path back through the pines. The side of the house was dark, but I could see the back porch light shining at the top of the steps. When I got to the top, Miss Gumpfrey opened the door. She was waiting for me, just as she had been when I first came.

When I told her I'd decided to go out to South Dakota, she gave me this big smile. "Your father will be so surprised," she said. "Pleased, I'm sure."

I laughed a little at that. "Well, he'd better be," I said.

She actually rolled her eyes. She looked younger somehow.

While I'd been out walking, Miss Gumpfrey had made supper. "You must be hungry," she said. "I made *Les Oiseaux Sans Têtes*. It was one of Mr. Biettermeir's favorites."

"I'm sure he was a wonderful man."

"Yes, he *is*," Miss Gumpfrey corrected me, and I let it go. I guess she was saying that the people we love are always with us… and maybe she was right.

"You said before that I need to learn to forgive. But how do I do that?"

"As I said, dear…swallowing pride is a start. But since you've asked, it's really about having empathy. You know what empathy is, don't you?"

"Yeah, it's like…walking in someone else's shoes, right?"

"Well, yes, that's one way to put it. In the case of your father, we know some things that happened to him, but not everything. We know he lost the love of his life in an instant, and that it made him lose his way. The rest of his story is his alone, until you give him a chance to share it with you. And for that, you need an open heart. You need to be able to put his feelings first, instead of your own—at least for a little while."

"I…I hope I can do that, but it doesn't sound all that easy."

"The important things in life never are, my dear. Now! I think we should eat before dinner gets cold."

"May I ask you one more question?"

"Yes, dear."

"What was it you said we're having for dinner?"

Her laugh sounded like a little bell ringing.

"Oh dear, of course! *Les Oiseaux Sans Tetes* means *birds without heads*. They are a treat, I promise you. We'll have a nice dinner, then it's off to bed with you. You are staying the night, aren't you?"

I liked the sound of that.

Jim

JUNE 21, 1993

29

Hanging safely in a steel basket six hundred feet up alongside the face of Crazy Horse, I was smoothing out one of his pupils with a 3,000-degree jet finishing torch. I was covered with granite granules no bigger than peppercorns. My two-way radio crackled to life.

"Jim. You there?" I snapped off the torch.

"Yeah, Marge. What's up?"

"Thought you'd want to know…some girl named Sarah called looking for you. From some place in Wisconsin. Clay Town, maybe? Anyway, she said to tell you—and these were her exact words—'Tell him his daughter Sarah called.' She sounded…I don't know…kind of *mad*, actually. Hey, I didn't know you—"

I clicked off the radio.

I turned around to gaze over the rough emptiness of the Black Hills and grabbed the cold rail of the basket to steady myself. I drew in a deep breath of the crisp clean air. I said the name *Sarah* on the exhale and stood up, dazed. My mind blurred. I felt like I had just awakened after a deep sleep.

Using the intercom, I hailed Clyde, the cable operator. "Haul me up."

Once topside, I climbed out of the basket and without a word, headed for the elevator. When I reached the ground, I walked to the parking lot, jumped into my truck, and headed for home, or what passed for home. I'd been living in a travel trailer for years, ever since arriving in South Dakota.

I closed the door of the trailer behind me and sat down on my one and only upholstered chair. How did I allow myself to disappear from Sarah's life? Just like my dad disappeared from mine. Big difference—my dad had no choice in the matter. I did. How the hell did I do that? How could I have blocked all that out of my head?

I thought about the reason why I'd run away—from everyone and everything. Why does anyone run away? Because life becomes impossible. At least that was my excuse. Because staying was just too painful. Yes, I had friends. Friends whose eyes brimmed with sympathy. Who wanted like hell to help me out. But what could they do? Could they bring my Anna back? Could they bring our unborn child back? Could they keep little Sarah from being taken from me?

The cabin, our tract of woods, the birdsong, the crinkly sound of the breeze through the trees. All that had once defined my life became just reminders of my loss. How was I supposed to deal with that? I didn't think I had any choice but to run away—from myself, my life, my memories. So I headed west, shedding all of that along the way.

Through all the years that I worked on Crazy Horse, my former life was something I pruned from my being like dead branches from a dying tree. Now, hearing that Sarah had tracked me down, that dying tree was springing to life, one fresh green leaf at a time. And it was wrenching.

The tin-can trailer home had somehow become my sanctuary. But now it felt more like a prison cell. Hardly any room to do more than eat, piss, and sleep. Even after all that time I've lived there, there's nothing personal to be found—not a photo or homey touch. Certainly nothing to remind me of Anna or Sarah.

I got out of my chair and decided to search the place from front to back, hoping I'd find something to jar my memory. I found two things that did just that. One was an old, crumpled piece of paper jammed in the back of a small drawer between the sink and the refrigerator. It read, "Mail note to Miss Gumpfrey." I remembered that this was about the sympathy letter I forgot to send to her after I learned that Hans had died.

That recollection opened a floodgate of scenes that flickered randomly through my mind: Hans's house; dear Miss Gumpfrey and her potato pancakes; the night Anna crawled into my bed for the first time; our make-believe marriage ceremony; all the work on the bus. I cast my mind even further back, to the Stein Works; Mom in her pleated skirt; Sal's crunchy rolls and *scamutz*. On and on, my mind unspooled snippets of memories I'd worked so hard to keep down, until I heard myself say aloud, "My chisels? Where are my chisels?"

I found my tool bag in a cabinet under the settee. In my haste to get at it, I busted the cheap framing, sending pieces of wood skidding willy-nilly across the floor. Once keen and bright, my precious chisels were covered with a coating of light rust. Without even thinking about it, I dug in the bag for a little can of oil and an old rag, and I began wiping them down, laying each one in turn on the dinette table. I hefted the maul, and felt its thick hickory handle warm to my touch. Suddenly, in the corner of my eye, Sal appeared. He was looking right at me, posing with his left hand bent to his waist, the right straight-arming a hefty wooden carving block. *Jimmy Boy,* he whispered.

All this sent me straight to the cabinet above the stove where I knew a bottle of whiskey was waiting. I took a long swig. Then another. And then another.

I sat, hefting my tools one after another and drinking, trying to make some sense of what had become of my life and what to make of it all. I got up and paced the aisle of the trailer, still gripping the bottle by the neck. Eight steps from front to back, back to front. I downed the last drop of whisky and sent the bottle skidding along the floor before it shattered against the wall gouging the cheap wood paneling. Half crazed, I threw open the door. It was chilly. Getting dark. I took a piss against the trailer, writing indecipherable graffiti on the oxidized aluminum sheath. The last few dribbles landed on my bare feet and I staggered into the darkness, tripped and fell, bloodied my hands on some sharp gravel. I rolled over onto my back. Choking on my own spit, I turned back over and struggled to my knees. I puked and wiped my mouth with a quick swipe of my forearm. I knelt there for a minute or so, swaying back and forth, feeling as if the ground had turned into the deck of a rolling ship. When it stopped lurching under me, I got on my feet and began running through the underbrush surrounding the trailer. I ran myself out of breath, stopped and bent over, gasped like a dying man, dry-heaved because there was nothing left in my gut. I put my hands on my wobbly knees and began to cry. "Anna!" I moaned in a voice I didn't recognize.

"ANNA…!"

I dragged myself back to the trailer, flopped down on the couch and passed out. When I woke up, dawn was breaking over the Black Hills and somebody was yelling my name and rattling the trailer door. As I got up, a splitting headache and chills swept over me. I struggled to open the door to find Charlie Tiernan, my workmate on Crazy Horse.

"What the hell brings you here so damn early?" I asked.

"Eyes, Jim. Remember?"

"Eyes?"

"We're working on the eyes today. For the celebration tomorrow? That's on Friday! The last we talked, you wanted me to pick you up."

"Oh…yeah, I remember," I said, half lying. "C'mon in. I'll put some coffee on."

"You look like you could use more than that," he said, stepping into the trailer. "Maybe a little hair of the dog wouldn't hurt, either."

Looking at the remains of the whiskey bottle strewn about the floor, Charlie teased, "Party got the best of ya, huh?" I ignored him.

While the coffee perked, I took two Tylenol and swept up the remains of the bottle, and pieces of wood from the cabinet. Charlie parked himself at the dinette table.

"Where did you get these chisels?" he asked, picking one up. "First rate is what they are. First rate."

I poured two mugs of coffee and sat down next to my friend. "They're mine…from a long time back."

"It's none of my business, Jim, but now that you mentioned the past, I hear that you have a daughter. It's all the talk over at the monument."

"Oh, hell, Charlie. People have such big ears—and even bigger mouths. I'd rather not talk about that, if you don't mind. I'm still working through all that and, to be honest with you, my memory has a lot of holes in it. When I have it figured out, I'll let you know."

"Sorry, Jim. Didn't mean to pry."

"I understand," I said, and we both shut up and drank our coffee. After a minute or two, I waved my hand in the direction of the chisels and said, "I used to carve some pretty intricate stuff back in the day."

"Given these chisels, you must have been pretty good. Where did you get them?"

"From Sal," I said instantly, surprising myself at how clearly those days with Sal came flooding back. I topped off our mugs. For the next half-hour or so, I told Charlie all about Sal and how he'd taught me how to carve hidden messages. I told him about *Luce di Dio*. I described Sal's shop down to its smallest detail, including the foul smell of Perodie cigar smoke. I was talking more to myself than I was to Charlie. The more I talked, the more I remembered. I really bent his ear.

All he could say when I finally came up for air was, "Well, I'll be damned."

After we finished our coffee, I gathered up my chisels and put them in my old tool bag. I hefted it from the table and led Charlie to the door.

"Well let's go," I said. "Time's wasting."

"Why you takin' those along?"

"Oh, just because," I said. I closed the trailer door behind me, and he didn't pursue it.

Ten minutes later, we were at the monument. Outside the

locker room, Charlie checked the bulletin board for the day's work orders. "You're on your own," he said, heading for the locker room. "I've been reassigned."

Left alone, I took a moment to look up at the monument. Six-hundred feet above me, Crazy Horse astride his mount was emerging from a wall of sheer granite. For all the time I'd worked on this monument, I'd seldom stopped to appreciate the magnificent scope of the thing.

I took the elevator to the top. When I got out Clyde was there, as usual, sitting behind the controls for the lift. It had just two handles—one for up and one for down—but Clyde acted as if he were steering a submarine.

"You look better today," he said.

"Thanks. I feel better," I managed, but in fact I felt like I'd been run over by a Sherman.

"What's that?" he asked, nodding at my tool bag.

"Chisels."

"You don't need no chisels. What you gonna do, freehand?" Clyde laughed like a hyena.

Ignoring him, I got into the work basket. The heavy rumbling of the cable engine beat into the crisp morning air as Crazy Horse's forehead slipped by. I stopped in front of the huge right eye. I turned around and looked out over the vast, stark wilderness and thought about the Sioux dying by the hundreds just to stay on it. Crazy Horse died for his people at just thirty-four, literally stabbed in the back by some coward, after all the metaphorical back-stabbing of broken treaties and promises. Like good soldiers the world over, his braves fought and died by the thousands, eager for peace and desperate to preserve their way of life.

I left the finishing torch on its rack and grasped one of my chisels in my left hand, a mallet in my right. I rested the sharpened edge of the chisel against the rock face, struck it, and...the chisel bounced back. "Damn granite," I said, striking it again.

Nothing.

I looked at the chisel, rubbed my thumb along its dull edge. The last time I'd used it was a million years earlier, on my cairn. Compared to granite, limestone was butter. I'd need to re-sharpen. *A flicker of Sal. Pietra del diavolo—devil stone.*

"Haul-up," I called into the intercom.

"Roger that, chisel man."

The winding drum screeched to action, hauling the steel basket slowly upward.

"Sounded like a phone was ringing down there, man. Ya ain't gonna do shit with no chisel."

I ignored Clyde's attempts to get my goat and said, "Look, I gotta go do something. While I'm gone, how about rigging up for the left eye? I'll be working some more on that one, too."

"You some kind of eye man? One of them optimists or somethin'?"

"I think you mean *optometrist*," I said, heading for the sharpening shed.

"Yeah, whatever—smartass!"

Using a grinder in the maintenance shop, it took me about a half-hour to get my chisels sharpened for granite. When I got back to the top of the mountain, Darryl Peterson, the supervisor was waiting.

"Say, Jim," he said, trying to sound casual, "Clyde tells me that you're planning to do some hand work on the eyes? They look pretty good to me, and right on target for the official opening, too. I'd rather you let them be, unless you have a damn good reason to change something."

"What do you mean, 'official opening'?" I asked, vaguely remembering something Charlie had referred to earlier.

"You know…the big event," he said, shaking his head. "How the hell come you don't know about it? Someday, you're gonna read the bulletin board. Anyway, lots of donors coming, the Lakota are having a powwow, the Chief's coming…things gotta go right."

"Sorry…musta missed that notice," I said, feeling kind of stupid about it. "But when you say, 'opening,' you mean—"

"The *eye*-opening, Jim. It's big stuff. A great moment to show off what we've all worked so hard on."

"All I want to do is put some finishing touches on those eyes," I said. "I'd feel a lot better if the granite was smoother."

"Mmm…OK, I guess. But no shiny stuff. We don't want his eyes reflecting the sun or anything."

"I'm not going to polish them, dammit. Just do a bit of chisel work."

"Chisel?" Peterson laughed, pointing to the parade grounds 600 feet below. "Any marks you make with a chisel aren't gonna mean crap to people standing down there."

"I know, Darryl. It's just…something I have to do," I said. I was thinking about Sal's belief that hidden messages carved in stone can affect the way people feel. Whether my hand carving will have any effect at all was beside the point. I was doing this for me. The old me, that is.

Peterson flashed me a shit-eating grin.

"So, after all these years just following orders, old Crazy Horse is finally getting to you? I gotta tell you, Jim…I never really thought your heart was in it. You're a good worker and all, but you never once showed any interest past getting a pay-check—and now this…*mission* to make the eyeballs perfect?"

He was right. Over all my years out there, I was pretty much phoning it in. I could've been working on the Notre Dame Cathedral and I wouldn't have cared one way or the other. I'd been treating this like line work: get the job done and go home.

I just shrugged, and Peterson said, "Well…never too late, I guess. You've put in your time. Earned the right to do what you gotta do—but make it quick. And I'll see you tomorrow morning at five, sharp. Don't forget!"

"Five o'clock!?"

"Geez, Jim! I know you musta been briefed on this. Are you okay?"

"Yeah, I am. Just fill me in." The truth was I was not okay. I was hell bent on finding Sarah.

Peterson said "Here's the plan. While it's still dark, you and Charlie Tiernan are going to be let down in the baskets, one on each side. When I give you a signal, you'll crack the torches and hit some rock with them. The boss wants to see sparks. You know, so the people think that we're somehow *opening* the eyes right then and there. Just as the sun comes up."

"Just like fireworks on the Fourth of July," I responded sarcastically.

"C'mon Jim. This is serious. Think of it as a bit of theatrics. A little reenactment to excite the crowd. There'll be lots of people here, some who are paying your salary. Are you up for this or not?"

"Don't get all hot n' bothered, Darryl… I'll be here. Five sharp."

"Great, Jim," he said, slapping me on the back. He turned

and headed for the elevator.

I had Clyde lower me down to the right eye and I began my work. When I finished, I switched to the left eye. Twelve hours of carving left me exhausted, but it was worth every second.

30

That night, I stirred more than I slept. I got to the site at four AM and found Charlie already at the winding shed. We took the elevator to the top, readied the finishing torches, and loaded them into the work baskets. Charlie would be at the right eye and I would be at the left. We got into our respective baskets and Charlie said, "You know Jim, this morning when I got to work, I looked up at Crazy Horse and even though it was dark, I felt like...well, I'm not sure how to put this. But it was like he was real. Like at any minute he was going to charge right off the mountain. Am I going nuts or something?"

"No, Charlie, You're probably not."

Once we were in position, I yelled over to Charlie, "Look closely at the upper part of the l eye, just below the eyebrow and tell me what you see."

Things went quiet for a moment, then Charlie yelled back, "It says, *"It is a good day to fight."*

"You got that right" I said.

I looked at my work on the left eye. "Mine says the rest: '*It is a good day to die.*' "

Charlie yelled "How the hell…"

At that moment, our two-way radios crackled to life. Darryl gave us the order: "Hit it, you guys! Time for the sparks!"

Our torches shot pressure-driven hellfire into the granite. Below us, we heard the crowd oohing and aahing as the sparks flew into the distance. Then came the sound of the Lakota beating drums, echoing through the Black Hills.

When we came off the mountain, Charlie and I grabbed a couple of donuts and some coffee and made our way over to the employees' picnic table just outside the locker room.

"The trailer's yours if you want it," I said. "I'll be getting along."

"What do you mean? You leavin'?"

"Yes, Charlie, I am."

"Jeez, Jim, are you sure?"

I took a minute to answer. "As a matter of fact…I'm going to look for my daughter. Her name's Sarah." That was the first time I'd said her name to anybody in a lot of years.

"Good god, Jim. I…guess I'm surprised! I mean, how long have I known you? Over a decade's my guess, and you never said *boo* about family, let alone a daughter."

"That's because…well, the story of me and my family hit a dead end a long time ago. I ran so far and so fast I figured I'd never have a prayer of circling back to all that, even if I wanted to—which, for a long time, I didn't."

"Sounds like quite a story, my friend."

Maybe it's time that story was told.

I sat down across from Charlie and it all poured out of me. I starting with meeting Anna at the dance and ended with Marge telling me about the phone call the day before. But there were some big gaps in the middle—things I still couldn't quite get a grip on. Things I'd put so far out of my mind that I couldn't get them back.

"Jesus, Jim, you went through a bit of hell, didn't you? But I'm still not clear on how you ended up way out here."

"That's a bit of a mystery to me too, Charlie. It's like, at a certain point, my mind just closed up. I guess that I just went nuts with grief."

"Yeah, I can believe that. So…where are you going to start this search?"

"Sarah told Marge she was in Clayton, Wisconsin. I'll head right there."

We sat in silence for a few minutes, each of us knowing that this was our last time together. Standing, Jim and I shook hands. "Well Jim, I best be getting back to the grind. I sure hope you find your daughter—and whatever else you're looking for."

"Thanks, Charlie. Say goodbye to everybody for me—and give your family hugs all around." Charlie gave me a wave and disappeared into the locker room.

I said my goodbye to Marge and told her that I'd give her a call about sending me my last paycheck. She gave me a hug and wished me good luck.

"I sure will."

The sun was throwing long, early-morning shadows across the parking lot. It would probably take a few hours for the rays to reach Crazy Horse's eyes. "Go get 'em," I said, looking up at the massive warrior emerging from the mountain.

I spent a few hours packing and cleaning up the trailer. Leaving the ownership papers on the table for Charlie, I jumped in my pick-up and was on my way to Clayton and hopefully a reunion with Sarah. I thought about calling Oscar but decided against it. Showing up unannounced might be risky, but trying to explain my whereabouts and the life I was living was not going to work with a phone conversation. I'll just trust that he's still alive and willing to listen. My mind drifted to thoughts of Anna and me pulling up to his parking lot on that cold December day so long ago. A blast from a trucker's airhorn probably saved my life. I had fallen asleep at the wheel and was on my way to crossing the divide on Interstate 90. I scared myself awake long enough to make it to the next exit where I got a room at a nearby motel.

Beth / Sarah

JUNE 23–24, 1993

31

Safely nestled in the luxury of Miss Gumpfrey's guest quarters, I slept until ten, then took a long shower. Before breakfast, I called Oscar to tell him what I'd found out.

Oscar listened to my story. But when I told him I was headed out to South Dakota, he must've gotten a little worried about me. He said maybe I should come back to Clayton first—that maybe he'd even come along with me to South Dakota. It was like when Heidi and Jake had wanted to go with me to Wisconsin. I thought it was sweet of him, but I told him I needed to do this myself. He just blew out a big sigh, like he was my dad himself. He told me to call him every night so he'd know I was okay. And that if Hussy broke down, to call him right away because he knew a lot of junkmen who could help.

Breakfast was another new eating experience. Those "birds without heads" had turned out be beef stuffed and rolled—thank God. Breakfast was Eggs Benedict, served on this beautiful blue-and-white china Miss Gumpfrey called *Delft*. She turned out to be one terrific lady. I was beginning to learn what luxury is all about and I liked it. Though I kind of hated leaving, I was pretty anxious to get to South Dakota. So we said our goodbyes and promised to keep in touch. She'd packed me a bunch of food for the trip, so I figured I wouldn't have to waste too much time making stops.

I made it to Mitchell, South Dakota, before I felt too tired to keep going. I had learned a lot about picking a good motel, so the one I found in Mitchell was much better than the one in Janesville. I remembered my promise and called Oscar. It felt good checking in. I decided to think about him as my honorary grandpa, though I didn't tell him that. I thought maybe I would when I got back to Clayton.

The shower was pretty clean and the room was quiet, so I fell asleep quickly. I did wake up once—not sure what time it was—to the sound of some idiot snoring away like a wart hog. It was coming from the wall right behind my bed. I rapped hard, but nothing changed. I shoved my head under the pillow—no use. But I must've fallen back to sleep at some point, because the next thing I knew it was morning.

The motel had a free continental breakfast so I ate right there. I wondered what Miss Gumpfrey ate when she was alone. I promised myself I'd go back and visit her once I got things straightened out. She wasn't exactly the *grandma* type, but maybe she could be my other honorary grandparent?

I reached Rapid City just before noon, then picked up Route 16 and headed for the Black Hills. *Hills?* Bullshit. More like mountains. Whoever named the place must have lived in the Himalayas or something. I'd never been in mountains before, so I had to get used to going around those high, nutty curves. Hussy didn't seem to mind, though—just stuck to the road like a mountain goat.

I made it to the Crazy Horse Memorial around one o'clock. There were only a couple cars in the parking lot. I followed signs to the Visitors' Center. Sure enough, Marge, the receptionist I'd talked to two days earlier, was sitting at the counter. I knew it was her because when I asked if Jim Robertson was around, she said, "Oh, you must be the girl from before. I told him you called!"

When she didn't offer any more information, I said, "So… do you think you can tell me where to find him then—*please*?"

"Well, honey, here's the thing," she said, looking kind of pouty. "Like you asked me to, I told Jim that you called right after you hung-up. That was on Wednesday. Anyway, the next day, that was yesterday, he put in his quittin' papers. He was good with staying till after the eye opening, which was early this morning. He was gone just after sunrise. You two could've crossed each other on the highway."

Leaning over the counter, I said, "Let me get this straight, Ma'am—"

"My name's Marge," she said. "You can call me Marge because that's my name."

"Okay, then, *Marge*…"—I leaned in closer, planting both palms on the counter—"you're telling me that my father left here this morning?"

"Right after we had the eye-opening ceremony. The one I told you about on the phone, remember? You said you couldn't make it in time. Well, you sure missed something, honey—it was a sight! Jim stayed for that, of course. In fact, he was way up there on the monument, helping to make it happen."

Pushing myself to the far edge of the counter and trying

to keep myself under some kind of control, I said, "You know, Marge, I really don't give a rat's ass about the ceremony or anything else. What I need to know is where my father is! Do you understand that?"

Marge moved back from her side of the counter, and said, "Well, I just don't like your tone of voice. You're a very disrespectful young lady. So, you can leave now."

"I'll leave when I get some answers. Where did he go?" I knew I was being ugly, but didn't care.

"I don't know. He just left. Maybe he just doesn't want to see you. I wouldn't blame him for that."

That stopped me cold. Marge was right. He didn't want to see me. Otherwise, why would he run? I slid back from the counter, inadvertently sweeping a packet of brochures onto the floor. I felt bad about how I was acting in front of this poor lady who had nothing to do with the fact that my dad didn't even want to see me. I bent down, picked up the brochures, and set them back on the counter.

"Maybe you're right, Marge. Maybe he doesn't want to see me. I'm sorry to have bothered you. I didn't mean to be so nasty." I started heading for the door.

"Wait," Marge said, and I turned back around. She'd come around from behind the counter. "I didn't mean to hurt your feelings, honey. Why, you've come all this way...you must be pretty disappointed. I'm not a mean person. I'm Lutheran, you know, and I wasn't brought up to snap at people like that. Maybe there's something I can do to help."

"I'm not sure what that would be," I said, my voice trembling a little. The reality of what was happening was starting to sink in. *I had a father but he didn't see himself having a daughter.*

"I have an idea. If anybody knows where Jim might be going it's Charlie Tiernan. He's been working with your father for years. Why don't you have a seat and I'll go find him."

"To be honest, Marge, I don't know if I want to keep chasing him."

"Well, I understand that, but at least let's hear what Charlie has to say."

"Okay…why not," I said. I sat down on a chair off to the side of the counter. "Might as well finish what I started, even if I don't like the ending."

"Alright then, that's better," Marge said. "There's a fresh pot of coffee over behind the counter," she said. "Help yourself to a cup. I won't be long."

I didn't want the coffee. What I wanted to do was go back to Clayton. Maybe jump-start my life. Maybe go back to Indiana, go to college and be done with it. Ten minutes or so went by before Marge came back with a heavy set man dressed in dust-covered overalls. He came right over to me. Marge busied herself rearranging things on the counter so she wouldn't seem like she was eavesdropping, but I could tell she was dying to know what this guy was going to tell me.

"You must be Sarah. I'm Charlie," he said.

I stood and we shook hands. Charlie reminded me of Jake— an older Jake, but with the same powerful workhorse build.

"Marge tells me you're looking for your father."

"Yes, I am. Do you know where he is?"

"Well, I'm not sure where he might be exactly at this moment, but I know he set off looking for *you*."

"WHAT? He did? But I thought—How do you know that?"

"Because he's my friend, and that's what he told me he was

going to do. And lordy, you look just like him." He looked down at the floor for a couple of seconds, then said, "You know…I've known Jim for a lot of years and he never talked about having a family till two days ago. I hope to hell you two find each other."

"It would help if I knew where he was going. Did he say anything about that?"

"Wisconsin is what he told me. Somewhere in Wisconsin."

"That's such a big help! Thank you," I said, giving Charlie a big hug, dust and all. "Is there a phone I could use?"

Charlie called over to Marge, "Sarah here needs to make a call. Long distance! That okay with you?"

"You bet, Charlie. Sarah, you go on ahead and use mine.

Jim

JUNE 24–25, 1993

32

By late morning I hit Minneapolis. I picked up Route 8 which bisects the upper third of Wisconsin, a direct beeline to Clayton. The minute I passed through Lindstrom, Minnesota, I had this recollection of driving with Anna through this very town.

Familiar sights began triggering buried memories. It was almost like looking through a family photo album. I passed a coffee shop in Turtle Lake and thought, *That's where Anna and I used to stop on our way to Minneapolis for her viola lessons.* Snippets of recitals, practice sessions, even Reger's Suites came tumbling into my head, linking themselves together until my life with Anna became real again.

The more I drove, the more my past roared toward me, a jumbled mix of Mom, Sal, Hans, Miss Gumpfrey, Clay Rodell, Al Poncelli, Mabel, Oscar. Images flashed through my head like snapshots. Sleeping in the bus; carving messages to my dead soldiers; lying in bed in the cabin, my head resting on Anna's swollen belly…the storm…the trial… But I still couldn't, for the life of me, figure out how I wound up working on Crazy

Horse. That was a gap that still needed filling in.

I could have easily made it to Clayton but felt that I needed to take some time to get myself ready for meeting Sarah. I took a room at the El Rancho Motel in the town of Ladysmith which was only about fifteen miles west of Clayton. Staring back at me from the bathroom mirror was a bedraggled, half-bearded, wind-wrinkled, unkempt recluse, not the Jim Robinson I pictured in my journey into the past. Whatever was going to happen, I sure as hell wasn't marching into the future looking like that. I took a shower and headed into town where I bought some new clothes, got a haircut and a shave, had my pick-up cleaned and washed. All-in-all, making myself presentable.

Following a good night's sleep, I lay in bed to give some thought to the day ahead. The branches I had pruned from my memory were sprouting overtime and I was more than a little anxious over it all. I had no idea what Sarah was looking for, or what she'd be like. Then there was Oscar. The longer I laid in bed the more nervous I got. The "what-ifs" mounted a full-blown attack until I took charge of myself and got out of bed. A long hot shower, a change into my new clothes, and a hearty break-fast, and I was in my truck heading to Clayton. I was ready to do what I had to do to make this work.

Nearing Clayton, I saw a billboard: GOLDEN'S SCRAP IS GOLDEN. 2 MILES AHEAD.

Wham! There we were, Anna and I pulling into Oscar's yard in the dead of winter eighteen years ago. With that precious memory, I knew that I was not alone. Anna would help see me through whatever the day might bring. I took a deep breath, got out of the truck, and went inside.

I recognized Frank Toilsen right away. He was half asleep, slumped in his favorite worn-out chair. "Hello, Frank," I said.

Bony and looking like road kill, old Toilsen weaseled out of his chair.

"Good-god-a-mighty!" he declared. "If it ain't you then call me dead blind. Jim Robertson, for chrissake! I knew there was a reason I lived this long! Good to see you, Jim!" He gave me the biggest hug he could muster, then backed away to look me up and down like he still didn't believe his eyes.

"Good to see you, too, Frank," I said quietly. "Been a long time."

"Seems like just yesterday to me," he said. Turning aside, he yelled in a raspy voice, "Hey, Oscar, come out here and brace yourself! You won't believe what the cat's dragged in."

When Oscar saw me, he froze in his tracks.

"Where in hell have *you* been?" he snarled, but he couldn't hide the smile blooming under his whiskers.

"Away," I said. "Far away, Oscar."

Oscar stayed put.

"You didn't write or anything. Left us all wondering whether you were alive or dead!"

"I guess I…couldn't," I said. "Kinda lost track of myself for a long time…" It wasn't much of an apology, but it was the best I could do.

"*Couldn't!* Goddammit, Jim! We were your friends."

I pondered that for a moment. He was right. I'd turned my back on my life and everyone who'd cared about me. It was all in the past tense now. Maybe there was no going back. I turned and walked toward the door.

"Hold on," Oscar commanded. Lowering his voice, he said,

"Before you decide to slip away again, there's something you oughta know. Sarah was here."

I stopped dead in my tracks and turned to eyeball him. "When?"

"Three days ago. She was looking for you. Didn't know anything about you till I told her a few things. Then she went off to Milwaukee to visit some lady named Mrs. Gumpy or something."

"*Miss Gumpfrey*?! Is Sarah still with her there, Oscar?"

"I think that'd be up to her to say."

"Listen, old man. If my daughter is trying to find me, I've got a right to know!"

"Don't tell me about your *rights,* Jim. You gave those up a long time ago, when you just up and vanished on all of us!"

Frank Toilsen jumped in like a scolding preacher. "You two better pipe down before you say stuff you'll be sorry for. That young lady wants to see her daddy and he wants to see her. Maybe it's time to sort all that out. Damn young'uns, you don't know shit from Shinola."

Oscar swallowed hard. "Hmpf. Maybe so. You want to talk, Jim? Then let's talk."

He walked toward the back room. I followed.

Oscar was torn between anger and understanding. The anger side came out first: "To keep the property from being sold or auctioned off, I paid your mortgage to the VA. At least you could've sent me a check once in awhile. So the first thing I'm going to do is figure out how much you owe me, adding in the taxes that covered these past fifteen years. That is if you want the place. Which by the way I kept as good as it was the day you left. How does that suit you?"

"I understand. I'll make good on it."

"That's good to know." He said. "Now, how about Sarah? You know you could have made a deal for getting parental rights to visit had you stuck around. Why the hell did you take off like you did? We searched like hell and it was like you dropped off the face of the earth."

I said, "Look Oscar, if it's an apology you're after, it's not going to happen. What I can tell you is I don't know what happened. Once they took Sarah away, life became a blank space. I still can't put all the pieces together. When I heard that Sarah was looking for me, it was like my past life came tumbling back. A past that I know I have to deal with. I know that I'm going to need help and I hope you will join me to put things right."

"Well Jim, if you put it that way, of course I'll help you. But it doesn't erase your obligations."

I grinned and said, "That's the Oscar I remember.

Beth / Sarah

JUNE 24–25, 1993

33

Oscar answered on the third ring.

"It's...a long story, Oscar, but I'm out here and...I think my dad is headed toward *you!*"

"Already here," he said.

"You're telling me that I'm out in this wasteland and my father's in *Clayton?*"

"Yep. I guess you two passed each other on the road without even knowin' it. It's kind of funny when you think about it."

I didn't see the humor. Before he could say anything else, I told him I was going to head back—but not to tell my father I was coming. "Please, Oscar. Let me just get back there before you say anything. Maybe by then I'll figure out exactly what I want to say to him."

But Oscar refused to play that game. "I can't do that, Sarah. Either you tell him you're coming or I will."

Ugh. Well, maybe it's better if he's prepared.

"OK, Oscar, have it your way. You go ahead and tell him. But I don't think I'm ready to talk to him yet."

Oscar went mum for a bit, then said, "That's fine...but try to calm down a little about all this, Sarah. It won't do any good coming in with your guns blazing. I had a long talk with Jim, and let me tell you, he's been to hell and back over all this. Maybe you should start by hearing his side of things."

"What about me, Oscar? Did you tell him what *I've* been through?"

"You know, Sarah, I think I need to back out of things here... it's for the two of you to work out. I'm just saying keep in mind that, whatever happened in the past, you need a dad and he needs a daughter. And there isn't much point in wasting more precious time now, is there? All that anger you've got saved up is stuck in you like a fish hook. It's gonna be painful to pull it out."

"I'll...think about what you're saying, Oscar. I have some time on the way back to sort things out, I guess. Thanks for... everything." I hung up and came out from behind the counter.

Charlie walked with me over to the parking lot. Before getting into the car, I looked up. "So my dad helped do this?"

"Yup, he did."

"Crazy Horse looks like he's going to tear right out of that mountain. Maybe settle some scores..."

Smiling at me, Charlie said, "Sounds like something your dad would say."

I thanked him and took his number on a scrap of paper— "in case you need me for anything"—and got right back on the road. I stayed over at a Holiday Inn this time, and treated myself to a steak dinner with all the trimmings. The room was blissfully quiet—no snoring, even.

Before checking out the next morning, I called Oscar. I told him I would probably be in Clayton by the afternoon and he told me to take my time, drive carefully. He said that Jim would be at the yard waiting for me. "You might want to come around back," he said, then gave me directions ending with "park by the stack of old refrigerators."

When I started Hussy, I noticed how perfect her motor sounded, humming like she was waking up from a nice nap. I thought about how I'd felt when I left Indiana. The rush of traffic. Wondering if I'd make it. Saying goodbye to Jake and Heidi. It really seemed like ancient history, but it had only been a week! I honestly felt older. Maybe Einstein was right and time really is an illusion. I had to thank my science teacher, Mr. Edmunds, for that one.

I was on the road for about an hour before I thought about Miss Gumpfrey. She'd be dying to hear all that's been going on, and I thought how nice it would be to talk to her. To hear her *grandma* voice. Who says you can't pick your relatives? Maybe she'd help me figure out how to handle things. I wanted to love my father. My real father. Could I love him if I didn't forgive him, or did I have to forgive him before I could love him? Maybe that was a dumb question, but I figured Miss Gumpfrey would have some kind of answer for it. Probably involving a baby bird or something.

I stopped at a roadside rest and called her. She said she was *tickled pink* to hear from me. I told her that I was heading back to Clayton to meet my dad, and she told me she was proud of my courage. When I told her I didn't feel brave at all—that I was scared to death—she said, "My dear child, *courage* doesn't mean *without fear.* Courageous people are afraid, but get on with things anyway. And that is exactly what you are doing. And I am proud of you for it."

I asked her the thing about forgiveness and love.

She didn't say anything for a moment, then said, "Love and forgiveness are much the same thing. Do one and you get the other. Fail at one and you fail at both. The important thing is not to let anger get in the way. You must put that aside in order to experience the rest."

"You sound just like Oscar," I said.

"Oh, I think most any older person, anyone with some life experience, would tell you the same thing. Reaching a certain age does come with some advantages, you know." She got quiet after that.

"I love you," I said. It came out of nowhere, I swear. I didn't even know I was going to say it.

"I love you, too, dear," she said quietly. I know she had tears in her eyes.

I promised that I'd call her once I got things settled. And I'd call Pete Paulson, too.

Back on the road, I tried not to think too hard, just look at the scenery. The Pixies singing *Gigantic*, a song from my middle-school days, came on the radio. I didn't feel like listening so I switched it off. It was past three when I got to Clayton. I drove right around Oscar's place to the back like he said to do. I parked Hussy behind the pile of old refrigerators and shut off the engine. "You're a good pal," I said, patting her dashboard— thinking how strange it is that we can get attached to a machine as if it were a person.

I felt nervous. Not scared or anything like that. It was more like hoping for no more surprises. No more secrets. I reached deep into my pocket and withdrew my mom's stone. I got out of the car and clutched it to my heart. "I have spunk," I said to myself heading to the back door of Oscar's place. It was open. I peered into the grayish gloom. Shelves laden with old machinery parts lined the walls. And there he was, arms at his side, standing in front of a stack of rusting iron.

"Hello Sarah," he said quietly.

I walked over to him and said softly, "Hello Dad."